Shadow Assassin

Sher Kyweriga

Silva Publishing
Minneapolis, Minnesota

Cover design by Renee Kyweriga,
Graphic Designer and Owner of Vintage Recreations

ISBN-13: 978-0615993041
ISBN-10: 0615993044

Chapter 1

9:25 p.m. Murder was just like anything else. To succeed all anyone needed was a plan, and he had a plan that rocked. No way would the cops figure this one out, because his plan was KISS all the way. That would be Keep It Simple, Stupid for the uninformed.

Besides being simple, his plan had a twist to it that would keep the cops chasing their tails in every direction but his. They'd be looking for a connection between the murders, and the beauty of it all was that there was no connection.

His plan was brilliant—a hell of a lot better than his partner's half-baked plan. He was no stupid fuck in spite of what his partner thought. Besides, he was taking all the risks, and it was his right to make at least some of the decisions.

He laughed out loud, and then quickly looked from side to side, hunching his shoulders up and down a few times and glancing out of the corners of his eyes to make sure he was still alone. He caught a glimpse of himself reflected in the glass covering a large photograph hanging on the wall. He stopped dead in his tracks to check out how he looked. Rockin', that's how. Purely rockin'.

When he'd seen the black leather biker's jacket earlier that day, he knew he had to have it. He watched his reflection in the glass, turning a little this way and then a little that. Finally, with a Keanu Reeves à la *Matrix*-like smile, he smoothed back his thick brown hair, swung his left shoulder around and sauntered on down the hall.

9:25 p.m. "Mama, isn't my daddy ever gonna wake up?" Christopher Emerson, known as Kit by those who mattered, rested his small chin on the edge of the hospital bed, focusing thoughtful brown eyes on his father.

Paul Emerson lay unmoving beneath the white coverlet, his body a shadow of what it had been after more than two years of inactivity.

Lani looked at her ex-husband for a moment. She took a deep breath, turned to face her son, and looked directly into his eyes.

"No Kit, the doctors say your daddy can't ever wake up. His brain was hurt too much in the car accident. But, you know what? I think it helps him when we come to visit, and I know he likes to hear the sound of your voice."

"Are you gonna die?" asked Kit, looking up with a frightened expression.

Now, she'd done it. Lately Kit had been expressing all kinds of fears. Fear of the dark, monsters under his bed, snakes popping up out of the toilet, pretty much anything seemed to frighten him these days. She hoped his fears were a natural part of his development and that she wasn't doing something wrong.

"Don't you worry, Honey Bug. I'm not going to die until I'm old and creaky, and you're all grown up."

Kit chuckled, "Old and creaky like Jonathon, right?"

"Yep, like Jonathon." Lani walked around the foot of the bed, leaned down and hugged her son until he squeaked in protest. "In fact, I'm going to love you forever, even when you're all grown up with a family of your very own."

"Mama, you're squeezing me to bits and pieces."

No longer worried about his mother's eminent demise, Kit wriggled out of her grasp and chattered on to the next subject.

"Jonathon is my very best friend. Did you know that? I think I should go see him right now. Daddy's sleepin', and he won't miss me. Jonathon likes it when I visit him. He said he would show me his seashells again. Did you know the shells whisper to you, Mama? I keep tryin' and tryin' to hear what they're whisperin' to me."

"Okay, but only for a few minutes. It's kind of late, Kit, so be really quiet and poke your head in to see if Jonathon is still awake. If he's sleeping, don't wake him up, okay? He needs his rest so he can get better and go home."

"I won't wake him up. I promise."

"Do you remember his room number?" Lani dropped a kiss on the top of Kit's dark red hair.

"Yep, Room 1111. That equals four, just like me."

"That's right, just like you. If you're not back in fifteen minutes, I'll come get you, okay? We've got to be getting you home for your beauty sleep, don't you know?"

"Ah, boys don't need beauty sleep." Kit grabbed his *Star Wars* light saber, shoved it down the back of his shirt, and dashed out the door to visit his old friend.

9:33 p.m. He checked his watch as he strolled along. The halls were empty—exactly as he'd planned. Even though White Oaks Nursing Home in Edina looked more like a swanky hotel with its plush, hunter green carpeting and designer wallpaper, visiting hours still existed. They ended every night promptly at 9:00 p.m., which fit into his plan perfectly.

Yes sir. If you had a plan, you never got caught, and if anyone would know about getting caught it would definitely be him. But, that was all in the past. He'd learned a few things over the years. He plan was definitely KISS with five, simple steps.

Step one: Check to be sure the hallway was empty in all directions.

Step two: Enter the target's room.

Step three: Slide the pillow out from under the target's head with one smooth movement.

Step four: Place the pillow *over* the target's face.

And step five? Lean on the pillow until the body beneath stopped writhing and twitching. A piece of cake.

He cradled his motorcycle helmet in the crook of one arm. In case anyone did happen to see him in the hallway, they'd assume he was on his way out. He hunched his shoulders up and down again and smiled. No doubt about it, he'd planned for everything.

He tripped as he walked into Room 2153. Straightening up, he frowned at the figure lying still beneath a mound of blankets. Joseph Wurlitzer was 75 years old. He had Alzheimer's. His daughter visited every day, in spite of the fact that she had two teenagers and an executive husband who expected her to entertain at a moment's notice.

Actually, he was helping her out quite a bit. Now, she would have more time to entertain. Joseph didn't even struggle. When the deed was done, he thoughtfully rearranged the pillow beneath Joseph's head, exited the room, and glided on down the hall, doing a snazzy spin and quickstep along the way.

Room 2145 belonged to Louise Curtis. Louise slept, snoring gently, face cradled in her pillow, a small string of drool dripping onto the pristine white of her pillowcase. Yuck.

Louise, who was sixty-five, had fallen and broken her hip. Her son, a surgeon at North Memorial Hospital, had insisted on White Oaks Nursing Home for her recovery because it was the best and nothing was too good for his mother. Hmmm, too bad for Louise. What a shame her son had insisted on the very best.

Trotting down the staircase at the end of the hall, he went in search of room 1115 and his third victim. The name on the door read Jeannie Bartlett. She was much younger than the others. He had selected her because of her youth and circumstances and because in spite of what his mother used to tell him, he did have a conscience. He felt terrible about Jeannie Bartlett's situation, really terrible. She was only thirty-two years old, mother of daughter Lisa, now nine years old; son Jeffy, six years old; and baby Kimmy, three. Yep, he'd done his homework, and he knew everything he needed to know about Jeannie.

She'd been quite a looker before her body wasted away. He glanced at the photograph on the bureau next to her bed, showing her strapped into a harness on a catamaran, leaning out over the water with her toes gripping the edge of one pontoon. With a wide, all teeth showing smile on her face, she was facing into the wind, long golden hair blowing out behind her. His eyes slid to a pause at her chest, which not even the best designer lifejacket could disguise. Whew! What a rack. No wonder her husband was jealous.

Story was his jealousy was unfounded, but you never knew. Maybe Jeannie really was bonking every male in sight. That's what her husband thought at any rate. Because late one night, he got out of bed and walked over to the closet in his underwear to extract his officially registered 9mm Glock automatic. He pumped one round into Jeannie where she lay sleeping in their bed. Then, he'd put the gun to his own head, pulled the trigger, and died before he hit the floor. Jeannie should have died, too. But her little girl Lisa knew how to dial 911, and help arrived in time to save her life.

Now, poor Jeannie was paralyzed from the neck down and had a whole host of associated ills that ensured she'd never again live on her own. The state subsidized her care, and a wealthy relative kicked in some bread as well so she could stay at White Oaks. In the end, the punishment her husband dished out was even harsher than he intended because Jeannie would spend the rest of her life paralyzed, her children farmed out to a number of relatives. Hell, the murderer thought, I'm doing her a favor.

Unfortunately, Jeannie didn't agree. As he lowered the pillow over her face, her eyes shot open in panic and confusion. She opened her mouth to scream, but she was powerless against his strength. It was over in a few minutes. He smiled and hummed softly as he straightened the covers over Jeannie's body, a fine line of sweat beading his brow. When they looked into his face before he killed them, a thrill coursed through his entire body. He liked it.

Well, three down and one to go. He pulled a package of Clove chewing gum out of his pocket, and shoved a stick into his mouth, relishing the spicy flavor as it bit into his tongue.

As he reached the doorway of Room 1111, he stopped to adjust his motorcycle helmet before he made the kill. He thought he'd try something different this time. He reflected for a moment, tilting his head, getting into his persona. In the scheme of things, this murder should be the hardest of the four. It wasn't every day that a son did in his old man.

His laugh was sharp, short, and quite impressive he thought, until he snorted accidentally. Looking around quickly to make sure no one had heard, he pushed the door open and glided into the room.

9:40 a.m. Lani leaned back in her chair, gazing at the man lying in the hospital bed. In spite of the fact that Paul Emerson was barely 30 years old, his face was gaunt and gray and his eyes as sunken as a man twice his age. Although the nursing staff worked hard to keep his limbs pliant, the muscles in his arms and hands had atrophied, curling up tight against his chest. His long legs remained straight, but only because early on, the doctors had recommended severing the muscles that would otherwise have atrophied over time as well, causing his whole body to curl into a fetal position. Since Paul would never walk again, the surgery had made sense.

The familiar sadness washed over her. Paul Emerson could have had it all. In spite of everything—even the incident with Kit—she was still fond of him. She would always be fond of him. She cleared her throat uncomfortably. Fond. Such a bland word.

Lani yawned. She was so tired.

"Hey hon, how's he doing?" Beth Kazmarik, one of the

supervisory nurses, poked her head in the door.

Lani's eyes followed Beth as she entered the room and started to review the chart hanging from the end of the bed. "Oh Beth, I don't know. It's so hard to tell, isn't it? I wish I could communicate with him somehow."

"I know, honey."

"What scares me most is thinking that Paul is aware of everything that is going on around him, but that he's locked inside his head and he knows he's locked inside and always will be." Lani's voice dwindled away, and she swallowed hard. Crying accomplished nothing, and so she never allowed herself to cry. Not ever.

Beth reached out to pat Lani on the shoulder as she walked briskly over to the side of the bed. She slid the aural thermometer into Paul's ear, and when the instrument beeped, she answered the question Lani had been afraid to voice. "His temperature is 103, honey. It doesn't look good at the moment. He's stopped responding to the antibiotics, and we're having trouble controlling his fever."

Lani scrubbed the heels of her hands against her eyes. She knew that pneumonia was a real threat to anyone who was immobile, and she'd known that Paul's doctor was worried that this current bout was getting out of hand.

"Have you called his parents?" At Beth's quiet nod, Lani stood and began to gather her things. "Well then, I'd better get out of here before they arrive. You don't need another scene, that's for sure."

Beth's pleasant round face tightened at Lani's words, and she lifted her chin, soft blue eyes sparking with anger. "Don't you worry, hon. When we called them no one answered at either the home number or when we left a message with Mr. Emerson's answering service. So, you can sit right back down and relax for a while more. You look exhausted, and you've as much right to be here as anyone."

"Just for a few more minutes, then." Lani sat back down in the chair, yawning. "You know what I miss the most? I miss his laughter. God, Beth, I wish you could have heard him laugh. The wonderful thing about Paul was he could make everyone around him laugh. I miss his laugh so much sometimes. I wish Kit could have known the best side of Paul instead of the worst."

Beth looked around the room. "Speaking of angels, where is Kit?"

"He went to visit Jonathon Sutton. That man is so patient with Kit, and they play at *Star Wars*. I think Jonathon is supposed to be Obi Wan or something, and depending on the day, Kit is either Han Solo or Luke Skywalker. They seem to both get a kick out of it."

Beth grinned. "Jonathon mentioned to me once that Young Kit, as he calls him, reminds him of his son Michael. He's been waiting for Michael to come into town and visit. I hope he comes soon. That poor old man could use a boost."

"Well, he sure has been good to my son." Lani felt a pang. "You know, a few minutes ago, Kit told me that Jonathon was his very best friend. I'm glad they're close, but Beth, he needs friends his own age too."

"Kit has plenty of time to make friends. He's a special little guy, and after one of his visits, Jonathon really perks up. Well, I'd better be moving along. You have a good night, now."

Beth paused on her way out the door when Lani spoke her name.

"Beth? Thanks. Thanks for everything. I want you to know, all of you here at White Oaks, how much I appreciate the care you give to Paul—and to Kit and me as well," she added in a low voice.

"Well, then. No thanks are necessary. You take care of yourself, you hear?" Beth's voice was gruff, her eyes stern. "Say, how is that new business of yours going, anyway? I've got to get over there and try a cup of that designer coffee you're selling."

"Oh, but we sell so much more than designer coffee, Beth. If all you want is designer coffee, you can get that at Starbucks or Caribou. If you come to the Tropical Bean Coffee Shop, you get the whole enchilada."

Lani sat up straighter in her chair, and grinning at the chance to talk about her new venture, she launched right into her marketing spiel, her voice taking on a sing-song quality.

"At the Tropical Bean, you can listen to the sound of ocean waves breaking against the shore, the music of jungle animals, and thanks to my partner Rachel's artistic genius, you are surrounded by a mural of the ocean, sand, and tropical flora and fauna much like you'd get if you took a vacation to Maui. *Plus*, you get the designer coffee. You can't get all that at Starbucks. The best part of all? You don't even have to leave Minneapolis."

Beth grinned back at Lani. "Now, this I gotta see. Expect me for ambiance, waves, and coffee on my next day off. But don't you work too hard, you hear?"

Lani nodded, waved goodbye, and yawned again. Because of Rachel's chemistry final, Lani had worked a double shift, straight on through to 8:00 p.m. She yawned again and then smiled. It didn't matter how tired she was because things were working out fine. Six months ago, she'd gotten her MBA, and the next week she'd opened The Tropical Bean Coffee Shop. She sympathized with Rachel, who was still finishing up her master's degree. At least Lani didn't have to spend hours studying every night. All she had to do was make The Tropical Bean the success she knew it could be.

Life was what you made it. She had all the right ingredients. All she had to do was just hang in there and make things happen. She looked at Paul lying motionless on the bed. Her smile faded.

"Oh, Paul, I have nothing to complain about. I wish things could have turned out differently for you."

Lani reached for Paul's hand so that in case any awareness lingered in his brain, he'd feel comforted by a human touch. She lay her head down on the comforter, still holding Paul's hand. She would rest her eyes for a moment, just for one moment, she told herself.

9:45 p.m. Two rooms down, Kit sat cross-legged on the end of Jonathon Sutton's bed. "But Jonathon, how does the sea get its voice into the shell to talk to me?" He looked up at his old friend, a large conch shell held tightly to his left ear.

"Well, that's a very good question. I guess it's magic, Kit." Jonathon lay propped up against a mound of pillows, his eyes following every move Kit made.

"But what is it saying?" said Kit, his eyes wide open and staring at nothing as he listened to the faint, rhythmic roar trapped deep within the creamy whorls of the shell.

Jonathon smiled. "Close your eyes Young Kit," he instructed. "Listen with your heart, and then tell me what you hear."

Kit obeyed, closing bright, chocolate brown eyes and screwing his face up tight in concentration. A moment later his eyes popped open in surprise and delight. "Jonathon, I think I heard it. I really did. I could hear the sun and water and birds all talkin'—and they're talkin' to me too." He laughed out loud.

Jonathon smiled again, reaching out to place his hand on Kit's shoulder, giving it a little rub, and then as though even that small movement exhausted him, he leaned back on his pillows. "You have a good heart and mind, Kit. You'll make a wonderful Jedi warrior."

Kit smiled and reached over his shoulder to pat his *Star Wars* light saber. He shook the great shell and put his small ear against it to listen once more.

He looked up. "Do you want to listen?" But Jonathon's head was turned on the pillow, and his eyes were closed. Kit lay the big shell down on the bedspread and wriggled off the bed, taking care not to disturb his old friend. He knew Jonathon needed to sleep a lot in order to get better.

A collection of smaller seashells marched across the ledge near the window, beckoning to Kit. He picked up a starfish, chuckling at how the rough sea creature tickled his fingers. He picked up a clump of white coral, but quickly set it down again. The coral was really pretty, but it was prickly to hold. He carefully lifted a fragile sand dollar and shook it next to his ear, listening for the rattle of the doves that lived inside. One day when Kit was visiting, Jonathon had taken a sand dollar and broken it apart to show Kit the tiny doves that lived inside. Kit had them sitting on his windowsill at home.

Next, he reached for a spikey shell with a smooth pink center. Kit turned the shell over and over in his hand, feeling first the sharp points and then the pearly soft inside. He put the shell to his ear, and although he could hear the barest whisper, the sound from this smaller shell was so faint he could barely hear it. He wondered why. Pursing his small lips, and wrinkling his brow, he pondered the problem. Finally, his brow cleared as an idea came to him.

Maybe, thought Kit, if I put the shells in water, their voices will be louder and I'll be able to hear them better. He picked up a large clamshell. Filling it with the smaller shells, he carried them down a short hall to the bathroom. Nudging the door partway shut with his butt, he moved over to the sink, which hung low on the wall so that residents in wheelchairs could reach. The height was also perfect for a four-year-old who loved to play in the water.

Kit tripped the stopper in the bottom of the sink and filled it with cold water. He could see fine from the mellow light cast by a small nightlight set into the wall above the sink. Carefully, so that he would break none of the fragile shells, he slid them into the sink.

The hallway door whooshed open, and Kit froze as he heard someone enter Jonathon's room. If it was his mother, he knew he was in for a scolding for getting Jonathon's shells all wet. He was only a little worried about his mom though, because she knew that Jonathon let him play with the shells. If it was a nurse, he was a little more worried. She might not understand, and he might get in big trouble.

Silent as a small creature of the night, Kit peered around the edge of the bathroom door as the light in Jonathon's room clicked off. From where Kit crouched next to the sink, he could no longer see the bed, only its shadow with Jonathon's form lying still in the center. He could see another shadow moving across the room to the bed. The shape was big and scary. It didn't look like his mother. It didn't look like a nurse either. The shadow was so tall, it reached almost to the ceiling of the room. The shadow stretched long spindly arms up over its head and pulled a funny, square hat down over its face.

Kit's eyes grew wide. The shadow looked like, like ... suddenly Kit knew exactly who the shadow was. It was Darth Vader from *Star Wars*. He shrank back against the bathroom counter as the shadow pulled the pillow out from underneath Jonathon's head and placed it over his face leaning hard with long, shadowy arms.

Kit saw Jonathon's arms shoot up and push at the shadow, but the shadow wouldn't let go. The shadow was hurting Jonathon. Kit's heart pounded. His mouth was dry. He didn't know what to do. He wanted his mother, but he was afraid the shadow would get him so he crouched small and silent as the shadow replaced the pillow under Jonathon's head, straightened the blankets, pulled the funny hat off his head, and glided out of the door.

Kit gasped in fear. He shot across the room and out into the brightly lit hallway, his heart pounding in a frenzy, screaming in the high shrill way that only small children experiencing deep terror can scream.

9:45 p.m. Lani blinked at the sound of voices and sat up straight in her chair. She must have fallen asleep. When she realized that these were not just any voices, but those she most dreaded hearing in all the world, she opened her eyes. Realizing that her face expressed all the distress she was feeling but unable to do anything about it, she looked up as a tall, thin woman fluttered into the room followed by a stocky man.

"Richard, what I want to know is why they didn't call us earlier. You would think that with the enormous amount of money we pay this institution they could keep us better informed about how our son is doing." Judith Emerson's cultured voice was sharp with annoyance.

"Judith," said her husband with more patience than he displayed to any other human being on earth, "they did try to reach us, honey. We were at the symphony and I had my cell turned to vibrate only for some reason … "

His honey was in no mood to listen. "Yes, and that's another thing, Richard. You really should be better prepared for emergency situations like this."

Judith's long, black velvet evening gown swept against her legs. Diamond stars studded each ear and the famous pearls looped around her throat, accenting a thin, elegant face. Silver hair clustered fashionably around her head in a mass of soft curls, not plain gray hair either, but that dark, almost tarnished silver with bright glints throughout.

Lani thought she looked like a soap opera queen. Judith finally noticed Lani sitting next to Paul, holding his hand. As usual, her sharp black eyes started at the top of Lani's head and traveled all the way to her feet. As usual, Lani immediately wanted to smooth her wildly curling red-gold hair, adjust her clothing, and apologize for her appearance. She resisted the urge, but was sure she had a smudge on her nose, ripped panty hose, spinach in her teeth or something out of place. Judith Emerson did it to her every time. No, she amended quickly, she allowed Judith to make her feel inadequate. Lani straightened her shoulders and sat up in her chair, determined to be polite and in control, no matter what Judith said or did.

A tall man in a black cashmere coat entered the room behind

the Emersons, followed by one of the most beautiful women Lani had ever seen. The man she didn't know. The woman she did.

Oh great, thought Lani to herself. This is so not what I need. An audience. This particular audience had never been a treat during the best of times, which this definitely was not. For a moment, no one spoke. She looked with annoyance at the man, wishing he had the decency to go wait in the lobby. He didn't. Instead, he stared right back at her, steel gray eyes taking in every detail as he looked first at her and then at Judith.

"Long time no see, Lani," said the woman next to him with the amused smile and drawl that had never failed in all the years they'd been acquainted to make Lani feel as though she were three inches tall.

"Jennifer, if you would like to visit for a time with Jonathon, we can pick you up when we're through here," said Judith with a regal air.

Jennifer Sutton was Jonathon Sutton's adopted daughter and Paul's ex-girlfriend, but in Lani's private thoughts she would always be Jennifer the Perfect Female or JPF for short. She knew that from day one, Paul's mother and father had compared the two of them and found Lani to be sadly lacking.

"Not tonight," said Jennifer. "I'll stop by tomorrow. He's bound to be sleeping by now, and I don't want to disturb him." Looking up at Mac, she explained, "Remember, I mentioned the other day that my father was paralyzed in a skiing accident? Another time, I'd like to introduce you to him."

Leaning against the doorsill, hands in her pockets, Jennifer's amber eyes drifted from Lani to where Paul lay in the bed. A look of discomfort, quickly masked by a bored, but socially appropriate expression crossed Jennifer's beautiful face, as though she wished she were anywhere in the universe instead of where she was. Lani looked in awe at the flawless makeup and the smooth, perfectly styled dark hair. Again, she resisted the urge to smooth her own hair and reach for the nearest lipstick.

"Hello, Jennifer." Lani returned her attention to her ex-mother-in-law. She braced herself for what she knew was coming.

Always the gracious socialite in any situation, Judith Emerson said in a stiff voice, "Well, good evening, Melanie. I have to say that I'm surprised to see you here. We only this minute received word ourselves that Paul is not responding to his medicine, and we rushed over as soon as we could. But I see that somehow the nursing staff thought it was more appropriate to inform you first about my son's condition." Judith Emerson was clearly overwrought, or she would never have overtly criticized Lani in front of strangers. Her tactics were usually much more subtle and painfully pointed.

"Jennifer, you of course, are already acquainted with Melanie," she said turning to the couple standing inside the door. "Mac, please allow me to introduce Melanie Emerson, my son's ex-wife. Melanie divorced Paul after he was injured."

Oh good, thought Lani. The implication was clear. Lani was a schmuck who had abandoned Paul instead of staying by his side as any faithful, loving wife would have done. Only, Judith left out a few of the rather pertinent details, details she'd refused to believe, even when Paul confessed what really happened that last awful night. It was easier for her to believe Lani was a schmuck.

She took a deep breath. Judith Emerson never failed to have two effects on her. The first was that no matter what the situation, or how well Lani thought she had prepared for it, in the end she always felt inappropriate and gauche.

"Well, Lani, perhaps you could leave those of us who are still Paul's family alone with him." Judith gestured toward the door. She looked around the room for a moment, and then asked, "Where is Christopher? Don't tell me you left him alone again with a babysitter."

Oh shit. Lani closed her eyes in surrender. Another implication. An implication that Lani was a wild woman who had three things on her mind: sex, drugs, and rock and roll, and her son was a poor little soul, neglected and left alone to fend for himself.

In spite of her good intentions, the second effect Judith Emerson always had on her kicked in, and Lani opened her mouth and let her thoughts fall out—pure and unadulterated. It happened every time they were together. No matter how hard she tried, Lani could never keep her mouth shut and the words boiling inside unspoken.

"Well, in the first place, Judith, I couldn't afford a babysitter even if I wanted to use one, and of all the people in all the world, you know exactly why. In the second place, I know exactly where Kit is, and for your information he has my permission to be there. Besides, as far as where my son is at any given moment—that really isn't any of your business, is it?" Lani spit the words out with fury and then with fury was immediately humiliated at her lack of restraint. It happened every time.

Judith reached out a trembling hand to Richard who stepped forward, his mouth pressed into a grim, angry line. Paul once said to her that when his father was really upset his lips entirely disappeared—and then he had demonstrated in such a comical way that Lani had whooped with laughter. Well, she wasn't whooping now.

She looked at Paul's mother who was clearly very upset at his condition and was immediately sorry for her outburst. "Oh, Judith, forgive me. I know you're upset about Paul ... "

Richard put an arm around his trembling wife. "I think you'd better leave now, Melanie. You don't belong here, and you're upsetting Judith."

Cheeks flaming, Lani raised her chin high, picked up her purse, her coat, and Kit's ski jacket, and walked with as much dignity as she could to the doorway. Wave after wave of heat flooded her face as she approached the couple standing in her way. The man looked back at her impassively, while Jennifer looked from Judith to Lani, one perfectly plucked eyebrow raised in commiseration.

Lani raised her chin even higher, looked directly at Mac and said, "Excuse me," as politely as she could. His gray eyes looked into hers, invading her privacy. She shut down behind the surface of her eyes, allowing him no access to her thoughts or feelings and moved past him into the hallway.

Upset with the Emersons' treatment of her, and even more upset with her own lack of control, Lani never even saw the young man with the motorcycle helmet tucked under one arm as he moved quickly toward her down the hallway. Nor did she register the fact that he stopped near the drinking fountain and while he pretended to drink, watched every move she made.

Right before she reached Jonathan's room, Kit shot out of the doorway, his *Star Wars* light saber in one hand screaming, "Mama, Mama, Darth Vader hurt Jonathon. We've gotta help him. Quick. Come on."

He pulled at her hand. Although, she was usually sensitive to Kit's imagination and willing to play along with him, Lani had one thought in her mind at that moment and it was to get out of the nursing home. She followed Kit's small form to Jonathon's room and looked through the doorway. Jonathon lay quietly in his bed. He often fell asleep during Kit's visits. His stamina was poor.

"Hush, sweetie, hush. Jonathon's sleeping."

"No, no, he isn't sleeping. Darth Vader hurt him."

Lani herded Kit back down the hallway. She looked up to see Mac, standing in the doorway to Paul's room, watching her with Kit, a strange look on his face.

Once again, she raised her chin and looked him straight in the eyes. Ignoring Kit's exhortations that they go back and help Jonathon, she finally scooped him up in exasperation. He dropped his light saber and reached for it, throwing his mother off balance in the process. Lani was a small woman, and even though Kit was also small, she staggered to support his weight as she struggled to reach the toy he'd dropped.

Automatically, Mac moved to help her, but a lazer look from

Lani stopped him in his tracks. She bent awkwardly, picked up the toy, and with as much dignity as she could assume, she raised her chin and walked away.

As the automatic doors to the nursing home swung shut behind her, she breathed a sigh of relief. Finally, she was out of there. She failed once again to notice the same strange young man lurking around the side of the building, watching her load Kit into the old Toyota Tercel.

9:56 p.m. Damn, damn, damn, fumed the young man moving out of the shadows. She saw my face. She saw my face, and so did the kid. He knew from everything he could get his hands on from the Internet, the library, and the bookstore, that a good assassin never let anyone see his face. Now, he had another job to take care of. No way was he going to get caught. No way, José.

Then he relaxed. All he needed was a plan. His handsome face crinkled charmingly as he thought about how he could begin to control the situation. He breathed a sigh of relief. That's right. He needed a plan. But first, the research. A good assassin never took a step without doing the research.

Pulling a small black notebook and pen out of his pocket, he jotted a note.

He climbed onto his Harley, fired it up, and pulled out of the parking lot, shivering in the cold. Shit, he was going to have to start driving a car until the weather warmed up. Ahead, he could see the taillights of Lani's Tercel as she turned right at the corner. He smiled again. A single chick and a little kid? No problemo.

Chapter 2

How did that old song go about working in a coal mine? thought Lani with dark humor. Something about five o'clock in the morning, up, gone, and exhausted before the day began. Well she could definitely relate to the exhausted part. Oh Lord, was she ever tired.

It was six o'clock in the morning in Lani's world, and she had just opened for business. She was a little peeved at her partner Rachel, who had called in to say she would be late—again. Thank goodness she'd found a building with an apartment upstairs. Otherwise, she would have to worry about getting Kit up, dressed, and off to some day care every morning. In a lot of ways, she was really lucky. She could keep Kit with her when she worked. Her customers were used to seeing the small boy playing with his toys in the corner of the shop and many greeted him by name.

Lani was tired though, and definitely running out of steam working both ends of the shift. She needed to talk to Rachel about taking on more hours, or they would need to break down and hire someone. Problem was? They were finally beginning to get out of the red, and Lani wanted to meet the sales goals she'd set. Besides, she had rigid standards about how to treat her customers, and she was uneasy about bringing on a stranger at this point. Rachel was quite a bit less rigid and had been pushing for some time to bring on extra help. Lani sighed. Maybe Rachel was right. They needed to talk.

The wind chimes over the door pealed musically as one of her regulars came in.

"How are you this morning, Mr. Ambrosiak," Lani greeted him with a smile. "Do you want your usual? A small latte in a ceramic mug?"

The slender accountant shivered and rubbed his hands together. His glasses were all fogged over. He pulled them off and wiped them clear with a large, white handkerchief. "I'm freezing today, Lani. The radio announcer said that it's 30 degrees below zero with this wind chill, so let's make that a large latte for once, okay?"

"A large latte it is, then."

Mr. Ambrosiak stopped in every morning on his way to work. As many of her regulars did, he would order his coffee and settle down to enjoy it while he waited for the bus. Right now, he peered through his glasses at the fresh pastries she'd set out this morning. Her goal was to encourage as many customers as she could to add a scone or Danish to their coffee orders to increase her sales. "Hmmm, what are those biscuits called?"

"These are my new mandarin orange scones, and they're really good, Mr. Ambrosiak. I'd definitely recommend them, and besides they go especially well with a latte."

"I'll take one. You know, Lani, your little Tropical Bean Coffee Shop is an oasis in my day." He pushed his glasses up his nose and smiled shyly at her. "If you only knew how much I look forward to coming in every morning."

"Thanks for the feedback, Mr. Ambrosiak. You're one of my very best customers, and what you think means a lot to me." Lani knew that Mr. Ambrosiak's wife, Carole, had died several years earlier from breast cancer. He had become one of her first regulars, and she suspected that he came into the shop every day as much for some human companionship as he did for the coffee. He often stopped by in the evening as well and sat reading the paper for a while before returning to his empty house. The fact that he called The Tropical Bean an oasis in his day filled her with satisfaction. It meant that her vision was working.

Lani had worked on her business plan the entire time she was completing her master's degree, refining her vision and trying to come up with a unique selling proposition that would differentiate her coffee shop from the competition.

For example, one way of describing her vision would be that she crushed little brown beans in a grinder, poured hot water through them, and sold cups of the resulting beverage to whoever walked in off the street. Her own vision went far beyond the mere making of a beverage, as she'd described the previous evening to Beth. Her goal was to create a relaxing, unique atmosphere in which customers would want to return again and again for social interaction and to be part of a community. The coffee and treats she sold were part of the deal.

She had modeled her vision after Caribou Coffee because she believed those owners had done a phenomenal job in creating a deep woods cabin atmosphere for customers. In fact, Lani had been an avid customer of Caribou Coffee when she was in college, often going out of her way to go to a Caribou Coffee Shop instead of to another with less atmosphere. She wanted to emulate their success, but from a different angle.

The way she figured it, she was starting her business in the upper Midwest. For most Midwesterners, snow and ice were challenges they faced a hefty portion of each year. In the middle of the winter, the urge to go somewhere warm and tropical was a dream harbored by the majority and yet realized by a minority who had the money to travel. So, Lani had worked hard to create an atmosphere for her shop that would provide people with the illusion of the tropics.

A bright mural of a tropical ocean scene stretched around two sides of a 30 x 20-foot room. The mural blended cleverly with the interior decor, making it appear as though the shop itself was the interior of a hut built of bamboo with a series of wide, open arches overlooking the ocean. Rachel had cleverly painted the mural so that it looked as though you could walk right out onto a patio leading down to sparkling turquoise water.

Lush, painted tropical flowers and plants blended with real potted white and yellow orchids on slender stalks, while orange and fuchsia hibiscus the size of small trees and a variety of other flowering plants added depth and reality to the mural. More orchids and plants hung from the ceiling where several fans revolved in lazy circles, while tall palm and ficus plants provided privacy between clusters of glass-topped wicker tables.

Rattan chairs beckoned customers with their bright green, yellow, and orange flowered cushions. In one corner next to a small rattan coffee table, a hanging chair lured single customers to relax in its depths with a good book. In another corner, a pair of Peacock rattan chairs invited intimate conversation. The hypnotic sound of the ocean ebbed and flowed in the background, occasionally mixed with the music of macaws, small tropical birds, and other jungle animals.

Lani couldn't have been happier with the results, and figured an added bonus was that she got to spend her working hours in such a lovely atmosphere.

As Lani gave Mr. Ambrosiak his change, he looked around the shop. "Where's Rachel this morning? I thought she worked the early shift?"

It was no secret that Mr. Ambrosiak had a not-so-secret crush on Rachel who never failed to flirt shamelessly with him every time he came in. But then, Rachel never failed to flirt shamelessly with any male who came within a hundred yards of wherever she happened to be.

Lani smiled gently. She knew that Mr. Ambrosiak was quite genuinely smitten with Rachel, and unlike her carefree friend, she tended to be very careful to respect his feelings. "She got held up this morning, but I expect her soon."

The chimes pealed again, and Lani's morning took off like a rocket. For the next 90 minutes, she greeted and served her customers nonstop. Lani always had a big smile for everyone. If a customer looked sad or tired, she wished them a happy day and tried to add a special word of encouragement. Her regulars came in as much for Lani's smile and her kind words as they did for her coffee and pastries.

Rachel breezed in at about 7:00 and pitched right in. With her dark brown hair hanging to the middle of her back in symmetrical cornrows, her smooth cinnamon brown skin, and sparkling black eyes, she fit right in with the tropical theme. When the mood hit her, she'd even greet customers with a lovely Caribbean lilt to her voice, and since she'd practiced the accent quite a bit, to Lani's ears it sounded quite natural, and the customers loved it when she went into one of her routines.

The mandarin orange scones were a huge success. One out of three customers tried them and several placed orders for a half dozen or more. Lani was delighted.

Traffic finally died down about 8:30, and Rachel dropped into one of the high-back rattan peacock chairs, fanning herself frantically. "Lani, quick, I need a double mocha cappuccino or I'm going to expire from exhaustion. Such a night I had, you wouldn't believe. But Jeremy is absolutely gorgeous—and he is worth every bit of exhaustion. I just need a few decades to recover."

Lani automatically reached for the stainless steel milk steamer and a large glass mug. Then she stopped, shaking her head in disbelief, and put both items down on the counter to turn and face her shameless friend.

"Rachel, you wretch. Get your butt over here and make your own cappuccino. I'm not even supposed to be on duty until noon today."

"You're right, Lani. I know you're right." Rachel smiled with the tiniest trace of contrition. "You know, I never mean to be a jerk, it's hard trying to fit in work, school, painting, and everything else altogether." Everything else was dating every respectable male in sight, and occasionally some who were not so respectable.

Lani immediately felt guilty for snapping at her best friend. "Oh Rachel, you're not a jerk. I never meant to imply that. In fact, if it wasn't for you investing in this shop, I'd never have had enough capital to get it going."

"Enough, enough already. The Tropical Bean is a fabulous idea, and we're going to be soooooo rich. I'm lucky you counted me in." Rachel jumped up, gave Lani a quick hug and busied herself at the counter. She set two mugs out and filling them both, dragged Lani over to one of the small glass topped tables, pushed her down into the soft, brightly cushioned chair, and set her coffee in front of her. "There, drink up and relax. I'll take over now. Where's the Kit kid? He's sleeping kind of late today, isn't he?"

"He had a bad night. Actually, we both did," said Lani, blowing on her cappuccino to cool it. "We went to see Paul. He isn't doing so well." She sighed.

Rachel frowned. "You know, Lani, I'd never tell you what to do, well yes, I guess I probably do tell you what to do a lot, don't I? Anyway, don't you think maybe it's time to get on with your life? I mean after all, you divorced Paul more than two years ago, and yet you go visit him every week. Then you come home sadder than you were before you went. It's time to start over, girlfriend."

Lani's spirits lifted, and she grinned at her friend.

Encouraged, Rachel raised both eyebrows and wiggled them suggestively. "I've got just the guy for you. In fact, I've got a few I don't need any more that you can choose from. Who knows, you might even like one, and God knows I can't take care of all of them myself. I need help."

She fanned herself with one hand, feigning exhaustion, but

when Lani didn't smile immediately in response, Rachel reached out and silently squeezed her hand.

Lani blinked some suspicious moisture from her eyes, suspicious because she claimed she never cried anymore. Instead, she gave a husky little laugh. "Oh Rachel, you've always got the perfect guy lined up. If I went out with every guy you claimed was perfect, I'd never have time to do my nails." She held up small, capable hands, sporting short unvarnished nails. "Oh yeah, I don't have time to do them anyway."

"You're avoiding the issue," said Rachel sternly. "As usual. And as usual, I'm ignoring the fact that you're ignoring the issue. Know what I mean? Hey, I'm your best friend. Come to think of it, at the rate you're going, I'm your only friend. Talk to me baby, talk."

"Oh Rachel, you know I can't leave Paul all alone. He was there for me when I was so lonely and needed someone."

Rachel snorted. "Yeah right, he was always high when you were so lonely and needed him is what I remember. I don't know that he was ever there for you."

"Yes, he was, and, he made me laugh. He was my friend. In fact, besides you, he was my only friend. I don't know any other way to explain it. Except for that one time with Kit, he never tried to hurt either one of us. In fact, to this day, I don't know what he ingested to make him behave that way. I know the two of you never really got along, but I truly cared for him. I still do." Lani cleared the huskiness from her voice.

"You're a good friend, Lani. Most people would have abandoned their spouses in that situation, let alone their ex."

"Well, the reason I went over last night was because Beth called. You remember Beth, right? She's one of the nurses. At any rate, Paul has pneumonia again, and he isn't responding to the antibiotics, so I went to check on him. So did his parents," she finished in a flat voice.

"Oh shit. I wish I could have been a fly on the wall during that visit. Did the Old Bitch do her usual once over? Was she wearing velvet and diamonds? That is her usual attire for visiting at a nursing home, is it not?" Rachel may not have liked Paul very much, but she detested Judith Emerson. The few times they'd come into contact, Judith's snubs were more evident than ever as was her annoyance with Rachel who deflected them with flip, dry humor.

Lani remembered one particular occasion shortly after Kit was born. She was exhausted from getting up every three hours during the night to nurse Kit, carrying the infant in a sling to class every morning, and studying every minute in between. She tried to do the natural thing, from breast-feeding to cloth diapers. She was determined to be the perfect mother.

One day, when she was feeling particularly exhausted, Judith showed up at her door unexpectedly. Lani hadn't slept more than an hour or two the previous night. She answered the door still wearing the old T-shirt she wore for sleeping. Her hair was hanging around her head in tangles, and Kit was cradled in one arm, screaming because his breakfast had been interrupted by the doorbell.

Judith swept in and took one look around at the dishes piled in the sink, the dust bunnies lurking in the corner, and the unfolded laundry heaped high in cloth mountains on the living room couch. Books and papers, pens and pencils covered the kitchen table.

"My God, Lani, what's wrong with you, look at this place."

Lani had been speechless. She knew that Judith had had a housekeeper when Paul was born, and she understood that Judith wasn't trying to be cruel, she was just being, well, Judith. But then, suddenly fatigue and the pressures of new motherhood rolled over Lani in one huge wave. A large tear welled in one eye, and no matter how hard she tried to hold it back, it rolled right down and off her chin to plop on Kit's screaming, little red face.

Judith, trying to be kind, but somehow missing that particular gene, walked over to the couch and in her fastidious Judith-like way used two fingers to pluck a cloth diaper from the pile waiting to be folded.

"Lani, these are awful. Why don't you let me pay for a laundry service? You can't put that darling baby into these awful yellow diapers. The service will pick them up every few days and replace them with fresh, clean white diapers. Let's do it."

The darling baby screamed louder. Lani's breasts responded to her baby's cry by leaking quite visibly, and Judith looked away in embarrassment, having previously made her point about the superior, far less messy merits of bottle-feeding. Another tear rolled down Lani's face.

At that moment, Rachel sauntered into the apartment through the open doorway. It was obvious she'd heard every single thing that Judith had said. She walked over and hugged Lani, dropped a kiss upon her godson's distressed little face, and drawled, "Well hot damn, there you have it Lani. That's what we've been doing wrong all these weeks."

Lani and Judith looked in surprise at Rachel, not understanding where she was headed with her comment. Rachel shook her head, gazing at the pile of unfolded diapers. She pointed at them.

"The diapers. All this time, we've just been hangin' 'em up and lettin' 'em dry. We were supposed to wash them first." She slammed her hand against the side of her head. "How dumb could we be!"

Lani laughed out loud at both Rachel's words and the funny, but ludicrously fake expression on her face. To this day she believed that Judith had never forgiven her for laughing. Their relationship, which had never been strong to begin with, deteriorated from that day on no matter how hard Lani tried. After a time, she quit trying very hard at all.

Today, feeling lighthearted at the memory and warmhearted at all the unwavering support Rachel had provided her over all the years of their friendship, Lani laughed out loud again. "Yes, she was wearing velvet and diamonds."

At Rachel's hoots of disbelief, she laughed even harder, tears forming and spilling out of her eyes. "Rachel stop, stop, there was a reason for the velvet." She gasped for breath. "There was a reason. They had come directly from the symphony and … "

"Oh yes, of course, the symphony. Lah di dah! What was I thinking of?" said Rachel, raising her nose into the air and striking a pose. "One always does wear velvet and diamonds to the symphony. How silly of me to have remarked upon it." She held her hand up, "But wait, I must know. The pearls, was she wearing the pearls?"

Now Lani was roaring with laughter, and she could barely catch her breath. "Yes, yes, she was wearing the pearls. Rachel, stop it, you wretch. It wasn't funny at all last night. She swept into the room, griping away at Richard like she does, and when she saw me, I swear she'd have dropped her teeth if they'd been fake. God, I was so embarrassed. Then, she looked around for Kit, and when she didn't see him, she implied that I always left him with babysitters. She made it sound like all I did was carouse around looking for men."

Rachel nodded in approval, "Well, that's what you should do. Not the part about leaving Kit alone, the part about carousing."

"Ha, ha. That would give Judith and Richard all the ammunition they need to try and take Kit away from me."

Rachel stopped laughing. "They didn't bring that up again, did they? No judge in his right mind will take a child away from his mother and give him to the grandparents. No way. Not in this day and age."

"No, that wasn't the issue last night." Lani gave a short, angry laugh. "You know, I don't understand why I let her get to me like I do. Last night I was so embarrassed. They weren't alone, you know, that was part of it. They must have invited Jennifer and some really stuck-up guy to the symphony with them. You should have seen him. He looked right through me as though I were no more important than a mosquito."

"Well, what did he look like? Was he cute?" Rachel raised her eyebrows high and flung out both hands in question.

Lani looked at her for a moment in irritation. "Cute? I don't know. He stood around listening to everything Judith was dishing out. In my opinion, he was being really rude. I wanted him to go away and stop listening in on what was obviously a private conversation. I didn't particularly notice whether he was cute or not. He was tall. That's all I remember."

"Lani, everybody is taller than you. That's all you noticed? Sheesh, we're gonna have to work on your perceptive capabilities." Rachel sighed dramatically, shaking her head in disbelief at Lani's misplaced priorities. Lani went on ignoring Rachel's dramatics. She'd seen them all before.

"I especially liked the part when Judith asked me to leave the room so that Paul's family, the family who hadn't deserted him you know, could be alone with him. She made it sound like I divorced him after he was injured. As if I would ever desert anyone who was hurt," Lani said indignantly. "Well, between making me out to look like the worst mother in the world and a disloyal bitch of a spouse who ditched her sick husband the moment he was defenseless, I'm sure I have no reputation left in this town at all. And then, Rachel, when I went looking for Kit, he ran out of Jonathon Sutton's room, with that silly lazer thing you bought him, screaming about Darth Vader."

She turned a stern look at her friend. "By the way, I wanted to talk to you about letting him see scary movies. His imagination is big enough as it is. Now, he's having nightmares."

"Light saber, not lazer thing," corrected Rachel absently. Not fazed at all from Lani's scolding, and catching a glimpse of the young man in question peeking around the edge of the door, Rachel asked again, "Where is that Kit kid, anyway? I may have to go and wake him up by tickling him to bits and pieces."

"Here I am Aunt Rachel," said Kit with a sleepy smile. He had dressed himself in jeans and a blue and yellow sweater.

In one hand, he dragged his *Star Wars* light saber. He hadn't left home without it since Rachel bought it for him after they'd had a marathon *Star Wars* video sleepover the previous week. In his other hand, he clutched the baby blanket that Lani had crocheted for him—her one and only attempt at crocheting. The blanket was in shreds now, and he never pulled it out unless he was sick.

"Why there you are, Sweetie Pie. By the way, wasn't *Star Wars* the very best movie you ever saw?" At Kit's enthusiastic nod, Rachel looked at Lani with a sniff. "I suppose you would have preferred that I show him *Bambi* instead, a nonviolent children's movie if I ever saw one, in which the baby loses his mother after a demented hunter shoots her in the very first scene and then has to learn to fend for himself, hmmmmmm?"

"Bambi's mama dies, Aunt Rachel?" asked Kit with interest. "Can we get *Bambi* next time we get a movie?"

"Sure thing, you little ghoul." Rachel looked with speculation at Lani. "That is of course, as long as your mama says it's okay for you to view such violence."

"I like violence," said Kit, putting an end to that discussion. "Can we get *Bambi*, huh Mama?"

Lani gritted her teeth at her partner who smiled sweetly back in return. "We'll see, Honey Bug. We'll see, okay?"

The chimes pealed, and a young man with a laptop cradled in his arm entered. As Rachel got up to serve him, she leaned down to whisper in Lani's ear. "Hey, he's kind of a hottie, don't you think?" She turned her head towards the front window. "Hey Lani, there's your pet charity case. You'll have to serve her yourself, you know. She won't come inside for anyone but you. Go figure."

Lani jumped up and poured steaming coffee into a large glass mug, put a lemon poppy seed muffin and a mandarin orange scone on a small plate, and set them on the small glass-topped table closest to the door. Then, opening the door, she called out, "Ma'am, your breakfast awaits you."

A tiny woman dressed all in holey black, scuttled in and

perched on the edge of the chair. Her head bobbed up and down as she checked out every other customer in the shop. Finally, appearing to decide that all was safe, she picked up the scone in a torn-gloved hand and took a dainty bite. Patting her lips with the napkin that Lani had placed in front of her, she gave a regal nod approving the morning selection. She didn't speak, and Lani didn't try to engage her in conversation, she just smiled and rejoined Kit for breakfast at one of the tables in the center of the large room.

"I had a bad dream," said Kit. "Darth Vader got Jonathon again. Mama, it was real. I didn't make it up, and I need to go see him today. You know? To be sure he's okay. Oh, and don't be mad, okay, but I left his shells in the bathroom, and I have to put them back on his shelf, 'cause he can't do it himself. Jonathan won't care, though, 'cause he said I could play with the shells. Can we go see him?"

Lani reached out and ruffled Kit's hair. "I'm not mad, Honey Bug. Yes, after supper, let's go see Jonathon. In the meantime, instead of Cheerios this morning, how about an orange scone? It's my newest, biggest seller."

Kit's eyes were huge, with dark shadows. Last night when Lani tucked him into bed, he wouldn't let her go without first a story, then a glass of water, and then another story. He was really frightened. In the middle of the night, he'd awakened screaming and she'd finally snuggled him into bed with her. She'd concluded that whatever shadows he'd seen in Jonathon's room, they must have been really scary. Now, he smiled at their usual routine.

"Yuck, I want O's, Mama, lots and lots of O's."

"Okay, Cheerios it is." She smiled back.

"Don't get up. I'll bring the Kit kid breakfast special in a second," called Rachel.

Her customer settled down at a table in the corner with his laptop, and Rachel rejoined Kit and Lani at their table with a fresh cup of coffee and a big bowl of Cheerios. She fanned herself comically and wetting her index finger with the tip of her tongue, she touched it to her hip, making a low sizzling sound, rolling her eyes, and silently mouthing in an exaggerated fashion, "Wow, is he cute."

Lani rolled her eyes and grinned. Floods might come, riots clamor, but Rachel would always be Rachel.

"Hey kiddo, how're you doing? Got any big plans today?" Rachel was having trouble getting her usual response from Kit that morning. "Hey, what? You don't love your Aunt Rachel anymore? I'm crushed Kit Emerson, I'm really crushed. Now, I'm gonna have to find a new boyfriend darn it, and I was thinking I'd found the perfect guy—even if I have to wait twenty years for you to grow up." Rachel heaved a huge sigh, sniffled dramatically, and looked forlornly out the window.

Kit giggled, "Oh Aunt Rachel you are too funny." He slid out of his chair and wriggled into her lap. "I love you lots and lots and a million trillion gazillion."

Rachel hugged him tight. "A million, trillion, gazillion? Only a million, trillion, gazillion? That's all? How about a million, trillion, gazillion and twenty-nine?"

"Nope, I only love my mama that much. That's the most you can love anyone in the whole world, right Mama." He smiled confidently now across the table at Lani. A million, trillion, gazillion and twenty-nine was their own private joke. She silently blessed Rachel for turning Kit's thoughts away from the previous evening.

"Hey, who wants to come across the street with me to get more milk and a newspaper?" said Lani.

"I do, I do," shouted Kit, dancing and waving his arms all about.

"Well, let's get your snowsuit and stuff. From what everyone's been saying it's really cold out there today."

Rachel nodded. "It's so cold out there, the snowmen's tongues are sticking to their popsicles. You better watch out, or you'll freeze off your nose, Kit kid. No cheating today, it's gotta be mittens, hats, and the whole shebang."

The customer with the laptop bussed his cup and plate, and striding out of the coffee shop, he removed his red stocking cap, stuffed it into his pocket, and pulled out a dark blue face mask instead, settling it on top of his head. Then, he removed his reading glasses, pulled the wax out of his cheeks, and chucked it into the street. He smiled to himself. Keep it simple, right? A good assassin was always prepared, and when he was doing close-up wet work— he liked that term, "wet work,"—you never took a chance that someone might see your unaltered face.

He wished he'd been more careful the previous evening. He felt a momentary flash of anger. Everything had gone smooth as a French silk pie except for the damn kid and the coffee shop bitch.

He took a deep breath. Oh well, it was only a little fuck up. No big deal. Piece of cake. It was a matter of focus, that was all. Besides, his partner would never have to know, because he was taking care of business straight away. He climbed into the dark brown Mazda he'd parked near the shop and drove around the block to the top of the hill. Now, all he had to do was wait. He grinned. A kid and a single chick. No problemo. He had a plan, and it was so KISS it was beautiful. Borrow someone's car, wait at the top of the hill, and mow 'em down. He pulled the ski mask over his face and waited for Lani and Kit to exit the coffee shop.

Rachel waved at Kit as he and Lani trooped out into the snow drenched world. Turning back into the shop, she saw that Kit had dropped one of his mittens on the floor. She shook her head in disbelief. Kit hated wearing mittens. She and Lani could never figure out why, but today was not the day to mess around. The announcer on the radio said 30 degrees below zero wind chill. He'd freeze his little fingers right off if he wasn't careful.

Scooping the mitten up and shrugging herself into her own coat, she ran out the doorway to call them back. Outside the wind was howling. Trying to catch up, Rachel slipped on a patch of ice, and almost fell flat on her backside. As she struggled to regain her footing, she heard an engine roar and looking up the hill to her left, she saw a dark brown Mazda flying down the hill, headed straight for Lani and Kit. She stared for a split second in disbelief sure that the car would slow down. When it didn't, she screamed a warning.

"Lani, *look out!*"

Lani turned, a look of horror crossing her face.

Oh God, there was no time, thought Rachel, there was no time for them to get out of the way. The car roared louder, closer. Lani swooped to gather Kit into her arms, but as she turned to jump out the way, she slipped on the ice and fell. Rachel screamed. Lani didn't pause. She wrapped her arms around Kit, rolled up and over the curb and kept right on rolling down the small bank, her body covering Kit's. The car flashed past, roaring through the intersection.

Rachel streaked across the street. "Oh my god, Lani, Lani are you okay? That son of a bitch almost hit you. What the hell is the matter with him? I got part of his license, don't you worry. We'll call the police, and Lani talk to me. Please tell me you're okay." Tears streaked down Rachel's face as she approached Lani who wasn't moving at all.

She heard a squeak, and sighed in relief as Lani finally moved, rolling her weight off Kit. "Oh baby, did I crush you to bits and pieces?"

Kit looked up at Lani, his face white as the snow in which he lay, blood from a deep laceration spilling scarlet down the side of his face. "Oh Mama, I don't feel so good."

Lani's face turned green at the sight of her son's blood, and she looked sick to her stomach. "Let's get you to the clinic, Honey." Struggling to pick up Kit, she said through gritted teeth, "How stupid could I be to not watch where I was going?"

Rachel snorted. "Stupid nothing. That son of a bitch tried to run you over."

Chapter 3

"**G**ood morning, Shari. How are you today?"

"Beth, I thought you were working the night shift these days. I am excellent. How about you?"

Shari Peterson shrugged herself out of her coat, realizing she was late again, but chattering all the while, hoping to forestall any admonitions from the senior nurse before her.

"I'm working a double shift. The flu has really been making its rounds here, both in terms of patients and staff, and we're having trouble getting in enough help." Beth's normally pleasant smile was absent, her eyes direct. "That's why I need you here. On time. Shari, you are a fantastic aide and all of our patients love you, but you've got to clean up your act, okay?"

Shari sighed. "I'm sorry, Beth. I mean to get here on time, honest, but something always seems to slow me down in the morning."

She didn't mention that what had slowed her down that morning was the very warm, very male presence in her bed, but she smiled at the memory. Flustered at Beth's continuing regard, she stammered. "But, I'll do whatever it takes to get here right on the dot if not before from now on. I promise, cross my heart, and all that jazz."

"Okay, Shari, enough said, but I'm going to hold you to your promise, and that's a promise!" Beth patted her on the shoulder as she passed. "Now hop to it. Breakfast was delivered to the floor."

"You've got it."

Shari decided that she would do everything she could to keep that promise, but she also believed that some people lived to work, and some people worked to live. Now, take Beth Kazmarik for example. She definitely lived to work. White Oaks Nursing Home and its residents were her life.

As far as Shari was concerned that was fine for Beth, but she was different and fell securely into the second category. She worked to live, and her focus was on having a good time. It wasn't that she didn't take her job seriously, though, because she cared about her patients. She cared a lot. However, unlike many of her co-workers, she had no career aspirations to be anything other than what she was.

Shari liked to take care of people, and she thought most of her patients were darlings. She worked hard to always have a bright smile and to listen patiently as they told her about their worries and their aches and pains.

Her favorite patient was Jonathon Sutton. Shari knew that before his accident he had been the powerful CEO of a small software company, but he always treated her as though she were as important as any of the big honchos who came to visit him all the time. He would even ask her opinion about things he read in the paper or heard on the news. Jonathon made her feel as though she had diamonds in her hair and a graduate degree in her hip pocket.

A lot of other people in Shari's life treated her like she was a stupid bimbo. But she wasn't. Even her new boyfriend was starting to talk down to her. Never focused long on any particular subject, Shari's thoughts flitted to the new guy she was dating. Michael hadn't called her once all week, and then last night out of the blue, he'd called her about midnight and expected her to let him come over. Of course, like an idiot, she was so relieved to hear from him that even though she was pulling the early shift at the nursing home, she'd told him to come right on over.

The minute he walked in the door, his hands were all over her. Not that she minded. Michael was a hottie, and she liked where he put his hands. He didn't even want to talk. He grabbed her, pulled her into the bedroom, and the rest was history.

That was another thing. They'd been dating for more than two months, but he'd never once asked her to his place. She knew where he lived, though, and tonight he was in for a big surprise, because she was going to show up at his door with dinner. Shari liked to do special things for special people. She could hardly wait. Michael was the cutest guy she'd ever dated.

Humming as she pulled Jonathon's breakfast tray from the large aluminum trolley, she reflected on how lucky she was. So what if Michael didn't always call. As far as how he talked down to her? Suddenly she felt confident that once he understood how much he was hurting her feelings he would stop.

Shari was an avid reader of *Cosmopolitan* and *O Magazine*. She knew all about how important open and honest communication was. Maybe tonight after dinner, she and Michael could talk, really talk.

Shari pushed Jonathon's door open with her hip. He was still asleep, his head turned away toward the window. Her heart turned over at the sight of him sleeping. He tired so easily, and he seemed to sleep most of the time. When he wasn't sleeping, Jonathon talked about his business, about getting back to it. She knew he was worried about being away and frustrated with how slow his recovery was. Shari was impressed with how brave he was about the disability he would be working with when he did complete his recovery and returned to the workplace. She was even more impressed with his resolution to put as much of his life back into order as he could.

Several weeks earlier, she'd come into the room to find Jonathon holding a letter, the saddest expression on his face.

"Are you okay?"

"Ah Shari, be careful who you trust in this world. Things are not always what they seem, and people are not always who you think they are. I should have listened. I shouldn't have been so harsh. I need to make things right."

After he received the letter, Jonathon started asking almost daily whether his son, Michael, had called while he was asleep, or if he'd received anything in the mail. Shari always went to check with the front desk in case a message had not been put through, but his son never called or wrote. To her knowledge, his son had never visited Jonathon—not even once. The bastard. Michael. How funny. Jonathon's son had the same name as her new boyfriend. The world really was a pretty small place when you came right down to it sometimes.

Shari chuckled, bustling forward, with her usual bright smile.

"Good morning, Jonathon. Guess what I brought you for breakfast? Your favorite. Oatmeal with raisins and brown sugar."

Jonathon didn't stir beneath the coverlet.

"Jonathon," sang Shari, "it's time to wake up now. Jonathon?"

She moved closer, noticing a foul smell in the room. She edged around the corner of the bed, her head tilted, her eyes searching for any motion from the figure in the bed.

Then she saw his face. Shari might not have had a degree in anything, but it didn't take a rocket scientist to tell when someone was dead. She dropped the breakfast tray on the floor, and backed quickly out of the room, her hand held tightly to her mouth.

Poor Jonathon. Life just wasn't fair.

Chapter 4

"Okay, we're almost done. Just one more tiny, little stitch."

Mac MacIntyre pulled the final suture tight, knotting and cutting it off neatly. The little boy before him didn't move a muscle.

"Good boy, Jimmy. I'd say you're really lucky you've got such a hard head. The next time you fall off the top of a ladder, you may not be so lucky. So, I'm going to make a deal with you. Promise me that no matter how much you want something, you'll ask your parents for help instead, and I'll let you dig around in my grab bag for the very best toy you can find. What do you say?"

Jimmy Wilson nodded. At this point in his young career, he was ready to promise anything if only the doctor would finish up and let him go home. Janet Phillips, one of the nurses on duty, brought the grab bag over, and the child started to dig through it.

"Thank you, Dr. MacIntyre. Is he going to be all right, now?" Jimmy's mother looked almost as frightened as her son.

"Well, I'd say that's entirely up to you."

"I beg your pardon?"

"Well, Mrs. Wilson, your son is only five years old, and you have control over most of what he does. He was extremely lucky today. Another day he might not be so lucky. You will of course follow your own counsel, but I'd recommend that you enforce stricter rules if you want to keep him safe. You can take him home now." Mac's words were clipped and curt.

Janet shook her head. She could never figure it out. Mac was so good with the kids, but his bedside manner did not always extend to the parents. Whenever a child came in with certain types of injuries—cuts, broken bones, or burns, he always acted as though it was the parent's fault.

If a child had an illness it was another matter entirely. Then, he was as patient with the parent as he was with the child. Go figure. On the other hand, he was a favorite with all of his elder patients, always gentle, humorous, and caring.

Mac owned the Northeast Clinic. Although the neighborhood had always had its share of families with small children, Northeast was also the home of many eastern European immigrants as well. Ukrainian, Russian, and Polish families had settled in Northeast Minneapolis decades ago, and now many of the patients that came to see Dr. Mac were in their seventies and eighties. They loved him because he took care of their pains, made them laugh, and listened to their stories.

"Dr. Mac, there's a four-year-old with a scalp laceration in Room 4," said Janet.

Mac stretched as he walked the short distance to the next examining room. It was only 10:00 a.m. and already he felt as though he'd been working for three days straight. Lately it seemed as though he was always tired. He couldn't figure it out though. He got plenty of exercise, he'd never needed much sleep to begin with, and for the most part he ate fairly healthy.

He stretched again. He was just so damned bored all the time. The worst part was that he knew he had no excuse for being bored. He was only 36 years old. He was smart, healthy, and had plenty of money to do anything he wanted to do. Problem was, all he ever did was get up, go to work, come home, think about work, go to sleep, dream about work, and get up the next morning to start all over.

Maybe he should go see someone. He laughed. He didn't need a psychiatrist to tell him to lighten his load and refocus his energy on something besides the clinic he'd started up five years earlier. He knew his life was one dimensional, but he didn't particularly want to do anything about it. God, he was so bored.

Mac sighed again, plucked the chart from the hanging box outside Room 4, and opening the door, he walked in with his hand outstretched. He stopped abruptly at the sight of Lani sitting on the hard gray plastic chair waiting to see the doctor. Her son was curled into her lap, clutching a plastic, sword-like toy. He was sucking his thumb, and his eyes were wide and staring. Lani held a towel saturated with quite a great deal of blood against his head. She looked up when he entered. Surprise and something less than welcome replaced the relief that had crossed her face when he first walked into the room.

"You," was all she said before a wave of color suffused her face.

Mac hid his own surprise and the fact that his gut hadn't quite finished twisting at the sight of the red-haired child, bloody, and in pain. His stomach had done the same gut-wrenching twist the night before when he saw the child at the nursing home. "Yes, me. What the hell have you done to your son now?"

Lani's jaw dropped, and her eyes widened. "I haven't done anything to my son."

She swallowed, blinking, and then blurted out. "Let's get this situation straight right now, shall we? I'm the client, my son is the patient, and you're the doctor. My son is hurt, so why don't you just get your ass in gear and take care of him. Or, if your skills aren't quite up to the job, how about you send someone in here who can take care of things."

Lani glared up at Mac. Mac glared right back, disconcerted by his less than professional greeting to what amounted to an almost perfect stranger. Anger flashed back and forth between Mac and Lani, and the thing that really threw him was that he couldn't understand why on earth he had said what he did. The woman irritated the hell out of him. He looked again with discomfort at the red-haired child.

Janet Wilson had entered the room behind Mac with a stainless steel bowl and suturing materials, but now she backed out of the room in haste. Doubled over with what appeared to be silent laughter, she responded in a hiss to one of her co-workers, "The MacIntyre has finally met his match. A few seconds ago, a parent told him off, and boy did he deserve it. You should see his face." The other nurse's eyes widened in surprise, and sauntering past the door, she tried to get a peek in at Lani.

Out of the corner of his eye, Mac saw the entire interaction between the two nurses, but as Janet walked back into the room, she was all polish and professionalism. For a moment, he was disappointed. He wanted so very badly to take out his irritation on someone.

Mac turned back to Lani. He had heard all about her from Judith Emerson during Paul's long illness, and he'd been surprised to finally meet her. She was such a tiny, little thing. In fact, she resembled a small fox curled and ready to leap at him as she stood up with the heavy four-year-old child in her arms. Red-gold hair curled madly about her small head and fire spit at him from the greenest eyes he'd ever seen. Last night, he'd thought they were blue. As she stared straight into his, something connected between them, and he didn't like it one little bit. His own eyes widened and then shut down. He ignored everything she'd said, and reached out to take Kit from her and lay him on the cloth-covered examining table.

"Mama," said Kit reaching for her. "Don't leave me."

Lani moved to his side and took his hand. "No way, Sweetie. I'm not going anywhere. We're going to get you all fixed up, and then we're going to take you home. On the way, I'll call Aunt Rachel and ask her to run across the street and pick up a *Bambi* DVD from Redbox so that you can lay on the couch all comfy warm and watch it, okay?"

Mac rolled his eyes in disgust. Oh well, he supposed most mothers thought Bambi was the cutest cartoon around with all those fluffy little animals bounding about. Lani was watching him and it was though she was reading his mind.

Kit's eyes brightened in spite of his pain. "Oh good. That's the one where the mama gets shot by the hunter and dies, right?"

"Yes, baby ghoul, it is, and you can watch every minute of it. When you're done with that video, we'll put on *Star Wars* again, and you can watch the Jedi knights slaughter all the bad guys, okay?" She looked at Mac with a challenge in her eyes, and his lips twitched in spite of himself. What a little demon she is, he thought.

"No, Mama. I don't want to see Darth Vader. He's bad. He hurt Jonathon last night."

Mac turned to look at the child, remembering how frightened he'd been the evening before. He gently removed the sodden towel from the child's head and examined the wound. It was nasty, but as is so often true with head wounds, it looked much worse than it really was. He sighed in relief, and then turned on Lani.

"How did this happen? Did you leave him alone again?" He turned away, clamping his lips shut. He couldn't believe those words had come out of his mouth on top of his out-of-line greeting when he first walked into the room. For some reason, though, he was feeling really discombobulated and irritated as hell by the effect this small woman had on him.

"No, I didn't leave him alone. I didn't leave Kit alone yesterday. I didn't leave him alone today." She looked him straight in the face, cheeks flaming, words clipped and precise.

"Well, then how did … "

Lani didn't let him finish. "As I explained to my mother-in-law last night, I mean my ex-mother-in-law, I do not owe her, you, or anyone else an accounting for how I care for my son. For your information, we were almost run down by a car this morning. I grabbed Kit and jumped out of the way, but I'm afraid I landed too hard, and Kit took the brunt of the fall. Now, are you going to get on with things here, or do I need to go out there and find another doctor who knows how to handle the situation?"

Mac finally noticed the blood on Lani's face as well. At first, he'd thought it was Kit's, but it was evident upon closer inspection that she had been injured too. The world righted itself, and he was immediately embarrassed at his display of temper. He didn't know what had come over him, but all of his instincts as a doctor asserted themselves. He turned to Kit.

"Hey buddy, look at me for a minute, okay?"

Mac took a small instrument out of his pocket, and shone the flashlight on the end of it into Kit's eyes. "Good, pupils retract appropriately. I don't think concussion is a problem. Now, let's take a look at that cut, okay?"

For the next few minutes, he and Janet Wilson worked over Kit, sponging away the blood and shaving the surrounding hair so they could cleanse and treat the wound, injecting a painkiller so that they could stitch the gash closed.

Lani stood right at her son's side, and when he cried a little at the injection, she didn't apologize for him or tell him it wasn't going to hurt. She just held his hand tighter and told him that of course it hurt, and that if he wanted to cry it was fine with her. Then she told him he could squeeze her hand as tight as he wanted, and she wouldn't even twitch because she loved him a million, trillion, gazillion, and twenty-nine.

Mac didn't understand the smile that flitted across Kit's face when she told him that, but against his will he was impressed with how she talked to her small son. He was puzzled, because she didn't seem to match up with Judith's description of her at all.

He clenched his jaw. He'd been so out of line with her. He seemed to get that way with some parents. He understood exactly why he behaved the way he did, but understanding didn't seem to stop him. He also knew that his staff was confused by his behavior because, of course, they didn't understand, and he had no intention of filling them in about his past. He sighed. He really needed a break.

When he was finished with Kit, Mac picked him up and handed him to the nurse.

"Janet, will you take Kit out and show him our magic grab bag since he's been such a brave boy?"

Kit's eyes brightened at the prospect, and he didn't object when the nurse carried him out of the room.

Mac turned to Lani and pointed to the end of the table. "Now, let me take a look at you."

Lani looked surprised and then uneasy. "Why? I don't need a doctor, I'm fine. If you're through with Kit, we're out of here."

"Sit," said Mac, and to his surprise, Lani sat. He picked up a mirror and handed it her, watching as her eyes grew big. "You didn't even realize you'd cracked your own head open, did you?"

"No," said Lani in surprise. "All I could think of was getting Kit to the clinic. We've never been here before, because I usually take him to the family practitioner who delivered him. I was in a panic, though, and this was the closest place I could get help."

She held up the mirror to examine the gash on her right temple and winced as though now that she knew about the wound, it was finally starting to hurt.

"Look up," said Mac, shining a light in her eyes as he had done with Kit. "Good, I think your head is as hard as your son's." He probed at her temple, causing her to wince.

"Gee, you have some bedside manner," said Lani. "D'you think you could poke at me any harder? Isn't there enough blood for you? You have to squeeze some more out?"

"You have a smart mouth," said Mac his gaze drifting down over her face to the feature under discussion.

Lani opened her mouth and then closed it in confusion at his attention. A small pink tongue crept out and across her full upper lip.

Mac stared for a moment, wanting to rub his forefinger across those soft pink lips. No, what he really wanted to do was to touch them with his own lips to see how they would feel. Startled and embarrassed, his gaze flew back up to Lani's wide eyes. Now, they were a deep blue-green. He'd never seen such eyes before in his life. They kept changing with her moods and, he suspected, depending upon the colors she wore.

Today, she wore a worn green t-shirt that molded itself to the soft fullness of her breasts, complementing the warm colors of her hair and lips.

"I do not have a smart mouth," Lani finally shot back, raising her chin at him as he loomed over her, and looking him straight in the eyes. "I call 'em like I see 'em. I don't believe in prevarication. In my opinion, that's what's wrong with the world. No one says what they're really thinking. Everyone is playing some game or another, but since everyone is playing a different game with different rules, in the end no one really knows anyone else, and the world ends up being a pretty lonely place to be."

"Huh?" Mac's jaw dropped.

Lani tossed her head. "And so, I call 'em like I see 'em. If you don't like it, too bad, so sad." She looked at him with defiance.

Mac grunted in response. Part of him wanted to pursue the conversation. What a perfectly succinct description of the world. He had a million comments he'd like to make in response to her statement, and he found that he wanted to know more about her thoughts.

To cover his confusion, he responded more gruffly than he meant to. "You have a smart mouth, and you talk too much. Hold still, be still, and let me look at your head. I've got other patients to see this morning, not just you."

Lani's eyes sparked at him, but she pressed her lips tightly together and remained silent, even though Mac's probing was obviously causing her discomfort.

"I don't think you need any stitches," he said finally.

"Oh, what a relief for me, but what a disappointment for you," she muttered not backing down one inch as he pressed his lips tightly together in response to her jibe. Mac dabbed at her forehead, his touch gentle in spite of the anger on his face.

"So, what are you so mad about anyway? Or, did you bounce out of bed this morning and hit the wrong side with a great big bang?" Lani shot her question at him, and then as though she couldn't help rubbing his nose in something, she added with an evil little smile, "I bet you always get out of bed on the wrong side, don't you. That's why you always have such a sour look on your face."

She clenched her teeth and stared at him.

"What are you babbling about?" That comment got to her, thought Mac, first with satisfaction, and then with concern as her teeth started to chatter.

"I d-d-don't b-b-babble," she said throwing a furious look at him.

It was clear to Mac that the small woman before him had been scared out of her mind over the injuries to her son, and he knew that now the excitement had died down, her head was probably beginning to pound.

He gentled his probing, and Lani closed her eyes and seemed to relax for a moment. As she relaxed, she stopped shivering and took a deep breath, obviously trying to gather herself together. Then, she stiffened, and as Mac started to apply a butterfly bandage to close her wound, her eyes shot open and she glared at him. Mac gently pressed the sticky fabric to her brow, his hand dropping down to the side of her face and lingering a millisecond. He pursed his lips at her expression.

"Now what?"

She rolled her eyes, and pressed her lips together, obviously trying to hold back the words that were on the tip of her tongue.

Finally, she sighed and turned her head the smallest bit so that she could stare straight into his eyes, and Mac gazed back, caught and silenced by her expression and the desire to keep on gazing. For a moment, he had the impression he was looking right into her soul.

Lani broke the gaze and shifted her body as though she were suddenly uncomfortable.

A high, distressed voice came through the door.

"Oh my God, what happened to my grandson? I want to know instantly how he was hurt. His mother wasn't watching him again, was she? This keeps happening over and over, and I'm going to put a stop to it." It was Judith Emerson.

Lani's eyes narrowed, and she skewered Mac with a glance.

"How *dare* you call my mother-in-law! You had no right." She slid off the table, bumped into Mac's large body, and blushed fiercely as she moved away. Grabbing her purse, her coat, and Kit's snowsuit she stormed out.

Mac started to call her back, to explain. Judith didn't even glance at Lani. She swept into the examination room, shooting questions at Mac before he could even close the door.

Lani trembled, trying to ignore the heat suffusing her face and chest. Of all the self-satisfied, interfering jerks. For the past two years, her mother-in-law had dropped hints about trying to gain custody of Kit, and Lani didn't need any jerky stranger helping Judith collect information against her.

"Mama, I gotta go," said Kit looking up in concern at her anger.

Her anger melted away immediately. "Oh, Sweetie. No problem. Come on, the bathroom's over there."

"Is Grandma mad at me?" asked Kit.

"No, sweetie, she's not mad at you.

"Is she mad at you?" He asked, shadows drifting across his eyes.

"I don't think mad is the right word exactly. Let's just say that Mama and Grandma don't agree about some things."

Mollified for the moment, Kit went about taking care of more pressing business.

Downstairs in the lobby, Lani stopped to zip him into his snowsuit, wincing at the sight of the shaved patch of hair and the gauze covering his stitches. At his request, she stuck the *Star Wars* light saber down the back of his snowsuit so that he would have full use of his hands. She marveled at how quickly he'd seemed to recover. Remembering the sight of that brown car roaring toward them, she shivered, wishing she could recover as quickly herself.

Outside, the world crackled icy cold, and the musical ring of the Salvation Santa's bell rang clear and bright announcing to the world that no matter how bad things get, no one is ever truly alone, we're all in this world together.

Lani's heart swelled as it always did when she thought about how many people really did care about what happened to others. The Salvation Army was a good example. The world really was a good place for the most part. Everyone just had to help out and do their part, that was all. Even if you could only play a small part, she believed that every little bit helped to make a difference. She felt in her pocket for her last five-dollar bill. Kit was already ahead of her.

"Mama, Mama, can I give some money. Save a little, spend a little, and always give a little away." Already recovering from his ordeal, he chanted the lesson that Lani had taught him.

"Well, Kit, let me ask you a question?" said Lani, the five-dollar bill at the ready and already knowing the answer. "How do you feel about eating macaroni again for supper?"

"I love macaroni," he shouted. "It's my very best favorite."

"It's starting to be my favorite too, Honey Bug. Here you go, let's help somebody else."

The four-year-old walked up to the Salvation Army Santa and pushed the five dollars into the shiny red pot.

"Bless you son, and have a Merry Christmas," smiled the

volunteer.

Hand in hand and feeling good, Lani and Kit strolled off to find their car through the falling December snow.

Standing in the doorway to the clinic, Mac stood with his mouth wide open as he held the door for Judith Emerson.

She sniffed. "Such poor judgment. That woman never has enough money. My grandson deserves much more than he is getting."

Mac turned to look at her in silence. He had a great deal of affection for Judith Emerson. As a young boy, she had always welcomed him into her home. In fact, if it hadn't been for the Emersons, Mac would never have known how a real family behaved. He felt that he owed her a lot for the warmth she had always provided, especially for him. But he was getting some mixed messages about Lani. In spite of the warnings going off in his head, he wanted to know more about her.

"I'm telling you Mac, this is only one in an entire series of accidents that poor child has endured," said Judith Emerson. "I've asked Richard to start custody proceedings. Melanie isn't fit to raise my grandson, and I'm going to see that he doesn't suffer from any more of these little accidents."

Judith pulled one hand and then the other into a pair of black kid gloves, smoothing each finger carefully into place before looking up at him. "I'm going to need your help, of course."

Mac did not acknowledge her request for help. "There have been other, er, accidents?"

"Yes, many. Oh, she always has a good answer, but she can't fool me. At one time, she even tried to blame Paul for Kit's injury, but I know neglect and abuse when I see them. It's more than time that I took action."

Mac offered her his arm. "Come on Judith, let's go have lunch. You can tell me all about Lani and these, uh, 'accidents.'"

Chapter 5

An attractive man carrying a burgundy briefcase held the elevator door open for Shari, who was loaded down with two bags of groceries.

"Thank you so much for helping me get into the building. That old guy out by the desk would never have let me go up. You see, I'm surprising my boyfriend with dinner," she confided with her usual bright smile.

"No problem, Miss, my pleasure," Jason Madison smiled back.

Although he carefully kept his eye contact in the right places, Shari didn't miss the quick once-over he gave her as she set down the groceries and shrugged off her ski jacket.

She didn't mind. She liked it when men looked at her, and she knew she looked especially nice that evening. She'd dressed in a tiny black skirt, soft matching cardigan, and a fuchsia stretch tube top. A golden unicorn's horn hung from her neck on a fine gold chain, teasing the edge of her cleavage. She'd added height to her slender 5'6" frame by pulling her bright golden hair up on top of her head with a black clip so that a feathery topknot waved gently with every move.

Jason cleared his throat. "Jeez, ma'am, if I weren't already married, I'd ask you to fix my dinner."

"You're so sweet." A trill of laughter spilled from Shari's throat, and then suddenly remembering Jonathan Sutton's face, she went on in a low voice. "Mister, I really do appreciate your help, because it's been a horrible day. My favorite patient died last night, and I found him this morning when I brought in his breakfast."

Shari gulped. "I've never seen a dead person before. He looked just awful."

"God, what an awful experience. Was it a heart attack?"

"We don't know, but the thing of it is? He wasn't the only one who died last night. Three other patients died, too." Shari's voice dwindled away to almost nothing.

"The police think maybe it was murder. They were there for hours today, asking us the same questions over and over. That's why tonight is so important to me. I want to forget about everything and cook my boyfriend a really good dinner."

The elevator door opened on the fifth floor with a musical ping.

"What a world we live in." Jason said with a grimace, leaning forward to hold the elevator open for her. "Have a good evening, Miss, and good luck with your dinner."

"Thank you." Shari looked out into the hallway. "Ooooh, this is the most gorgeous place. I had no idea."

French blue carpet, thick enough to trip an unwary foot, spread out before her. Each entry contained its own small alcove flanked with tiny chandeliers. At the end of the hallway, a series of mullioned windows created a large bay filled with soft blue and green chairs and ottomans. Short bookcases filled with brightly jacketed books invited residents to sit and relax in the sunshine that would pour in through the windows during the day.

The man smiled at her and leaned forward with a whisper. "Wait until you see the apartments themselves. I promise you, you ain't seen nothin' yet. Say, how are you going to get in, anyway?"

"I have the code," said Shari, holding one hand high and rubbing her fingers together. "Anyway, thank you again for your help, Mister. Have a good one."

"You too, Miss," he smiled as he released the door and stepped back inside the elevator.

Shari breathed a sigh of relief as she put the heavy groceries down outside Michael's door. She'd had a brief hassle with the desk clerk in the lobby. It seemed that you couldn't walk in off the street and visit a resident of River Rock Tower condominiums uninvited. If the resident didn't answer and give permission for you to come upstairs, you had to wait in the lobby, which didn't fit Shari's plans at all. She planned to have dinner simmering on the stove when Michael came in.

She had almost decided that Michael might be The One, and she figured it wouldn't hurt to demonstrate what he could come home to every night if he played his cards right.

Shari, one of the middle children in a family of six, could cook like a dream. She knew, because her Gran had told her so, that the quickest way to a man's heart might not be through his stomach, but it was a close second. The more she thought about it looking around, the more she really did think that Michael might be The One.

She pulled a small piece of notebook paper out of her pocket and punched in the code to the apartment. Last night, while Michael was in the bathroom, she'd gone to hang up his coat, which he'd slung over the back of a chair in her small kitchen, and a notepad had fallen out of the pocket.

Of course, Shari had had to take a quick look to see what was in the notebook, and on the inside cover she discovered that Michael had written his address, his telephone number, and the code to his apartment. That's when she got the idea for the surprise dinner. Quickly writing down the information, she'd returned the notebook to Michael's pocket and hung up his jacket before he reentered the room.

Now, as she punched in the numbers, she held her breath, turned the knob, and opened the door. *Yes.* Until she'd actually gained entrance, she'd been afraid that the code wouldn't work and that she'd be locked outside with melting groceries until Michael finally came home. Not exactly the surprise she'd intended.

The man in the elevator was right. The inside of the condominium was even more beautifully appointed than the hallway. The kitchen was a dream. Feeling quite domestic in a luxurious kind of way, Shari set out all of her groceries on the enormous marble-covered island in the center of the kitchen, and started poking around in the cupboards to find the pots and seasonings she needed to complete her dinner.

Unclipping her charm bracelet, she coiled it in a small silver pool on the window ledge above the sink so that it would not interfere when she rolled out her piecrust.

Finally, once she had the au gratin potatoes and the apple pie in the oven, Shari gave herself permission to wander around Michael's condominium.

In all of her twenty-three years, Shari had never been in such a beautiful home. Everything was so incredibly neat, it was almost as though no one lived there on a regular basis. Who would have figured, she thought with a grin? Michael certainly had never given the impression either that he lived in such a place or that even if he did, he wouldn't be a complete slob. Shari frowned for a moment. Gosh, when they'd gone out together, he'd never been especially careful about picking up after himself. In fact, he was always tossing fast food wrappers on the floor of her car. She shook her head. Who would have figured?

French doors led off the living room and into a long sunroom. Pretending just for the fun of it, Shari opened the doors and walked out to sit on a cushy rattan sofa. If she lived here she would always drink her morning diet Pepsi in the sunroom so that she could look out over the trees to where the Mississippi flowed by. Even though the night was cold, the sunroom was warm and city lights twinkled like stars wherever she looked.

After dreaming for a while, Shari got up to check on her

dinner. Things were moving along fine, so she went on with her exploration. The condominium had two bedrooms. One was the master and the other was in use as a den. She started with the master bedroom.

Wow, the adjoining bathroom was larger than the bedroom she shared at home with her two younger sisters, and the tub was fantastic surrounded as it was with pots of orchids and greenery. Who knew, she thought with a smile, maybe they'd use the bathtub tonight—and maybe they wouldn't. Her smile deepened. It would all depend upon how nice Michael was to her that evening.

With a smile on her face, Shari wandered into the den, and for the first time since she'd entered Michael's home, she found clear evidence that someone actually lived in it. The wastepaper basket was filled to overflowing with paper and aluminum Coke cans. In addition, papers covered the desk. Suppressing a small pang of guilt, Shari sat down in the high-backed leather chair in front of the desk so that she could take a look at whatever it was that Michael had been working on. After all, if she were going to have a serious relationship with him, she'd have to know everything there was to know, right?

She'd barely registered that the papers contained some sort of plan, with times and diagrams sketched out in green ink, when she saw an award in the form of a crystal pyramid sitting on the corner of the desk. It read Jonathon Sutton, 1st Place, 1999 Engineering Innovation, awarded by something called the IAEE. Her brow creased in confusion and then cleared. Maybe the world really was a small place after all. Michael must be Jonathon's son, and this must be Jonathon's condominium, but then why hadn't Michael told her? She remembered all the questions Michael was always asking about the residents, and yes, now that she thought about it, he did seem to focus a lot on Jonathon.

Shari tilted her head in confusion. Then, why hadn't Michael visited Jonathon instead of just hanging around and asking questions? Yet she was sure that he hadn't come to visit because

Jonathon always asked whether Michael had left a message at the front desk, and surely if he'd stopped in, Jonathon would have said something about it.

Suddenly Shari heard the front door open, and her stomach felt as though a herd of butterflies had gone on a rampage. What if Michael was angry that she'd broken into his apartment? What if he didn't want company for dinner? Maybe he had a reason for not wanting her to know about his relationship to Jonathon. She stood up so quickly that the leather chair spun on its wheels, bumping into the enormous oak desk with a soft whump. Before she could move away from the desk, Michael appeared in the doorway. He stared at her with an odd expression on his face, and his eyes slid to the surface of the desk behind her.

"Michael," said Shari, forcing a bright note into her voice. "Surprise?"

Michael walked into the room. He said nothing, and his eyes were colder than Shari had thought it possible for brown eyes to be. She shivered, wrapping her arms tightly around herself.

"Michael, say something. I wanted to surprise you with dinner. Please don't be mad."

Finally, Michael opened his mouth to speak. "I'm not mad. Just surprised that's all. But that's okay, because I like surprises."

As he crossed the room with quick strides, his hands curving at his sides, a glimmer of wild excitement replaced the coldness in his eyes, and without understanding her sudden need to flee, Shari backed up, trying to move away. There was no place to go. The oak desk held her captive as Michael came closer and closer.

Chapter 6

Lani stirred the noodles in the pot and looked around her shabby kitchen. Her head pounded, even though she'd taken two ibuprofen. She needed to finish supper, get Kit into his snowsuit, drive over to White Oaks Nursing Home to check on Paul and Jonathon as she'd promised, then come back, work on the books a while, make a list for tomorrow—and darn it, she'd forgotten to turn the dryer back on, and Kit was out of underwear.

She wished she could relax in a chair and have someone bring dinner to her for a change. She grimaced. She couldn't remember a time in her life she could sit back and not have piles of worries and things to do stacked up before her. She shook her head, feeling guilty about the negative turn her thoughts had taken.

"Mama," said Kit absently as he lunged first to the left and then to the right, skewering dastardly aliens in the deadly rays of his light saber, "did you know that two twos are four and two threes are six?"

"Hmmmm," said Lani, her thoughts drifting to her morning's encounter with Dr. MacIntyre. She stiffened. What a jerk. She tried to remember the color of Mac's eyes. Gray. Definitely Gray. Granite, hard, not-one-ounce-of-understanding, I-know-it-all-gray. What a jerk.

"*Mama,*" said Kit. "I'm talkin', but you're not listenin' to me."

Lani turned at once, a smile on her face at the sight of her warrior son. "You're right, Honey Bug. I wasn't listening very well. I've got a lot on my mind today."

Her eyes took in Kit's battered appearance. He had a nasty scrape on his chin and nose. His dark red hair wasn't as curly as hers, but it had a definite swirl to it and the two stubborn cowlicks, one in front and one in back, usually caused her to want to smooth them down. Tonight, though, the shaved patch in front, sporting a large white bandage, caused her to want to gather Kit up into her arms and hang on tight. Lani caught her breath. Oh God, what would I do without him? she thought.

"I said," Kit repeated patiently. "Did you know that two twos are four? And, did you know that two threes are six?"

Lani smiled her megawatt smile. "Why Kit Emerson, do you know that you just did multiplication? How did you do that, anyway?"

"What's multi, multiplation, Mama?" asked Kit.

Lani was delighted. She hadn't taught him to multiply; the observance was his own. Kit's developing intellect never failed to fascinate her. She had no other children to compare him to, and although she realized the possibility existed that he wasn't really a bona fide genius, she was constantly in awe at the things he said and the speed with which he learned.

"Multiplication is a quick way of adding up numbers. Good job, Kit. Your daddy was really good with numbers, too. Later, I'll show you how it works, okay?" She grinned, delighted with her son's first foray into mathematics.

Math had been Lani's least favorite subject in college. In fact, that's how she met Paul during her junior year. One day when she was feeling hopelessly lost with an assignment, she'd gone in search of the math department's teaching assistant.

She explained her dilemma to the tall, brown-eyed man sitting behind the desk. The nameplate on the desk read Paul Emerson.

"Some of these principles you would have learned in high school algebra. So, all we have to do is build on what you already know," said Paul.

"You're talking about that value of X thing, aren't you? The problem is, you see," Lani had admitted with embarrassment, "I don't really care what X is. X didn't make sense to me in high school, and it doesn't make any sense to me now either."

"Ah, but knowing how to calculate X is an extremely important thing to know how to do," said Paul with his laughing brown eyes. He gestured at the whiteboard and said, "Here let me show you." He drew a vertical line on the board, and said, "Let's suppose you want to build a bridge across San Francisco bay."

Lani raised one eyebrow. "I think that's already been done at least a couple of times."

"Yes, of course, but you want to build a special bridge, one that will never fall down no matter what. Are you with me, so far?"

"Uh, yes, I think I'm following you, especially since X has not yet made an appearance."

"But, it's about to," said Paul, drawing several vertical arrows pointing down to the middle of his line.

"These arrows represent a bunch of cars crossing the bridge. Now, it's easy to calculate the amount of weight a certain number of cars represent. So, you already know to the pound how much weight is pushing down. See how brilliantly I've indicated the weight pushing down on the bridge with these red arrows? But what you really want to know is how much weight the columns of the bridge can hold up. The columns are represented by the blue arrows pointing up at the line," he confided as he grabbed the blue dry marker and demonstrated. "That unknown, how much weight the bridge can support, is X. Here's how you figure it."

He drew the formula on the board with a flourish, challenged her with another problem, which she was able to stumble her way through, and then asked her out for a cup of coffee.

Paul made her laugh that day, and he kept on making her laugh right up to the time he became so enmeshed in the drugs he was taking that he was no longer safe to be around.

Lani pushed out the negative memories with a shake of her head. She cleared her throat and called Kit.

"Come on, Honey Bug, it's time for supper."

She placed a plate full of macaroni and cheese and green peas in front of her son.

Someday, instead of noodles and cheese, she would buy whatever she wanted at the grocery store. She would choose Porterhouse steaks, lobster, ready-made quiche—all the groceries she couldn't afford at this point in her life.

When you came right down to it, you had to sell a lot of cappuccino to support even a family as small as hers, not to mention paying Rachel's salary as well. But on the positive side, the Tropical Bean had only been in business for six months, and they were already getting out of the red. She was projecting that the shop would be turning a profit after the first year, especially if she continued to introduce more retail items such as the hand-painted mugs and canisters that Rachel was creating between her more serious art.

Rachel worked fewer hours overall, because of the pottery she created to sell in the shop, and as a result, unless Lani wanted to continue to burn both ends of the candle, they really did need to hire someone to work part time. They'd have to talk seriously about finding someone.

Suddenly Lani grinned. She really had nothing to complain about and everything to celebrate. She didn't have to work for someone else, she got to choose her own workspace, and she was doing what she most wanted to do.

"Mama, tell me again about how you named me," said Kit licking a cheesy noodle off his spoon.

Lani dropped into a chair across the table from Kit and dug into her own plate of macaroni and cheese. When she was as hungry as she was that night, she loved it, too. With a sigh of satisfaction, she settled back in her chair.

"Okay. Here's how it was. There you were, just born. Your little face was all wrinkled and red, and you were screaming at the top of your tiny baby lungs. The nurse put you on top of my tummy so that they could cut the cord …

"My belly-button cord," prompted Kit.

"Yes, your belly-button cord." Never willing to miss an opportunity to teach Kit about the world, Lani added, "It's really called the umbilical cord. But anyway, there you were screaming away, and then, when the nurse put you on my tummy, you just sort of curled up against your Mama, stopped crying, and started to look around. You had the biggest, bluest eyes … "

"And now they're brown," broke in Kit.

"Yes, they are. Because most all babies are born with blue eyes, and then as they get older, some babies' eyes turn brown, like yours did, and some babies' eyes stay blue. So, anyway, there you were, so cute and little. I looked down at your tiny pumpkin head, and it was all covered with red hair, and I thought to myself, why my baby looks exactly like a baby fox, a little kit. So, I named you Christopher Peter Emerson for long and Kit for short."

Kit nodded his head vigorously, his mouth full to bursting with noodles. He swallowed. "I love that story. Do you know anyone else named Kit for short?"

"Nope, only you. I guess you're unique, Christopher Kit Peter Emerson," smiled Lani.

Kit took another big mouthful of noodles, obviously thinking hard about something. He chewed, swallowed, and then launched another question at Lani before she could finish even one more bite.

"What's that word you said I am? Unique?"

Lani laughed. "It means special. One of a kind. You're the only Kit I know, and that makes you unique."

Kit smiled back at her, and as he polished off his macaroni and cheese, Lani heard footsteps ascending the internal staircase leading to her front door. She looked up as Rachel gave a quick tap on the kitchen door and entered the apartment without waiting for an invitation. For once there was not even a hint of laughter in Rachel's warm brown eyes.

"Lani, there's a pol. . . er, an individual downstairs looking for you. It seems as though that story you were telling me about this morning might have a certain validity to it?" She waggled her eyebrows in Kit's direction and Lani caught on at once.

"You don't mean he's really ...?" Lani could feel the blood draining from her face at the implication that Kit may have been in danger the previous evening.

"Yep. That's exactly what I mean, and it may be that our young charge was the last to see him."

Kit, bored with the cryptic conversation, had wandered into the living room and was once more vigorously pursuing evil creatures of the empire.

Lani pulled Rachel out of the kitchen and onto the landing.

"Are you telling me that Jonathon Sutton is dead, and Kit was the last one to see him alive?" She hissed in a low voice.

"You've got it, and right now this very minute, there's a couple of policemen downstairs who want to talk with you. Look, it's quiet in the shop right now. How about I stay up here and keep the Kit kid busy."

"Thanks Rachel."

Lani was almost down the stairway before Rachel was done speaking. Jonathan couldn't be dead. She'd been so sure that Kit had been telling one of his stories the night before. What if she could have done something to save Jonathon? Lani's heart pounded, and she knew she had to be as white as the snow on the front step.

As she entered the back door to the Tropical Bean, a young policeman stood up. He'd obviously just taken a sip from the cup of coffee Rachel had given him, and as Lani came in he quickly wiped his hand over his mouth. The older policeman frowned as he pulled out a notebook, his coffee untouched on the table in front of him.

"You wanted to speak with me," said Lani without any formal introduction.

The young police officer also pulled a notebook out of his pocket.

"Yes, ma'am. I understand that you were at the White Oaks Nursing Home last night about 9:00 p.m.?"

"Yes, I was. Has my son seen something that could have put him in danger?"

The older policeman spoke for the first time. "Well, ma'am, that's one of the things we'd like to talk with you about."

Jennifer opened the door to her apartment and reached out to take one of the bulging sacks of Leeann Chin take-out from Mac.

"Mac, you're an angel. I couldn't think of going out, not with Jonathon dying, and ... " Her bottom lip trembled, and she dashed one hand across her eyes. "I feel so guilty about not stopping in to see him last night, but it was late, and I was so sure he'd be asleep."

Mac followed her into the apartment, took off his coat, and hung it on the polished cherry wood coat rack.

"Jennifer. I'm really sorry about your stepfather, but try to let go of any guilt you're feeling. From what you've said, he was a good man, and he would understand."

"It's not as though we were really close or anything. But he was always good to me when he was around." She laughed a short laugh. "Of course, he wasn't really around much because he was always working. I used to think that one of the reasons my stepbrother Michael always got into so much trouble was because Jonathon was too busy to pay attention to him."

Jennifer's eyes widened. "Oh gosh, I didn't even think of it until now, but I wonder if anyone at the nursing home knows how to get in touch with Michael. I haven't seen him in years, and I haven't got a clue where he's living."

Mac perched on the edge of the kitchen table, watching as Jennifer pulled crisp Chinese chicken salad, cream cheese puffs, Szechuan chicken wings, fried rice, and lemon chicken out of the paper sacks he'd brought.

"Wow, we're not going to go hungry tonight, that's for sure."

"There should also be some tuxedo cheesecake in the bottom of that second bag along with the fortune cookies," said Mac in an absent voice. "Did Jonathon only have the one son?"

"Yes, and even though he didn't spend much time with him, he thought the sun rose and set with Michael, which made it so much worse because he was always getting in trouble. I wonder if he still chews that awful Clove chewing gum and stutters as badly as he used to. He was a bit of a geek, that stepbrother of mine."

The telephone rang, and Jennifer spun toward the sound, almost dropping the container of fried rice she held in one hand. "Mac, it's probably the funeral home. They were going to call me back about when we could have access to the body, but the police said it would be at least another few days. They have to do an autopsy whenever anyone dies violently."

The telephone kept ringing, but Jennifer showed no sign of picking it up. She stared at it as though she wished it would stop ringing.

"Aren't you going to answer it?"

"Yes, of course. How about you wait for me in the living room and enjoy the fire. You don't need to listen to all these sordid details. I'll bring dinner in as soon as I'm off the telephone, and we can eat in front of the fireplace, okay?"

"Sure, I'm easy."

For whatever reason, it was clear to Mac that Jennifer didn't want to talk in front of him, so he wandered into the living room and settled his long frame down onto the black sofa, sighing as his body relaxed against the soft leather.

He gazed out the living room window of Jennifer's townhouse.

Backlit in shining gold and white lights against the winter sky, the Minneapolis skyline was magnificent. Outside, the snow had slowed to occasional hard, icy gusts against the building, but inside, the fire crackled with hot blue and golden flames.

As Mac's body relaxed, his thoughts drifted to the confrontation he'd had earlier in the day with Lani Emerson. What a little spitfire. His lips twitched in spite of himself.

Judith had certainly given him an earful about Lani over lunch. For a moment, Mac's thoughts drifted again as he silently experimented saying Lani's name. He liked the way her name felt against his tongue, like music.

He shook his head in irritation, recalling Judith's assertion that Lani was at best a negligent parent and at worst an abusive one. According to Judith, Kit was always having accidents, and she was becoming terrified that Lani was behind them. She'd asked him if he would be willing to examine the boy, but Mac had explained that he had no grounds without Lani's permission or a court order. Besides, although no doubt existed in his mind that Lani could give as good as she got, he remembered the look in her eyes as she'd hovered over her small son that morning, and there was no way that Mac could reconcile her behavior with any form of abuse.

When he'd tried to explain his thoughts to Judith, she'd snorted, well not snorted exactly, because of course Judith Emerson would never behave with such vulgarity. But she had definitely sniffed as she retorted that of all the people in all the world, she would have thought that Mac understood his moral obligation toward any child who might even remotely have been abused.

Her oblique reference cut through Mac like a razor. The memories from his childhood were dim—but not forgotten. So, he'd finally agreed that he would examine Kit if Lani gave her permission.

Placated, Judith had reached over and patted his hand, and then she'd changed the subject by dropping the bomb about the murders that had occurred right around the time they were visiting Paul the previous evening.

Jennifer drifted into the room balancing a large tray of food and wine in her hands and set it down on the low cherry wood table in front of the couch.

Mac's eyes moved over her elegant figure. Jennifer was probably the most beautiful woman he'd ever met, with her golden eyes and smooth swinging ebony hair. Then, even as he gazed at Jennifer, her image faded, and he found his thoughts drifting to red gold curls rioting over a small imperious head and fire sparking from slanted green eyes.

"Earth calling Mac, Earth calling Mac. Do you read me?" Jennifer dropped onto the couch next to him and shifted her body so that her hip fit snugly against his.

Pulling his thoughts into the present, Mac turned his head against the back of the couch and smiled down at her.

"Would you like a glass of wine?" At his nod, she leaned forward to pour a burgundy stream of Black Opal Shiraz into a glass and handed it to him.

"Hmmmm, these cream cheese puffs are one of my all-time favorites."

Mac picked up a crisp won ton and popped it into his mouth.

"I'm rather partial to them too," she said leaning against him and tilting her face toward him.

Mac looked down into Jennifer's face, and he knew she would respond if he kissed her. Instead, not even understanding why, he reached for another cheese puff and dipped it into the plum sauce before taking a bite.

He thought he saw a flash of irritation cross Jennifer's face, but a moment later was sure he had imagined it. Jennifer was unfailingly good-natured. Of course, he didn't really know her all that well, and this was only their second date. Judith had been trying to get the two of them together for the longest time, but his schedule had been impossible until lately. He was really glad that he'd hired an associate. He was just plain tired out.

Jennifer leaned back against the couch, and looked up through half-closed lids at Mac. Her dark hair fell back, framing her oval face. She smelled of something complex and musky. She lifted one hand and pushed a lock of Mac's hair off his forehead and then stroked his cheek. Jennifer lifted perfectly painted scarlet lips in an invitation to Mac. Hell, he thought, let's not be stupid.

As Mac bent his head to take advantage of the invitation, two things happened. He thought of another set of fuller, pink lips, and as his nose began to brush the side of Jennifer's face, he froze as his cell phone went off. Oddly grateful for the excuse to turn away, he pulled the small phone from his pocket and flipped it open.

"Hello, Mac here," he said in a brisk voice. His face went still as he listened to the person on the other end of the telephone. "Oh Judith, I'm so sorry. Of course I'll come, right away. Give me fifteen minutes." Mac flipped the telephone shut and turned to Jennifer.

"I've got to go. That was Judith Emerson. Paul died."

Twelve minutes later, Mac walked into Paul's room at the White Oaks Nursing Home to find Judith weeping quietly in Richard's arms. Paul's bed was empty, the covers pulled back in a silent indication that the occupant had gone on to another place.

"Richard, Judith, I'm so sorry," said Mac. "Was it the pneumonia?"

Richard nodded at Mac over his wife's head. "The doctor was just here. We'd appreciate it if you would talk to him, Mac, and get all the details. It's funny. No matter how prepared you think you are, when it happens you're still not ready."

Richard cleared some huskiness from his throat and resumed talking. "We want the boy, Mac. Judith and I can provide so much more for him than his mother can. Now, that Paul is gone, we owe it to our son to take care of his. Judith told me about your conversation at lunch. She said you were willing to help us prove that Melanie is an abusive mother."

Mac opened his mouth to refute Richard's comment, but before he could get a word out, he was interrupted.

"Well," said a familiar, furious voice. "I guess Dr. Mac can agree to whatever he pleases, but it doesn't mean he's going to find anything. Abusive mother. How can you say that when it was your own son who threw ... "

Judith pulled herself out of Richard's embrace and rose to her full height, which meant that she towered over Lani. Lani tilted her chin and looked up at her without flinching or backing down one single inch. Mac's eyes were riveted on the small woman, but she didn't waste a glance in his direction.

"Don't say another word, Melanie. That was history, and it's over. Paul can no longer defend himself. I never believed that story anyway, and in fact, I've always thought you made it up because you were tired of being married to Paul. You thought you'd married into money, but when we refused to support you and Paul, you got tired of your marriage pretty fast, didn't you? I told him ... I tried to tell him," and here Judith turned to look at the empty bed, and she broke down into sobs.

Lani turned also to see the empty bed, and her eyes widened, abruptly filling with tears. Mac stood silently watching her. She turned her back on all of them, obviously fighting the tears that threatened. She dashed the back of her hand across her eyes, pulled a tissue from her pocket and blew furiously.

Mac continued to focus on Lani, confused at the mixture of emotions that were coursing through him. He wanted to deny that he had conspired with Judith against her, he wanted to demand an explanation from Lani herself about all of Judith's assertions that she was abusing Kit, and he wanted to pull her into his arms, rest his chin on top of that glorious, soft curling hair, and tell her to cry her heart out. Her tiny sniff as she whirled once more to face the room caused him to take a step forward, but the disdain in her eyes stopped him before he moved again.

"When, when did Paul die?" she said to Richard, ignoring Mac completely. "Why didn't anyone call me?"

Judith raised her head and stared defiantly at Lani. "I told the staff last night that you were no longer married to my son and that they were not to call you about his condition."

"Oh Judith," said Lani sadly, all the anger leaching from her face. She reached out a hand but let it drop to her side when Judith backed away abruptly. Lani pulled the strap of her purse back over her shoulder and turned to face the three of them.

"I'm very sorry about your loss," she said. "But Kit is my son. Do what you must, but you'll never prove that I'm an unfit mother. Do you know why? Because I'm not. If you would like to continue to see your grandson, I would ask you to stop accusing me and start working with me instead."

"Richard, I refuse to give her money. Now that Paul is dead, his trust fund goes to Christopher. She isn't to touch one, single penny."

"Oh for God's sake," said Lani. "I give up." She raked her eyes over Mac, and as she moved toward the door, Kit peered around the corner. His eyes were huge and dark as he looked first at the empty bed and then at his grandparents.

"Mama?"

"It's okay, Honey Bug. Thank you for waiting in the lobby, but now it's time to go home. We need to talk, okay?"

Kit looked once again at the empty bed.

"But Mama, did Darth Vader kill my daddy just like he killed Jonathon? I need to know."

Chapter 7

Rachel hummed *This Kiss*, moving in time with the music as she wiped down the tables and counters at The Tropical Bean. It was 10:00 p.m. and time to go home for another date with Jeremy the hunk. She smiled as she planned a little late dinner, a little late chitchat, and a lot of *hootchka* if she had anything to say about it, and since Jeremy never seemed to complain about any of her suggestions, she was pretty confident that her evening was going to be pretty fantastic. She gave the counter a final swipe, rinsed the rag in the sink, and took a look around the shop.

Now, all she had to do was run upstairs and borrow Lani's psychology reference book so that she could study for her finals tomorrow morning.

A movement near the door caught her eye, and for just a moment, for no apparent reason at all, her heart started to pound. Odd. Rachel always felt completely safe and comfortable at the Tropical Bean. Northeast Minneapolis was as safe a neighborhood as any these days, and yet, for the past hour or so, she had had the oddest sensation that someone was watching her. Creepy.

The shadow at the door moved again. Oh, for heaven's sakes, thought Rachel. It's Lani's Letitia come to visit, only Lani's not here. Rachel chuckled over the incongruency of the name Lani had bestowed upon the homeless woman who would never come inside for anyone else. Although Rachel may have had her doubts about whether the tiny woman was a benefit in terms of drawing customers into the Tropical Bean, it was a mighty cold night. In fact, the weather for the next few days was projected to be well below zero, unseasonably cold even for Minnesota, and Lani had been worrying about the woman's plight and whether she could survive the winter.

Rachel poured a steaming cup of hazelnut coffee into a large paper cup from the air pot she had prepared for her dinner with Jeremy. She slid one mandarin orange and one white chocolate raspberry scone into a paper sack. Although she could no longer see any movement through the front window, she was pretty sure that Letty was hovering in her usual, uncertain way outside. Rachel held the coffee and paper sack high above her head so that they were visible to anyone looking in the window. Moving slowly she unlocked the front door and placed her offering on the front stoop.

Ten minutes later, Rachel was in her car and on her way to an evening of vegetable lasagna and lust.

Shit, it was cold. He rubbed his gloved hands together as he hovered in the shadow of the gas station across the street from the Tropical Bean Coffee Shop. He had thought the sexy broad with the long brown hair was never going to leave. He could see her through the window, shimmying her shoulders and shaking her well-padded hips to a melody that he couldn't hear, while she cleaned up the place. Finally, when it looked like she was ready to go, some old hag started to creep around, peeking in the windows. So, of course, the woman inside stopped everything and put together some damn care package.

He watched as the old lady scurried away around the corner of the building and crouched beneath a patch of juniper trees as the other woman set a cup and paper bag on the stoop. As soon as she retreated into the shop, the old woman crept forward and snatched them up, holding the hot cup close to her face and chest as though all that stood between her and freezing to death in the night of a Minnesota winter was the warmth contained in that paper cup.

He stomped his feet. His toes were dead, his fingers were tingling, and his cheeks were numb. Shit, he'd never bargained for all this hassle. Damn that kid and his mother, anyway. Well, tonight was it. He wasn't going to blow it this time. He couldn't believe that he'd missed them that morning as they crossed the street. But when that blonde got out of her car to pump gas, he'd been distracted. Of all the rotten luck.

He had no trouble popping the lock on Lani's front door in about three seconds flat. He was a pro at breaking into places. He glided inside. Light from the halogen lights of the gas station across the street spilled in through the windows as he carefully maneuvered through the tables and chairs to the door at the back of the shop. For a moment, he was blind when he entered the pitch-black hallway and headed for the steep staircase leading to the apartment above. No problem, he had a flashlight.

As usual, he had every detail planned out. He didn't know the layout of the apartment above, but he did know about the back hallway and staircase, because earlier in the day when he'd come in for a cup of coffee, he'd pretended to be confused about where the bathroom was. That woman with the waist-long hair had looked at him pretty suspiciously for a minute, but really, what could she do in the end but believe him. He was pretty smooth, he thought to himself, and he had his plan and his explanation ready. No problemo. A piece of cake. You simply had to know what you were going to do, plan every little step, and then go do it.

His partner was always nagging him about the time and effort he put into his plans, saying that he was obsessive. Well, he hadn't been caught, no sir, not once, since he'd learned to develop a system and a plan for everything he did. Besides, since the risk in this whole situation was a bit one-sided, and that one side happened to be his, he was going to do things as he saw fit—no other input needed or wanted, thank you very much.

The old house creaked and groaned all around him as he crept up the steep stairway and entered the tiny kitchen. He shivered as his body adjusted to the warmth of the house, his stomach growling in response to the leftover aroma of macaroni and cheese. Carefully, so the beam of his flashlight could not be seen from below, he explored the small apartment, determining how he would make his move. He thought for a moment about Lani's curvy little body. Damn, it would be nice to take a little time and sample the wares, but not in front of the kid. He was definitely not going to be able to get his rocks off if he eliminated the kid first. He shuddered at the thought. Who said he wasn't a sensitive man?

A door slammed below. For a moment he panicked. He wasn't quite ready. Then, he took a deep breath and calm kicked in. After all, he had every move planned out. First the woman, and then the kid.

Rachel turned up the heat and the radio, the first to soothe her body and the second to soothe her soul. Gosh, she was hungry. She salivated at the thought of rich tomato sauce and hot, melted cheese, with a bottle of that Turning Leaf Pinot Noir to wash down the lasagna. For dessert, she thought with a rowdy grin, we'll have a little cannoli, thawed from the freezer, but still quite tasty. Yeah, for dessert, a little cannoli and a little of this and a lot of that.

Then, she'd get up about six o'clock and study for that psychology test. Oh shit! thought Rachel, I forgot Lani's book. She slammed on the brakes, turned into the Quarry shopping center and did a U-turn right in the middle of Target's parking lot. Three minutes later, she pulled up into her usual place against the curb outside the Tropical Bean Coffee Shop.

Frustrated at her forgetfulness and in a hurry to get home,

Rachel ran up the steps and burst into Lani's apartment short of breath and panting from the exertion. She stood still for a moment to catch her breath. Somewhere in the apartment a board creaked.

It's only the wind, thought Rachel. Another creak, and the hair rose on the back of her neck. The apartment felt wrong. She looked around the dark kitchen, shadows looming all around, eerie rose-yellow lights streaming in from the gas station and store across the street. She wondered how Lani could sleep with all that light.

Rachel flipped on the kitchen light, chasing away the shadows. With their departure, her heart slowed, and her courage began to trickle back. She shook her head in disgust. She was only reacting to some innate fear based on the murders at the nursing home and from the scare Letty had given her earlier. For heaven's sakes, she scolded herself. Get a move on. Jeremy's waiting.

Rachel moved through the apartment, refusing to turn on any more lights in an effort to prove to herself that she had nothing to fear. She hummed out loud to dispel the lingering unease.

Squatting down before the oak bookcase in the living room, Rachel searched the shelves for the psychology reference book Lani had described to her. A photograph sitting on top of the bookcase caught her eye. She grinned. It was a new photo of Kit wielding his light saber as he fought off legions of *Star Wars* bad guys.

Suddenly, a dark reflection in the glass of the photo frame moved, and all Rachel's internal alarms went off. She tried to turn, but before she could move, a swish of silk flipped over her head, tightening against her throat with lightning speed. Hard hands jerked her back against a harder body increasing the pressure around her throat and cutting off her oxygen supply.

Rachel's nails dug furrows in the soft skin of her throat, as she clawed at the noose, trying to loosen it so that she could gasp even one breath into her aching lungs. The blood, trapped in her head, throbbed and pulsed. Black spots jabbed at her eyes, and her legs buckled beneath her. Writhing and kicking with every ounce of her draining strength, Rachel's foot connected with the bookcase, and several books tumbled onto the floor with a crash. She shoved her elbow back into an iron-hard midriff.

"Uhhhhhh. You damn bitch." The murderer almost dropped her when her elbow connected with his stomach. In response he tightened his grip on the silk scarf, pulling as hard as he could.

Mac gripped the wheel of his car as he sat in the parking lot of the nursing home, waiting for the engine to warm up. Lord, it was cold tonight. He breathed as slowly as he could to avoid fogging up the inside of the windshield.

His mind was going a mile a minute, no ten thousand miles a minute, he amended, as Lani Emerson persistently invaded his thoughts. Irritated at the memory of Lani's face as she first stared in disdain at him and then ignored his very presence, he consciously dragged his thoughts in another direction.

Poor Judith and Richard. A wave of sadness engulfed him for a moment. He remembered Paul as a little kid always wanting to tag along with his big brother, David. Mac couldn't even remember the number of times they'd ditched Paul when they were kids so they could go about their business.

Richard was so hard on those boys when we were growing up, he thought. It was as though he expected them to take on the entire world. It was no secret that David had signed up for the Marines because Richard had been a Green Beret in the early days of Vietnam. If American machismo were personified, Richard would have been the poster boy.

Although Richard served as Mac's mentor, and clearly wanted Mac to be successful in all that he did, he never expected the same level of perfection that he demanded from his sons in everything they did from sports to scholastics. David had been a natural athlete, but Paul wasn't as coordinated and always had to work hard to try and keep up.

Then David was killed in an accident that should never have happened during a routine exercise two months after joining the Marines. Richard turned all his attention to Paul, who chose to evade any pressure by entirely rebuffing his father.

Over the years, Mac lost touch with Paul, and although he hadn't known about the drugs until after Paul's accident, he believed that Paul used them as a coping mechanism, to feel good about himself. Now, Paul was dead, too. He wondered if maybe that was why Richard was so bent on getting custody of Kit.

Well, that just went to prove his own point. Even parents with good intentions screwed up their kids. He intended to take care of the problem by avoiding the whole marriage and kid thing.

Mac put the Toyota Camry into first gear and pulled out of his parking spot. He'd promised Jennifer that he'd return. He sighed. He was in no mood to be sociable. His thoughts drifted again to Lani Emerson. He grimaced. What was it about that little hell-raiser anyway? She was trouble with a capital T. No, she was terrible trouble, with a double capital T, and he wanted no part of her. He had no doubt that the feeling was mutual. If she could have eviscerated him with a glance, he'd be dead on the floor right now, steamy entrails piled up next to his corpse.

He remembered the child's words. "Mama, did Darth Vader kill my daddy just like he killed Jonathon?"

Mac's skin crawled. According to the police, no one had seen anything. Four murders in a public place, and no one saw a thing. Mac had answered some questions, but it was soon clear to the police that he had seen nothing of merit. What the police didn't know was that Kit had run screaming from Sutton's room the previous evening. The kid had been terrified out of his wits. Maybe he really did see something. Then that morning some crazy driver almost ran both the kid and his mother down in the street. What if that accident wasn't an accident at all?

Mac knew the location of The Tropical Bean Coffee Shop

because he drove past it on his way to work. From comments Judith had made, he also knew that Lani and Kit lived in the apartment above the shop. Making a sudden decision, Mac drove past the exit leading to Jennifer's townhouse and turned onto East 394.

He pressed his foot on the gas pedal, the speedometer moving steadily from 55 to 75 miles an hour, a sense of urgency building within him. He didn't even like Lani Emerson, and yet all of a sudden he wanted nothing more than to be sure she and her small son were okay.

Lani pulled into her driveway and parked. Kit was fast asleep buckled into his car seat in back. Every muscle in Lani's body felt as though it had been beaten twice with a lead pipe. She ached all over. Paul's death on top of the murders at the nursing home and the accident that morning had left her drained and longing for nothing more than a good book and a hot bath. Kit had been tired and confused at the nursing home and had fallen asleep almost as soon as the car started moving, but in the morning she would have a lot of explaining to do.

Walking around the car to pull Kit out, she looked up and saw that lights were on in her kitchen. Odd. She was sure she'd turned them out. She hesitated, and then locking her sleeping son into the car, she moved quietly toward her house. The back door was unlocked. She stopped cold. She may have forgotten to turn out the lights when she left, but there was no way she would have forgotten to lock the door.

A crash from above caused her to flatten her back against the wall entry. She gasped out loud. Suddenly a man slid through the open door. Lani gasped again and then recognized Mac.

"What the hell are you doing here?" she asked in a furious whisper.

Mac moved toward her. He could think of no good reason to

explain his presence. He barely knew the woman. He wasn't sure why he'd followed her home.

Another crash caused both of them to leap up the remaining stairs and into the kitchen. Looking through the arch to the living room, Lani could see a long shadow against the wall struggling with a smaller, rounder shadow. The small figure collapsed. Rachel. Lani yanked open the door to the closet located off the kitchen and scrabbling inside, snatched out an old, oak baseball bat. She ran forward and lifting the bat high over her left shoulder, she swung it with all her might across the back of the larger figure.

The figure screamed, dropped Rachel's body, and swung an arm out knocking Lani against the wall. She fell to the floor gasping in pain and crawled to where Rachel lay in a sad, small heap. Desperately she unwrapped the silk scarf from about her friend's neck.

"Rachel, Rachel, please be okay." Lani cradled her friend's head in her lap. "Mac, help me. Please help me." A thick groan from Rachel caused Lani's face to crumple, and she tightened her arms around her friend.

Mac barreled into the fleeing figure, bringing it to its knees. Light flashed off a silver blade, Mac yelped and let go, and the figure flew out through the kitchen, crashing down the stairs.

"Kit," screamed Lani. "He's outside in the car." She struggled to her feet and would have followed the figure down the stairs. Mac grabbed her and pulled her into his arms.

"Stop it, Lani. Stop it. I'll go. You don't know if he's still down there. Call 911." He gave her a little shake. "Now. 911. I'll get Kit."

Lani thrust the keys at him and ran for the telephone.

The telephone rang at 11:30 p.m. He ignored it. The telephone rang again at 11:45. He ignored it. The telephone rang again at midnight. He sighed. *Damn* it.

"What?" he snarled into the telephone.

"Don't 'what' me, you senseless jerk," said the voice on the other end. "I thought you said you could take care of everything. Is this what you call taking care of things? We've got four dead bodies at the nursing home, and from what I can tell, we've got two potential witnesses."

"Yeah, yeah, yeah," he answered turning to look into the mirror for the fortieth time since he'd returned home. A welt the size of Texas and California all rolled into one swelled in an ugly red and purple mass across his well-muscled shoulders. He could barely pick up a coffee cup in his left hand, and to top it all off, he had a killer headache. He was not in the mood to take any shit from anyone.

"What were you thinking of? I'd like to know. I thought you said you had a plan. You and your plans. Some plan. I'm expecting the cops to come knocking on my door any minute. I'm connected to all of this, you idiot. Don't you understand?"

The voice was getting hysterical as it did from time to time with him. Never in public, though. In public, the person behind the voice displayed total control at all times. He knew how much of that control was pure pretense. Acting, so to speak. But the person behind the voice was really good at the acting, and no one ever seemed to suspect. He knew better.

The aspirin he'd popped when he walked in the door began to take effect. As the throbbing in his shoulders eased off, his cockiness and good humor began to return.

"Chill. Let's review the facts," he ordered. The voice on the other end of the telephone became silent. "Do the police have a clue yet about who was supposed to be the intended victim?"

"No, I don't think so."

"Exactly. That was my plan. Did anyone at the nursing home see me or anything suspicious?"

"Only the child, and now his mother is suspicious. I don't care about the mother, but I don't want that child hurt. Do you understand?"

"Yep, clear as a crystal bell. The mother saw my face. I have no choice but to take her out. The kid I'll leave alone," he lied, neglecting to mention this evening's fiasco. Even now, he couldn't believe he'd tried to kill the wrong bitch. Oh well, no harm done. She'd never had a chance to see his face, so she was a harmless witness. That Lani woman was another story. She'd seen his face the other night and all she had to do was put two and two together in terms of timing and her kid's hysterical exit from Jonathon Sutton's room.

As far as the kid went? He didn't know what the kid saw. It really didn't matter, though. By the time he'd completed his plan, both the woman and the kid would be history. In the meantime, he had no intention of showing his cards to anyone—especially his partner.

"Look, we've got to meet. I haven't seen you for a week." The voice was getting hysterical again.

He didn't really want a meeting yet. It wasn't part of the plan. He needed to complete his work. Then they could meet as often as his partner desired.

"I tell you what," he said. "I've got it all figured out. I've modified my plan, and starting tomorrow, I'll have complete access to that Lani woman. So don't worry, okay? I'll fix it so that no one ever knows she was hit. That's a promise."

Chapter 8

Lani unlocked the door to the Tropical Bean promptly at six o'clock. She was stiff and sore from her bounce against the wall the previous evening, and she was confused and terrified about why anyone would have singled out her apartment for a burglary. Because, she thought trying to comfort herself, that was all the attack on Rachel had really been. She walked in on a burglar, that's all.

The police believed it was a random breaking and entering, and she also wanted to believe it was random. She wanted to believe it with all her heart. Yet, Mac thought ... and here her thoughts became chaotic because she was entirely confused, both about her reaction to Mac and his thoughts that there might be some connection between what Kit claimed he had seen and Jonathon's death.

Her mind shied away from that possibility. That would mean her son was a witness, which meant he was in danger. That meant the accident with the car was deliberate. No way. Her accident yesterday was only that. An accident. A random accident? Just like last night was a random breaking and entering? A chill chased itself up and down Lani's spine, and her stomach turned over. Yeah right.

Lani wrested her thoughts from the "accidents," but then they drifted immediately to Mac. Another unwelcome set of thoughts. She frowned fiercely. Yesterday he'd kept staring at her mouth until she'd begun to wonder what it would be like to feel his mouth against her own. Even a day later, that thought sent warm feelings pulsing all through her body in a way she hadn't felt since she left Paul.

She sighed with a sense of relief. *I'm just a horny broad who hasn't been laid in a long time.* That's all this was, she decided. Because, she detested Mac MacIntyre. She did, and, it wasn't because he'd called her mother-in-law behind her back.

After her first explosion of anger, she'd known that he hadn't called Judith. He couldn't have, because he was with her the entire time. She just blew up at him because of the famous Lani temper. She kept thinking she was getting that temper of hers under control, but then something happened and she lit off on someone like lightning. She wasn't proud of her temper, that was for sure. But the gall of that man, agreeing last night at the nursing home to help Judith prove she was unfit as a mother. She looked down at Kit where he lay sleeping in a little nest she'd made from a comforter and a couple of big pillows. No way was she going to leave him alone upstairs.

The chimes pealed.

"Lani, honey, are you okay? I saw the police cars outside your house last night," said Mr. Ambrosiak as he made his way to the counter.

Lani's face softened. Northeast was a great neighborhood. People really cared about each other. It was the main reason she had chosen to open her shop here.

"I'm fine, Mr. Ambrosiak. Thanks for asking. I had a break-in last night. I'm afraid Rachel was hurt."

At his look of concern, she rushed to explain that Rachel was going to be fine and that she was hospitalized for observation for a day or so.

The chimes pealed again, and for the next sixty minutes, traffic was nonstop. Mr. Ambrosiak settled with his paper in one of the tables by the window so that he could watch for the 7:00 a.m. bus to take him into the city. Sally Denison trooped in, big clunky tennis shoes and all, and ordered her usual large cup of coffee with a morning glory muffin. She settled in with her novel to wait for the bus as well. Before long, Lani had twenty customers spread throughout her shop, some chatting, and some simply enjoying an hour of quiet before the workday began. Bending down to replenish the pastries in the glass case, she heard the chimes peal, but because of her position, she couldn't see who had entered the shop.

"Good morning," said Mac. Lani stood up so fast she cracked her head against the side of the counter.

"What are you doing here?" Some of her customers looked up at the sound of her voice. Embarrassed, she smiled at them to indicate that everything was okay before turning to glare at Mac again. She raised her chin.

Mac didn't seem to notice her anger. Dark blue eyes stared into hers for a moment before drifting down to her mouth. He smiled and looked into her eyes again. Lani blushed, which torqued her off enormously.

"So," she hissed at him. "Have you come to see what a bad mother I am? Let me help you out. I wouldn't want you to work too hard in helping Judith prove that she and Richard are more fit than I am to raise my son."

She extended one small hand, counting off on her fingers with the other. "First, I let my child witness a murder. Second, I barely prevent him from being hit by a car. Third, he's almost present when his mother was supposed to be attacked by an intruder." Lani raised haunted eyes to Mac. "It was supposed to be me, not Rachel, wasn't it?"

Mac gazed into Lani's eyes and she knew he could read the fear and uncertainty she felt. She did not look away. He leaned on the counter, and his hand crept across the space between them to touch her hand. She stiffened and grew still. Mac's thumb stroked the back of her hand in a gentle caress. Lani's eyes widened. She gasped, and a hot wave of color washed across her face as she abruptly pulled her hand away. She glanced quickly around the Tropical Bean to see if anyone had noticed the exchange. Nobody was even looking their way, and so she resorted to her usual tactics. She raised her chin and glared.

"Well," she challenged taking up right where she'd left off. "Do you have enough ammunition to get me yet?"

Ignoring her anger, Mac asked in a low voice, "Why do you always tilt your chin at the world? Maybe everyone isn't out to get you. Did you ever stop to think about that, Mighty Mouth?"

She frowned at him. "Don't call me Mighty Mouth. I don't like it."

"Hmmmmm, and you expect everyone to do exactly what you like, is that it?"

"Of course not." Another blush suffused her face. "You make me sound like such an egomaniac."

Again, without any conscious thought on Mac's part, his hand crept across the counter and wrapped itself around Lani's where it lay inert on the counter. He winced at the movement.

Lani shuddered as she remembered the intruder's flashing knife.

"How bad is it?"

"Just a scratch. I didn't even need stitches." Mac leaned closer. "Lani, about Judith. She is going through a bad time. She just lost her second son, and I think she and Richard believe that if they can raise Kit, they can redeem some part of their mortality. That doesn't mean they have the right to raise him—only the desire."

Lani jerked her hand away again, her temper rising as she cut off his words. "Look, I didn't ask you here. I suggest you leave. You're free to gather whatever evidence you wish against me, but don't expect me to like that fact or you."

"Oh Mighty Mouth, I never said I was going to help Judith. She made the claim, but I never made the offer." Mac looked down at the sleeping form of her son as he curled into his makeshift bed behind the counter.

"Yeah, right." Lani had no intention of trusting Mac or anyone else when it came to Kit. She raised her chin at him and opened her mouth.

Before she could say anything, Mac pulled a five-dollar bill out of his pocket and laid it on the counter.

"You sell coffee. I'm in the market for a cup. Are you going to serve me, or do I have to feel discriminated against? Perhaps you don't serve doctors in this elite shop, is that it?"

His raised eyebrows were so comical that she almost laughed out loud—almost.

"All right, what will it be?" Lani smiled in satisfaction at the confusion on Mac's face as he perused the dozen or so selections listed on a wooden board behind the counter. His confusion seemed to grow as he read about cappuccinos, lattes, au laits, and all the variations in between.

"Uh, where's the regular coffee?"

Lani smiled sweetly. "I'll bring you a cup. Go. Sit." With a slender forefinger, Lani pointed him toward the hanging basket chair, swaying in the bay window at the front of the shop.

Mac looked at her suspiciously, and then without another word, he went, and he sat.

With a devilish smile, Lani put together a Snickers bar mocha cappuccino complete with chocolate and caramel syrup swirled across a mound of whipped cream, all of it topped by crushed peanuts and a maraschino cherry.

Dusting her hands off on the back of her jeans, she carried the hot beverage across the shop to Mac, set it on the table next to him, and presented him with fifteen cents in change.

"What the hell is this? It looks like dessert, not coffee." He looked in disbelief at the change she presented to him. "You're charging me $4.85 for a cup of coffee? My God, woman. You must be making money hand over fist. I thought doctors charged an arm and a leg—no pun intended, but it's clear to me that coffee shop owners are going to beat our charges blind."

Lani's lips twitched, but "Enjoy," was her only response as she turned and walked away.

Mac watched Lani sashay her way across the shop, his eyes fixed on her curvy little figure. In spite of how small she was everything about her was in all the right proportions. Mac dragged his eyes away, fully aware that he was staring again. He wasn't pleased at all about how much Lani Emerson was on his mind. He didn't even like her type at all. She was bossy, arrogant, and rude.

He leaned back in his chair and sighed as the soft cushions gave in all the right places beneath him. Mac's first appointment wasn't until 8:30 a.m. He decided he had plenty of time to sit and relax for a change. Lifting the coffee drink to his lips, he took a tentative sip. Not bad. He didn't particularly like sweet coffee, but the blend of the chocolate, caramel, cream, and coffee was soothing and—not bad.

Suddenly Lani stood up straight, eyes squinting against the glare of sun on snow, as she peered out the front door. An enormous smile lit up her face. Mac was entranced. He'd never seen that smile before. He'd never seen a smile of that magnitude on anyone before.

Lani turned and filled a tall, clear mug with cream and coffee and put a freshly baked pastry of some sort on a plate. She carried them to a small glass table to the left of the front door. Moving very slowly, she walked over and opened the door, causing the wind chimes to tinkle with the movement. A freezing gust of air entered the shop as Lani stood and in a low, careful voice said, "Good morning. Your coffee is waiting for you."

The tiniest woman Mac had ever seen entered the coffee shop, slowly looking all around as though to ensure she was entering a safe place.

From head to toe, the little woman was dressed in black. Torn gloves tied on with white string, enclosed hands no larger than a child's. A black wool coat several sizes too large for her small form bulged over what were clearly several layers of clothes beneath it. Her hem, spattered with salt laden slush from the frozen streets dragged a scant inch above black rubber galoshes, covering feet that were surely several sizes smaller. Her black felt hat drooped in holey folds around her head, shading her face so that he could see nothing but a small sharp chin. An enormous spray of dirty, fuchsia roses hung from its floppy brim over one eye, waving whenever she moved her head. His back prickled for some reason as he looked at the woman. She seemed familiar somehow. He shook his head, embarrassed at his thoughts. How absurd.

Obviously, this was a person of the streets, but Lani ushered her in as though she were royalty. Not a penny exchanged hands as the small woman sat back and enjoyed her coffee. Every time the chimes rang in a new customer, she would tilt her head and close her eyes as though she were absorbing every sweet note. She never spoke and rarely moved. She just sat and enjoyed her coffee and pastry.

So, the little spitfire has a soft heart, thought Mac, remembering the money he'd seen she and Kit stuff in the Salvation Army Santa's kettle the day before.

Mac leaned back in his hanging basket chair, pushing himself gently to and fro with one foot as he sipped his coffee. All around him, customers came and went. Lani seemed to know most of them by name and never failed to greet everyone with an enormous smile and a few words. For some of her customers, she offered encouragement, as was the case with the young man who was on his way to a job interview. With others, she expressed concern, as was the case with the older woman whose husband was recovering from a heart attack. It didn't seem to matter who came in the door,

Lani had something positive to add to their morning. He'd never seen anything like it. How could she ever learn all that she seemed to know about a group of total strangers?

More to the point, what really struck Mac was that she even took the time to bother with all these people. Over the past few years, it seemed as though the world was becoming populated with more pain, confusion, and loneliness. The escalating information explosion, the workaholic schedules that so many people willingly subjected themselves to, and the isolation of trying to get from one day to the next was breeding a world of strangers. And yet, thought Mac, Lani treated none of her customers as a stranger.

Mac learned a lot about Lani Emerson that morning. He watched her fix her son breakfast when he woke and noticed how Lani's regular customers called Kit by name and asked him the sorts of questions that caring adults always ask children. Even the tiny street woman sat up and watched every move Kit made.

Mac sat for a full hour, watching customers, listening to the soft music and the background of ocean waves pounding against the sand. He hadn't been this relaxed for months.

Finally, Mac glanced at his watch, sighed, and stood. It was time for him leave. He stretched and sauntered over to leave his dirty mug on the stand provided for that purpose. Turning to Lani who was carefully avoiding him from her position behind the counter, he said, "I'll be back," in his best Arnold Schwarzenegger imitation.

Mac was disappointed at so how not-thrilled she looked at the prospect.

Lani thought he would never leave. She hadn't felt so self-conscious since the first time she ate dinner at a boyfriend's house and bit into a taco, also a first, only to have all the ingredients spill down the front of her new blouse.

She could feel Mac's eyes on her as he watched and listened to every word she uttered to every customer. What a pest, and yet, after he left, the shop seemed empty without him. Go figure. She sighed and glanced at the clock. Eight twenty, near the end of her morning rush.

She glanced around the coffee shop, which was pretty much emptying out. Only two tables were presently occupied. Her two retired lady customers, Shirley Dubrovnik and Dot Scheuneman sat at the table in the middle of the shop. They came in every couple of days on their way downtown to shop.

Dot and Shirley were having an animated conversation with Kit, who was demonstrating his light saber to them and explaining all about Jedi knights and Darth Vader.

Her other customer, a young man who looked familiar somehow, sat at a nearby table, clearly listening to every word Kit and the two ladies said. He seemed especially interested in the Darth Vader story that Kit was telling. Lani realized that Kit was regaling the ladies with his story of how Darth Vader had hurt his friend Jonathon and then kidnapped him.

Lani had tried to explain Jonathon's death, but Kit was too young to understand. She sighed. Later on that morning, she would also have to explain his father's death to him. She didn't know if she knew the right words to do that. She didn't know if the right words even existed.

She looked up as the young man left his book, his hat, and his coffee mug on the table and approached her.

He smiled a shy smile and ducked his head toward his right shoulder. Lani smiled at him, but he avoided her gaze for a moment, his eyes flitting this way and that. Lani waited patiently. Finally, clearing his throat, and raising the most beautiful, chocolate brown eyes to Lani, he burst into what appeared to be a rehearsed speech.

"Hi, I happened to overhear you tell a customer about your p-p-partner's accident last night and that you were going to have to hire someone to help out. I d-d-don't sup-p-pose you'd c-c-consider hiring me."

Lani opened her mouth to explain that she wasn't ready to hire anyone, but before she could say a word, the young man rushed into speech again.

"I m-m-may not have any experience w-w-working in a c-c-coffee shop yet, but I p-p-promise that I'll w-w-work really hard, and I'm a quick learner."

He stretched out a quick hand to shake Lani's and in the process, he knocked over three boxes of tea, a decorative mug, and a display of cookies. Lani quickly grabbed the mug with her free hand before it rolled off the edge of the counter and patiently stacked the tea and cookies in their respective places.

The young man's hand closed convulsively over Lani's. "I'm w-w-working on the clumsiness, and I d-d-don't usually knock things over unless I'm really nervous. And, I'm really nervous right now. Sorry," he said closing his eyes for a moment as though he wished he could take back some of his words. He opened them again, biting his lower lip. "Oh yeah. My name is Michael Sutton. So, what do you think? Would you c-c-consider hiring me?"

"Uh, well, I'm not sure I'm really in the market to hire, anyone just at this moment," said Lani, her heart going out in spite of herself to the clumsy young man. Even though she knew that she would have to hire someone eventually, she didn't want to hire any old body to fill the position as so many fast food and small shops did. She wanted to hire the right body. Someone who would buy into her vision. Someone who would be as interested in her customers as she was. She wanted to hire someone who wanted to help her business grow.

The young man started to get a panicky look on his face, which puzzled Lani. Why on earth would a job in her shop be so important to anyone? The name he'd spoken suddenly clicked.

"Wait a minute. Did you say that your name is Michael Sutton?"

"Yes, ma'am. I know you knew my father. He was k-k-killed

just the other day, and I hadn't b-b-been to see him for years." The young man's voice was quiet, his eyes dark with emotion.

"I'm so sorry about your father. He was a good man, and if you were to ask Kit, his very best friend."

"I know," he said with a wistful smile. "He used to write me letters, but I n-n-never answered him. Sometimes he talked about a little boy who would come to visit him, and then he asked me to c-c-come. Only I never d-d-did." An agonized looked crossed the young man's face.

Lani's eyes softened. "I'm so sorry. Time can get away from us sometimes." She straightened her shoulders. "Here's the thing, though, Michael. I'm not quite ready to hire anyone."

"Oh, please, let me t-t-try." He turned his head and his eyes darted about the shop. Only two tables were occupied at the moment, Shirley Dubrovnik and Dot Scheuneman at one and Lani's protégé, Letty, at the other, quietly finishing up her breakfast.

The intensity in his eyes increasing, the young man ducked behind the counter and scooped up a carafe that Lani had filled with her special breakfast blend. Before she could say anything he was across the shop and smiling at the two little senior citizens sitting in the middle of the shop.

"Good morning, la-la-ladies. May I pour you a complimentary cup of coffee this morning? After all, Ms. Emerson told me that you are two of her special customers, and so we want to take extra special care of you." Although his hand was shaking a little, his voice was cheerful, his stutter almost under control, and his smile couldn't have been any friendlier.

Lani noted the ladies' response with amusement.

Shirley put one plump hand to her even plumper bosom, her cheeks pink with what appeared to be pure pleasure. "Why thank you, young man. I'd love a refill. How very thoughtful of you."

Dot wasn't charmed quite so easily. After all, until that moment she'd never even laid eyes on this young man before, and it was clear she wasn't ready to get buddy, buddy with just any old person—even if he was offering her a free cup of coffee. She clapped her hand over her cup.

"Ma'am, d-d-do you know that you l-l-look like my Aunt Rita? She raises Siamese c-c-cats, the prettiest things you've ever seen, although they don't warm up to many p-p-people." Michael's hand was really shaking now, but it was obvious that he was determined to make an impression on Lani and that he wasn't about to give up. To her surprise, Dot visibly relaxed in her chair.

"Siamese cats, eh? Well, I don't have a Siamese, but I have the biggest, gentlest marmalade Maine Coon you've ever seen. I call him Edward." She finally smiled at Michael and held out her cup. "Don't quite know what I'd do without that cat. He's my best friend," she nodded at Shirley, "present company excepted of course."

"D-d-does he have an "M" mark on his forehead?"

"Yes, he does, the sweet thing."

Lani had to press her lips tightly together to keep from smiling. Of all the people in all the world, she would never have suspected that the regal Dot Scheuneman would refer to a cat as a "sweet thing." Just goes to show how little we know about people sometimes, she thought to herself.

Michael visibly relaxed and stood chatting with the two ladies for a few more minutes, while Lani shook her head in amusement. He certainly had a way with these two customers at least. Finally, the young man turned and looked around the shop again. The only other customer was Letty, but when he started heading in her direction, Lani's hand shot out as though she could pull him back from across the 15 feet that separated them.

"Michael, no, wait … "

But he didn't hear her low command to stop. Letty looked up in alarm as she saw the young man bearing down on her and shrank back against her chair. Suddenly, before he got any closer, he stopped about ten feet away, looked at her for a moment, and then abruptly turned on his heel to pluck a clean cup from the rack on the counter, fill it with coffee, and place it on an empty table.

Letty's eyes were flitting all about the shop, as though she was ready to bolt at any moment. Lani could see her small chest rising and falling as she struggled to control her breathing. Not for the first time, Lani wondered what had happened to the woman that could have caused her to shrink from contact with people as she did.

"Ma'am?" Michael's voice was low and calm. "In c-c-case you need it, here is a fresh cup of coffee. It's yours, if you'd like it." He backed away.

Letty didn't even look in his direction, but after he was standing next to Lani once more, she looked all around the room, and finally put two, tiny gloved hands down on the glass-topped table, stood, and without meeting anyone's eyes backed toward the table with the fresh cup of coffee on it, her shoulders all hunched together as she moved. When she could touch the table with her backside, she turned, snatched up the mug of coffee, and darted forward to dump the steaming brew into the paper cup that Lani always gave her in case she didn't choose to stay. Keeping her back to the room, the small woman clamped the lid on her cup. She reached into her pocket, and extracting several small golden discs, she set two down by her plate, paused for a moment, and then backed up once again to the table on which Michael had left her the fresh cup of coffee. Eyes trained on the floor, she dropped one more disc on that table before whirling around, gathering up her belongings and darting out the door.

"You're hired," said Lani without hesitation, her eyes following her favorite customer out the door.

Michael's head turned so fast from where he'd been watching Letty exit the shop to Lani, she swore she heard his neck crack.

"Huh? I mean, I am?" An enormous smile broke out across Michael's face, and he tripped over a chair as he made his way back to where Lani stood behind the counter. This time he didn't even apologize, he just righted the chair, gave it a sound pat with his hand, and kept right on coming. "D-d-do you mean it, ma'am?"

"Lani. Call me Lani." She smiled back. "Yes, I mean it. Do you know that Letty hasn't accepted food directly from anyone but me since I moved in? If my partner, Rachel, leaves her a packet on the front steps sometimes she'll take it and sometimes she won't, but she's never been that friendly toward anyone else. You must have bewitched her. If you can bewitch my favorite customer, I'm thinking you'll do fine with the rest of 'em."

"Her name is Letty? Does she talk to you then?"

"No, not really. I call her Letitia, Letty for short, because I think it's a beautiful name, and I don't know what her real name is. She never talks. She mumbles sometimes, and once I saw her crying outside the window. That was the first time I met her. She was standing right outside last summer while Kit, Rachel, and I were getting the shop ready to open. Her face was all pressed up against the window, and tears were streaming down her cheeks." Lani's own eyes glimmered with moisture at the memory. "I didn't know what was wrong or how to help her, but when I tried to ask her in, she ran away."

"She seems to b-b-be so scared," said Michael as though he could relate to her fear in some very real way himself.

"I know." Lani's voice was subdued, but threads of pure steel twisted through it. "I'd like to know why, because if I ever found out anyone was abusing that small woman, I'd have his head on a plate so fast he'd never feel it separate from his neck." She took a deep breath, turned to Michael, and smiled. "So, when can you start?"

He grinned, a look of delight, and something else as well on his face. Lani watched him, puzzled, wondering again why this job was so important to him. "I c-c-can start right now, ma'am. I mean Lani."

"Great. I'll show you how things work." Lani walked over to the table Letty had occupied, scooped up the two small golden discs and the dirty dishes, and then on her way past the table on which Letty had dropped the other disc, she scooped that up as well. She reached out and dropped it into Michael's hand. "Here, it's your first tip. Letty always leaves me one or two in payment for her coffee and rolls."

Michael looked down at his hand. "It's a beer bottle cap."

Lani grinned at him. "Yup. Around here, we take our thanks in any form it comes—even golden beer bottle caps."

Chapter 9

Lani walked into the hospital lobby and headed for the information desk to ask for Rachel's room number. Kit walked quietly beside her holding her hand.

"Mama?"

"What, Honey Bug?" Lani smiled down at him, holding his hand tightly in hers. No way was she letting him out of her sight, not for one solitary second.

"What happened to Aunt Rachel?"

Lani's mind raced. She didn't want to lie to her son. On the other hand, she didn't want to scare him either. Choosing her words with care, and hoping to distract him from the more frightening aspects of the story, she said, "Aunt Rachel scared away a burglar, and she got hurt. She's okay now, though, and we're going to bring her these flowers and make her feel better, okay? She will be so happy to see you!"

"Mama, was it Darth Vader? Did he hurt Aunt Rachel, too?" Kit whispered, sliding his thumb into his mouth.

Lani stopped in the middle of the lobby and went down on one knee so that she could look Kit squarely in the eye. She paid no attention to the people streaming by on either side, and didn't notice the young man hovering in the doorway, watching every move she made.

"Kit," Lani reached down and lifted his chin so that she could look directly into his eyes. "I promise you, Honey, it wasn't Darth Vader who hurt Aunt Rachel. It was a bad man, and you know what?"

"No, what Mama?" Kit spoke around the thumb in his mouth, eyes enormous, shadows lurking.

"Aunt Rachel told the police that she kicked that bad man really hard and made him swear. She's one tough cookie, your Aunt Rachel is."

Kit giggled, and pulled his thumb out of his mouth. "Aunt Rachel kicked the bad man?"

"You bet she did, and I bet he was so scared, he's still running far, far away."

Kit's grin spread. He tugged on her hand. "Come on. Let's go see her. I want to hear how hard she kicked that bad man."

The young man sank down onto one of the cushioned chairs in the lobby. He chose a chair in a corner grouping so that he was out of the main thoroughfare. No way could that Lani woman and her kid get by without him seeing them, but they wouldn't notice him back in this corner. He was taking no chances they'd recognize him.

He pulled out a small black notebook and started jotting down random ideas. He couldn't decide whether he should try to take out both the broad and her kid at the same time, or if he should grab the kid first and get the woman separately. After all, he wasn't sure she'd seen his face, but he knew for a fact that the kid saw him kill Old Man Sutton. If any of the adults got smart enough to really question what the kid saw, well that could be all she wrote for yours truly. Nope. He was taking no chances.

He glanced down at his notes, pursing his lips as he considered the possibilities. Nah, poison was no good. Too uncertain. Besides, he'd read that poison was a woman's thing. Recently in fact, some nurse had been arrested for poisoning terminally ill patients at Good Samaritan Hospital. Nope, no pussy assassin techniques for him. He was the real thing, and he was going to plan out every detail of his attack.

He tapped his pencil against his teeth. Maybe he could lure the kid into his car. He shook his head. Fat chance. Damn mother never took her eyes off that kid. He'd have to figure out how to separate them. He made a couple of notes. Maybe that wouldn't be so hard, especially since he was going to be so close to them from now on. Just like white on snow. Just like fleas on a dog. Just like grease on ...

He looked up in alarm, feeling eyes watching him. He smiled. Someone's eyes *were* watching him. Cute little chick on the other side of the lobby. She couldn't have been more than 16 or so, so no way was he interested.

Still, she was really cute. Dark brown hair caught up in a long, silky ponytail. Tiny floaty shirt that barely covered a navel pierced with a shiny stone that sparkled even from a distance. She smiled and then looked away obviously flirting with him.

No harm in flirting back he thought, sending her a big grin. He stood up and gave a languid stretch to show off his muscles. Then, trying to act cool and in control, he flipped his notebook shut, shoved it into his back pocket, and took a few steps in her direction. He stumbled, lost his balance, and reaching out blindly for something to break his fall, he grabbed a branch of the lobby tree rising out of a thigh-high ceramic pot right next to him. The branch ripped off in his hand as he struggled to maintain his balance, which in the end he did, but he felt like a fool holding a tree branch crotch-high. He figured he looked like Adam pulling up a fresh set of fig leaves.

The girl giggled. She smiled at him and then looked down at the floor a few seconds before her eyes slid back up to meet his across the space that separated them.

He grinned back as a trim woman in her forties walked out of the gift shop. Mama took one look at the strange man ogling her daughter and another at her daughter's silly grin and averted eyes. She spoke three words. He couldn't hear what they were, but the kid turned bright red, and although a defiant look crossed her face, she just pressed her lips together and flounced her way toward the door, ponytail twitching all the way.

He sighed. Oh well, he needed to focus anyway. Now, what had he been thinking before he was interrupted? Oh yeah. He was trying to figure out a no-sweat, sure-fire way to kill that damn Emerson kid and his mother.

He pulled his pencil from his pocket and jotted down a question. How can I eliminate the threat? As though in answer to his query, the idea popped into his mind wholly hatched and as easy as pie to execute.

He nodded his head. It would work. He was sure of it. He laughed out loud, and then looked quickly from left to right, but not one of the poor bastards coming or going seemed to have noticed his exaltation. He narrowed his eyes. Two birds with one stone, and no one would ever be the wiser.

He stood up, nonchalantly buttoned his leather jacket, and snugged his wool muffler around his ears. Wait a minute. He stopped in the middle of the lobby, ignoring the dirty looks he got as people swerved around him. He could get three birds with one stone. This time he smiled silently so that he didn't draw any unwanted attention. He flipped one end of his muffler over his shoulder and sauntered toward the door. He had places to go and things to do.

"Tell me again, Aunt Rachel. Did you really kick that bad man in the balls?" Kit stopped abruptly and covered his mouth with both hands. He turned to look at Lani obviously questioning his choice of words.

"Testicles is the word you're looking for, Kit." Lani said trying to keep her amusement from showing.

"Hey, that's one he didn't learn from me," said Rachel in a raspy voice. Her dark hair was spread across her pillows, and although she smiled at Kit, her face was pinched and pale, her throat bruised a livid green and purple.

Lani looked at her friend, and her heart turned over. She'd never seen Rachel flat on her back before and so defenseless. All she could think about was how close she'd come to losing one of the people she loved best in all the world.

"Kit, I think we'd better go and let Aunt Rachel rest. Rach, you look so tired. Try to sleep. We'll come back tomorrow, okay?"

"Wait, you didn't tell me what happened between you and that hunky doctor," rasped Rachel. "Hand me that water glass, and let me clear my throat. No way are you going anywhere until I get the full scoop."

"There is no full scoop. The man's a snake. He's going to help Judith and Richard prove I'm an unfit ... " Lani stopped abruptly looking at Kit, but she didn't need to say the words because as usual, Rachel was right with her.

"Well, if he's really going to help Judith, he's even lower than a snake, but don't you worry, Lani ... " Rachel's voice gave out on her. She stopped to take a sip of water, her eyes flashing.

"Haven't you ever heard about that 'presumed innocent until proven guilty' thing we built this country around," drawled a voice behind Lani.

She spun around to see Mac leaning in the doorway.

"You, you ... "

"Yes, Mighty Mouth, it's me. I thought I might find you here sometime tonight. I asked the nurses at the station to give me a call if you showed up."

Mac glanced with what appeared to be some concern at Rachel who was watching the interchange between he and Lani with interest.

"So, you're Doctor Mac," she said and then clutched her throat before sipping more water.

"I am." He crossed over to the bed and reached for Rachel's wrist. "I know I'm not your doctor, but try not to talk, okay? Your vocal chords are really bruised. You need to give them and the rest of you a break while things heal."

"Oh, so now I'm a beast who has no regard for her friend, is that it?" Lani's chin was tilted, and if the glance she directed Mac's way had been filled with sparks, he'd have burst into flames.

Mac turned to Rachel who was grinning from ear to ear.

"Did you hear me say any such thing? Don't talk, just nod," he ordered.

Rachel obediently moved her head up and down, grinning widely.

"You traitor," said Lani. "But even if he is a snake. . . "

"Uh, Mighty Mouth?   I think the exact term was, er, 'dirty snake' if I heard right."

"Well you did hear right. Only, I'd have added 'rotten' to the 'dirty' if I'd had two seconds more to think about it. And, how many times do I have to tell you not to call me Mighty Mouth."

"Mama? Don't you like Dr. Mac? He helped fix my head, 'member? I like him. That's okay, right?"

Kit looked from his mother to Mac, a question in his eyes, and then at Rachel's muffled gasp of laughter he turned to her.

"Do you like Dr. Mac, Aunt Rachel? I think he likes you, because he took your tempature with his fingers like my mama does for me when I'm sick."

Rachel's eyes were filled with laughter, but the strain on her face was growing.

"Oh Rachel, I am a beast. You need to rest. We'll come back to visit tomorrow, okay? Don't you worry about the shop either, because I hired someone to help out. I'll tell you all about it tomorrow, when we don't have an audience. Kiss Aunt Rachel goodnight, Kit. She needs to rest now."

"Aunt Rachel, today I love you a million, trillion, gazillion, and twenty-nine," whispered Kit, climbing up onto the bed to give Rachel a soggy kiss.

Rachel closed her eyes and hugged him tight.

Lani reached down and held her friend for a minute. "You get well fast, you hear."

Rachel nodded. Lani lifted Kit down from the bed, and gathering up his snowsuit and mittens, she gave Rachel a gay little wave.

Mac followed Lani down the hospital corridor. She got onto the elevator, and Mac jumped on board with her.

"Lani, I'd like to talk with you."

"Drop dead." She didn't even turn her head in his direction.

Mac looked down at Kit.

"Got any suggestions about how to get your mama to listen to me?"

Kit thought about Mac's question, a serious expression on his face. "Well, sometimes, when she's mad at me, I give her a kiss, and that always makes her laugh."

Lani choked.

Mac laughed, and the elevator door opened onto the lobby.

Lani practically leapt out of the elevator, pulling Kit behind her. When she showed no signs of stopping to acknowledge anything he'd said, Mac reached out and caught her shoulder.

"Don't touch me you … "

"Yeah, yeah, yeah, I know. I'm a snake. A dirty, rotten snake."

When Lani began to whirl away from him he started to talk fast.

"But Lani, we need to talk. I called down to the police station, and talked to one of my old buddies. He's a detective, and anyway, I told him about what's been going on with Kit … "

"You told him what? You called the police to talk to them about my son? You had no right." She tilted her head, eyes glaring.

"Lani, this isn't about right and wrong. I'm worried that Kit really did see something. Did you tell the police how he ran out of Sutton's room screaming about Darth Vader that night?"

"Of course, I didn't. Kit didn't see anything, did you Honey Bug?"

Kit looked from Lani to Mac, clearly confused by the conversation.

"Lani, you don't know that. What if … "

"Stop it. Stop it right now, and stay out of my life. I don't need you in it, okay?"

Lani whirled away, and then stopped short when she caught sight of a familiar figure standing in front of her.

"Lani, need some help? Mac can be pretty, uh, intense at times, I know." Jennifer Sutton, in all her easy elegance, stood with a smile on her beautiful face and a good-sized wicker basket slung over one arm.

"Jennifer, thank God," said Lani with vehemence. "Will you get this guy off my back?"

"I'd be happy to. In fact, that's why I'm here. Mac, Judith said you were doing rounds tonight, and I thought you might get hungry." Jennifer lifted the wicker basket to show off its contents. A crystal plate filled with some soft cheese that looked like Brie— Lani's own personal favorite—crackers, and salami nestled in the basket along with designer fruit juice and a baguette. A small container of what looked like olives and a miniature raspberry mascarpone filled out the corners.

Lani felt like drooling. For the price of the food in that basket, she could feed Kit for a week. Leave it to Dr. Mac, she thought viciously, to not only eat like a king, but to have a harem delegate deliver it to work.

"I'll leave the two of you alone to enjoy, your, uh, snack."

Mac watched Lani as she stood next to Jennifer. She barely reached the taller woman's ear and certainly didn't match her elegance in any way. Jennifer wore a black wool coat belted trimly at her waist, with a gold pin nestled in the collar of the fox-trimmed hood that framed her face. Shining leather boots covered her from toes to knees, and black kid gloves protected her hands.

Lani's slender form was engulfed in an old blue wraparound wool coat. A black knit cap anchored the hair on top of her head while the ends curled out from under the cap in a riot of red-gold. She helped Kit into his snowsuit, and then, pulling a pair of black wool mittens over her hands, she turned to go without a word.

Mac knew Lani was more scared than anything. Hell, he was scared, too. Throughout the day, he'd become more and more convinced that Kit had actually seen the murderer in Jonathon's room. That, coupled with the fact that someone tried to mow Lani and Kit down the previous morning, and then someone had attacked Rachel that same night in their apartment was more proof than he needed to believe they were in danger.

"Uh, Mac? I thought I could share your break with you." Jennifer smiled, but the smile didn't quite reach her eyes as she watched him watch Lani leading Kit to the hospital exit.

"Jennifer, how thoughtful of you. Could I take a rain check though? I've got to check on a couple of patients." Mac had one thought. He wanted to finish his rounds and go after Lani.

"No problem. Give me a call, okay?"

Nodding, Mac felt a brief pang at his cavalier treatment of Jennifer, but he pushed it aside. For some reason or another, all he could think of was a pair of flashing blue-green eyes and an imperious little head covered with red-gold curls. He didn't even notice the shadow that passed across Jennifer Sutton's eyes as she watched him walk away.

Lani pushed Kit's door open for what must have been the third time in ten minutes. He was still asleep. Of course he was asleep. Even more important, he was still safe in his bed. Where else would he be? She was becoming neurotic.

Lani yawned for the third time in as many minutes. She didn't understand what was wrong with her, but she could barely keep her eyes open even though it was only 8:30. She frowned. She'd gotten home from the hospital to find the front door of the shop locked and the "Closed" sign in the window.

Tomorrow morning, she'd have a thing or two to say to her new hire, Michael Sutton. She couldn't afford to close her doors early, and she couldn't imagine what would have been important enough for him to close up shop and leave.

Lani yawned again, a queasy feeling in her stomach causing her to clench her teeth hard. The one thing she didn't need was the flu, but clearly something was going on with her. Her head hurt, and she was having trouble collecting her thoughts.

Maybe she'd lie down on the couch for a minute, and then she'd feel okay again. Just for a minute, though. She had to ... but her thoughts seemed to collide inside her head, sliding from an image of Kit as he ran screaming from Jonathon's room, to Kit lying bleeding beneath her in the snow, to Mac's challenge about what had she done to her son, to Mac's eyes filled with laughter as he called her Mighty Mouth.

Lani curled up on the couch, swallowing to quell the nausea. She'd close her eyes for just one minute.

Mac swore at the red light. It had taken him more than an hour to finish his rounds. He knew he was feeling more anxious than the situation warranted, but even as he wondered why he was bothering to check into the well-being of a little spitfire who did nothing but tilt her chin at him, Mac stepped on the gas, a sense of urgency filling him as it had the previous night. Checking up on Lani was becoming a habit, but something was wrong. He felt it. Looking first to the right, and then left, and seeing no cars approaching, he drove through the intersection and stomped on the gas.

Mac pulled into Lani's driveway, killed the engine, and was out of his car and up the sidewalk in less than two seconds flat. The night was freezing, and the smell of cherries lingered on his tongue. He wondered why he always tasted cherries on his tongue in below-zero weather.

Mac looked up. Lani's kitchen window beckoned him with warm golden light. Silence filled the air all around him, but it wasn't the silence of a quiet winter evening. It was the silence before something happened. Mac's skin crawled. He pushed the doorbell, and although he waited as patiently a he could, peering through the small window in the door and up the staircase, no one approached.

His uneasiness increased. He knew Lani was home, because her car was in the driveway next to his. Why didn't she answer the door?

Mac leaned on the doorbell again and then took two steps back, looking up at the light glowing from the kitchen window.

Shit, he thought. Now what do I do?

He jumped at an explosion behind him, and then laughed. A backfire. Nothing more. He would ring the doorbell one more time, and if Lani didn't answer the door, he would go home to a quiet nightcap and a cool shower. Now, why the hell did the thought of a cool shower enter his mind? Whatever.

Mac pressed the doorbell one last time. He waited thirty seconds, and then as he turned to leave, another explosion filled the quiet night air. Mac stopped dead in his tracks, his jaw dropped, and as he saw flames licking at Lani's kitchen window, he applied his shoulder to the door. Once. Twice. Three times, and he was through the door and charging up the stairs.

Smoke filled the entry at the top of the stairway, and flames filled the kitchen. Heat drove Mac back from the doorway.

"Lani," he shouted. "Lani, where are you?"

Mac glanced around wildly, trying to find another way into Lani's apartment. The landing he stood upon stretched before him toward the front of the old building and Mac saw a second door about ten feet in front of him. Praying that the fire was confined to the kitchen, Mac put his shoulder to the door. This time he broke it down in one great heave.

The force of his attack on the door catapulted Mac into the hallway beyond, and although smoke stippled the room and clogged his lungs, he saw no flames.

"Lani," he shouted. "Damn it, where are you?" Pulling his muffler over his nose, Mac tore through the hallway and into the living room. Through the smoke, he could see Lani curled in a ball on the couch. She wasn't moving. Mac's heart stopped cold as he leapt across the room, and lifted her small form in his arms. God, she weighed almost nothing. Her face was still and white against his shoulder. What the hell was wrong with her?

In the distance, he could hear a siren. Thank God. One of the neighbors must have called the fire department.

Kit. He had to find Kit. Behind him lay a bedroom, but one glance told him it was Lani's. He turned to peer through the growing smoke and heat, and saw another room on the far side of a dining room, next to the kitchen. He laid Lani on the floor by the door leading out onto the landing, and ran through the house.

God it was hot. He could hear flames crackling ferociously as they ate through the old wood in the kitchen. He could feel his skin blistering from the heat as he ran past the kitchen door and into the back bedroom. Kit lay in a small mound beneath his covers, unmoving. Mac scooped him up, and was back through the living room in less than two seconds. Slinging Lani over one shoulder, he clasped Kit in his other arm. The smoke was so bad, it was almost impossible to breathe.

Mac staggered to the stairway and stood aside as a trio of firefighters surged up the stairway. The third took Kit from Mac, but he refused to release Lani, merely shaking his head and gesturing with his chin for the fireman to precede him down the stairs.

Mac drank in the fresh, cold night air, and laid Lani down on the snow. Pulling off his coat, he wrapped it around her small form. All around him lights swirled and spun amber and white, while the siren shrieked an accompaniment.

"Give me the boy. I'm a doctor." He reached for Kit, noting his blue face and heavy breathing. He quickly wrapped Kit in the blanket offered to him from the fireman, and snapped an order. "Oxygen. Give me a tank of oxygen."

The firefighter complied and held the mask over the child's face while Mac turned to Lani, and accepting a second tank of oxygen did the same for her.

In moments her eyes flickered and opened to look up into his. He saw the terror fill them and answered her question before she voiced the words.

"Kit's right here. He's okay, and so are you." Mac didn't even realize that he was holding Lani against his heart with one hand, while with the other he smoothed her tumbled curls back, looking into her eyes and murmuring all the while, "It's okay, Love. It's okay. I won't let anything happen to either of you."

He could not believe his eyes. That Lani woman and her kid had escaped him again. Unbelievable. What the hell was he doing wrong? He'd written everything down, planned every move he was going to take. His plan should have worked.

Across the street, firefighters trooped in and out of the building. A team on the ground held a steady stream of water on the roof. Paramedics slid the portable gurneys into the ambulance, one holding the woman and the other holding the kid, and lights flashing, they spun out of the driveway and turned in the direction of the hospital.

A small man ran up to him all out of breath. "What's going on? Is Lani hurt?"

He shrugged, turning away and hunching his shoulder to hide

his face. His movement was unnecessary, though, because the other man was focused only on what was going on across the street. Without waiting for an answer, the small man darted across and joined the crowd milling about in Lani's backyard.

Maybe he'd at least taken out the kid. It was possible, because even thought they'd hooked him up to all that hospital paraphernalia, the kid wasn't moving. With any luck at all he would buy it before the ambulance got to the hospital. It didn't matter to him how it went down. He wanted that kid dead, and it was about time some of the luck ran his way.

Damn. His partner was going to shit bricks at this latest development. No need. He'd figure out what to do. All he needed was a little time. That's all. Just a little time.

He didn't think the firefighters would find any evidence linking him to the fire or to that other little matter the fire was supposed to cover up. He hunched his shoulders up and down. Man, when this gig was over, he was going to blow this place and head south. No more snow and ice for him.

He turned away and headed toward his car. No way could he get back into the building with all the activity going on. But tomorrow, he'd be able to get back inside to take care of business—and nothing was going to stop him.

Chapter 10

Lani looked up from the hospital bed as Mac walked into the room.

"Hi. Can't you sleep?"

The clock on the wall read 4:30 a.m.

"Not any more. Every time I close my eyes, I get these horrible pictures of what might have happened if you hadn't come and pulled us out of that fire."

Lani's voice broke, and she tightened her arms to hold Kit closer and lowered her cheek onto his head so that she could breathe in the essence of small boy. Kit didn't move.

"Mac, Kit's going to be okay, right? You weren't just telling me that."

"He's going to be fine. I promise, Lani." Mac walked over and stood close. His hand twitched as though he wanted to reach out with it, but instead he shoved it into the pocket of his hospital coat.

Lani barely noticed as she looked down at her son. He looked so small in the big hospital bed, and he was so still. He'd woken up crying the previous evening. Lani had been there right next to him. The nursing staff had been unable to convince her to sleep in the room next door. She refused to leave her son's side, and Mac finally told them to leave her alone. Then, he'd turned to her and ordered her into the bed with Kit to sleep.

Lani looked up at Mac. "You saved our lives. I know that, but what I don't know is what happened. I couldn't wake up. I was so sleepy."

Mac opened his mouth and then closed it as though he'd swallowed what he'd been about to say. He paused, saying in a low voice, "The fire department finished their preliminary investigation. It was gas and accumulation caused the explosion."

"I noticed a funny smell when we got home last night. It wasn't all that strong, though, and I was so worried about Rachel, I just didn't pay any attention. We could have died." Lani's eyes were dull, her voice raspy from the smoke she'd inhaled the previous evening. "My good Lord, we could have died."

Mac sat down on the bed next to Lani and reached out to turn her face toward his. He looked into her eyes, his own dark with some emotion that Lani was too worn out to interpret. His hand slid from her chin to her shoulder. He could feel it tremble as he gripped her hard.

"But you didn't die. You're okay, and Kit's going to be fine too. He was closer to the fire, and so he inhaled more smoke than you did. Besides … "

"Besides," broke in Lani, her voice shaking. "He's so little."

"Lani, I want to keep Kit here for a couple of days, for safety purposes, okay?"

She closed her eyes, and leaned back against the pillow, her face the color of the hospital linen. "Of course, whatever you think is best. I'm not taking any chances with my son's health. Besides," her voice broke, "I haven't any home to take him to."

"Lani," Mac opened his mouth to say something, but she cut him off.

"I haven't any place to take him to. Oh God, what are we going to do? I know I should be grateful that we're okay, but what are we going to do?"

Immediately, Lani was embarrassed. She sat up and shrugged

her shoulder to dislodge Mac's hand, but he didn't let go. Instead, his large hand slid around to her other shoulder, and he pulled her close. Her head fit into the hollow of his shoulder, and for a moment she relaxed against Mac's solid body. It felt so good, and it had been so long since anyone held her like this. She breathed in the smell of clean hospital linen along with the fine wool of Mac's jacket. Something else, too. Something spicy with a tang of lime.

Lani turned her head. As Mac turned his own to look down into her eyes, she was surprised to find his mouth close to hers. His eyes darkened again, and he looked from her eyes to her mouth. His glance lingered for a moment, and then taking a deep breath his eyes returned to look into hers, and he lowered his face and rested his cheek against her forehead. Lani felt the rasp of his beard against her skin. He was so warm, and she was so cold. She shivered, and Mac tightened his arm around her.

"Lani, I want you to come home with me."

"Mac, I don't even know you."

"You know me." That's all he said. Although she didn't respond to his invitation, Lani lay back comforted against his warmth.

"Mac, how bad is my shop?"

He spoke against her hair, his breath stirring the curls on her forehead.

"It's not as bad as it could be according to the fire chief. Your kitchen is gutted, but thanks to whoever called the fire department, the fire was contained. The smoke pretty much damaged the rest of your apartment, though, and your things are going to need some pretty heavy-duty cleaning before you can use them again."

"What about my shop?" Her voice was a whisper. She cleared her throat and tried again. "Is my shop ruined?"

"No, Lani. Your shop is okay. The police chief said that you could open up shop again any time you want. His crew verified the rooms above the shop are sound. Since the damage was in the far back corner of your apartment, he said you didn't even have any smoke damage in the shop itself.

Lani relaxed against Mac's body. "I need to get over there."

"No. You don't. You need to rest."

"Mac, you don't understand. That shop is our life. If I don't open, I don't make any money. If I don't make any money, I can't afford to live. I've got deliveries coming at six o'clock, and I've got to be there to receive them."

Mac looked down at the small woman in his arms. With a sigh, he stood.

"Okay, I'll make a deal with you."

Lani looked up at him, suspicion clear in her eyes. She raised her chin.

"Oh Mighty Mouth, there you go again," he chuckled.

"What? What did I do?"

"Your chin. Whenever you want something or you're mad or challenging someone, you raise your chin at the world."

"I do not," she said unconsciously raising her chin. Pausing as she realized what she'd done, Lani acknowledged his point with a quiet little chuckle.

"Oh yes, you do," said Mac grinning, clearly delighted that he'd gotten her mind off the fire. "Okay, here's the deal. You rest for the next hour, and then I'll drive you over to the shop, okay?"

"Why are you being so nice to me?" asked Lani with a frown. "I don't like it."

"You'd prefer I was mean? I can try harder to be a bastard if that will make you feel better. You just let me know when I've got the right mix going, okay?"

In spite of herself, Lani grinned. "Okay, I'll let you drive me to the shop, but I want Kit moved into the second bed in Rachel's room. I won't leave him alone."

Lani unlocked the door, and as they entered the wind chimes peeled a musical welcome.

"Come on in. I'll make you a cup of plain coffee, at least, it's a special breakfast blend I have so it's not really plain, but I think you'll like it."

She shrugged herself out of her coat. Reaching for Mac's, she went into the back of the shop to hang them both on a hook in the supply closet. Closing the door, she moved behind the counter and started assembling filters, coffee, and cups.

"Will it have whipped cream and caramel?"

"Huh?"

"The coffee you offered me. Will it have whipped cream and caramel gooped in?"

"Nope, its plain, why?"

"Just curious about why you're offering me a plain cup of coffee today instead of another frilled up cup of dessert."

Lani grinned for the first time that morning. Mac's heart started to beat faster. She was so pretty, but it wasn't only the way she looked that made him want to watch her for hours. Everything about her felt familiar somehow. When he was with her, he felt as though he'd come home, which considering his background, was not only unlikely, but bizarre.

"Mac? How much do you think it will cost to rebuild my kitchen?" Lani shuddered and swallowed hard. "It's … gone. We are so lucky. You may annoy the hell out of me, but I'll never forget that you pulled us out of that conflagration. If you hadn't, we wouldn't even be alive."

"Oh Lani, don't think about … "

Lani walked around the counter until she was standing six inches from Mac. She put one hand on his chest and tilted her head so that she could look into his eyes. A light flowery scent emanated from her hair, and he wanted to bury his nose in the soft, bright curls. He gulped instead and took a deep breath.

Lani stood still, her eyes wide, a brilliant blue-green. Mac took another deep breath, his eyes drifting to her mouth, intrigued by her soft full lips, wondering what it would be like to lower his head and brush his own across Lani's. Behind them the coffee gurgled and spit as it finished dripping into the carafe. Lani didn't move. It was clear to Mac that she knew what he was thinking. Her own eyes drifted down to his lips and then back up with a question. Delicate color suffused her cheeks, brightening the color in her eyes even further. She hesitated and then took two steps back, resolution growing in her face.

"Mac, I have something to say. You saved my son's life, and you saved mine."

His face reddened. He searched for the right words—any words.

Lani held up her other hand and with a gesture stopped him before he could get one word out.

"No, don't say anything. It's true. You did. Thank you. That's all I wanted to say." She turned and moved briskly back behind the counter.

"You know something?" said Mac, a hint of frustration seeping into his words despite his best intentions.

Lani turned, a suspicious frown crossing her face. "No, what?"

"You are the bossiest small woman I've ever known."

Lani opened her mouth to respond, and Mac held up his hand. "No, don't say anything. It's true. You are. Now, where's my plain cup of coffee, hmmm?"

Another smile lit up Lani's face, and she made a ceremony of preparing a plain cup of coffee.

Mac accepted the cup she handed him and retreated to his chair in the window so that he could keep an eye on Lani and make sure she did not overdo things and wear herself out. He sank back deep into his chair, took a sip of excellent black coffee, and watched her move about the shop, thinking he could watch her forever.

The chimes above the door jingled, and a young man balancing several large bakery boxes in his arms entered. Outside, the sky was inky black before the winter dawn, but inside the shop was filled with warm, golden light and the fragrance of coffee freshly brewed. The smell of smoke, very faint, wafted through the room, but it was so faint as to be almost imperceptible. Mac sighed with relief. At least Lani could stay in business.

"Good morning. I'm Mike, the new deliveryman for Jake. It looks like you had quite a night. Everyone okay?" The young man set the bakery boxes on the glass topped counter in a line and didn't wait for an answer to his question before chattering on. "Oh yeah, Jake said to tell you that he was sending over a few of his new chocolate raspberry-filled croissants, no charge. He said to let him know if your customers like 'em, and if they do, he said to tell you that he'd give you a good deal."

Lani smiled. "Tell Jake thanks. I really appreciate the gesture. We're all fine. We just, uh, had a little fire."

The doorbell pealed again, and Michael Sutton held the door open as he stomped the snow off his boots before entering the shop.

Lani's eyes drew together, and she frowned. Before Michael could even get his gloves off, she spoke a curt, "Good morning. We need to talk."

Michael blushed, but he didn't look away. "You're upset because I c-c-closed up early last n-n-night, aren't you?"

"You're darned right I'm upset." Lani's face was pink and her eyes sparked, but then she paused and turned to the delivery man who was listening to the entire exchange with a wide smile on his face. "Anything else? Tell Jake thanks. I'll see you tomorrow."

She waited pointedly until the door closed behind him, and then she whirled around to face Michael. "Look, you said you wanted this job. I really need someone I can depend on now. Especially with the fire, and Rachel and Kit being in the hospital, and … "

"What fire?" At Michael's look of concern, Lani took a deep breath, obviously struggling for composure. He looked around. "Where's K-k-kit?"

"He's in the hospital, but he'll be okay. Look Michael, I've got to know if you really want this job."

"I d-d-do, I do want it. Look, I'm sorry, it won't happen again. Something came up, and I c-c-closed the shop 30 minutes early. It was an emergency. I won't d-d-do it again. I promise." He gulped over the word promise, striving to gain control of his stutter.

Lani looked at him for a long moment, and then shook her head. "Okay. Enough said. Let's get to work." She moved over to the counter and starting filling the glass case with quick, economical movements. Michael disappeared into the back of the shop to hang up his coat.

"Lani, are you okay?" Mac left his chair and crossed the room to where Lani was standing staring into space, her pastries forgotten. "Come here a minute."

He reached out his hand and was surprised when Lani reached back and took it, allowing him to pull her out from behind the counter. "Take a quick break and try one of these things."

Mac pushed Lani down into a soft chair, but before he could turn to get her coffee, Michael was there with a croissant on a plate and a large cup of black coffee. He set them on the table and touched Lani's shoulder. "Don't w-w-worry, Ms. Emerson. I can work as many hours as you need me to work. You just do whatever you have to d-d-do."

Lani smiled, and the young man visibly relaxed.

"Why is K-k-kit in the hospital? Is he okay?" Michael retreated behind the counter and started to set out the rest of the pastries.

Mac explained what had happened. He was surprised to see a shadow cross Michael's face, but even as he searched for what lay behind the expression, Michael looked away, his face blank and smooth. Mac's antennae sprang up. This kid would bear some watching. Something was going on that he didn't understand. Mac looked with concern at Lani, but she was finally relaxing. No way was he going to interrupt her peace of the moment. When he looked up again, he found Michael watching him. Although his face was inscrutable, he looked away the moment Mac's eyes met his.

The wind chimes over the door pinged with a flurry as Mr. Ambrosiak rushed into the shop. "Lani, Honey, are you okay? I heard the explosion last night, and I called the fire department right away. I came over to help, but they took you and Kit away in the ambulance. You're okay? What about Kit? Where's Kit?"

"He's fine. He's just going to stay at the hospital for the next day or so. He inhaled a pretty hefty dose of smoke."

"Thank God you're okay. First Rachel, and now you. What's the world coming to? You're both okay, though?"

"Yes, we're fine. Oh, Mr. Ambrosiak, you may have saved my shop, and you definitely saved the rest of my apartment. Your coffee is free for life. I don't ever want to see your money again."

Obviously pleased, the slender man took off his glasses, polished them vigorously, and then put them back on. "Well, that's really nice of you, Lani, but you're running a business. I'm not going to take advantage of you."

Lani ignored everything he said and jumped up to lead him over to one of the best tables in the shop. Still ignoring his protests she brought him the morning edition of the *Minneapolis Star Tribune*, a large latte, and knowing he had a sweet tooth, she also brought him one of the experimental croissants. The little man settled back in his chair with a sigh and a smile. He shrugged himself out of his coat and took a sip of his coffee.

"What happened? How did the fire start?"

"The fire chief said it was gas accumulating from my stove. The pilot light must have gone out, I guess." Lani's brow furrowed. "But I don't know why I didn't realize that it had gone out. Usually I have an excellent sense of smell, and I'm so careful about the pilot light. Last night, I was so tired."

Mac opened his mouth, but then hearing the stress in Lani's voice, he kept his thoughts to himself. He'd know soon enough if his suspicions were warranted.

"Oh, there's Letty." Without another word, Lani whirled to the counter. Michael was ahead of her. He filled a large paper cup with coffee and put two pastries into a sack.

Mac turned to look, and at the sight of the tiny woman pressed up against the front window of the shop, his heart started to hammer. He took a step forward to open the door, his brow furrowing. He couldn't see her face beneath the drooping brim of the hat, but somehow ….

"No, Mac, don't … " said Lani and Michael simultaneously. They looked at each other and laughed. Lani continued. "See, she's gone. She won't come in unless the conditions are perfect. I still haven't figured out what makes them perfect on some days and not on others. We can put her breakfast out around the edge of the door, and maybe she'll still come and get it."

"Who's Letty? Strange name."

"Oh, I have no idea what her name really is. I call her Letitia, Letty for short, because I think it's a pretty name, and the poor woman obviously has nothing. Why shouldn't she have a pretty name?"

"So, who is she?"

"I haven't a clue. She won't come in for anyone but me, and now Michael."

Lani pushed open the front door of the shop. Frigid air swirled inside raising goose flesh on Mac's arms. Lani didn't seem to notice the cold as she sidled quietly outside and laid her offering near the corner of the shop.

"I'm so glad it's warmer today. I worry about her."

"Lani, d-d-do you know where she lives?"

"No, but I wish I did. I'm afraid she lives on the street, although how she can survive, I don't know, especially this winter. They say it's the coldest one we've had in more than ten years."

Mac watched Lani's face in fascination. His little spitfire had such a soft heart. His brow furrowed again. Somehow, that old woman …, but as Lani pulled out one of the chocolate croissants and waved it in front of him, he sat and began to eat, enjoying the sound of the waves, the fragrance of the coffee, and the sight of Lani as she bustled about serving her customers.

As the door closed behind Mac and Lani, Michael breathed a sigh of relief. He'd been worried that Lani would fire him. He was so glad she didn't know what he'd done the previous night. His plans weren't solid yet. He needed more time. He poured himself a cup of Guatemalan coffee, inhaled the rich fragrance, and pulling out a crumpled piece of paper from his pocket, he settled down to study it between customers.

The tiny woman pulled her rags tightly about her, and curled into the nest she'd made. Strange thoughts coursed through her mind, confusion, blended with the fear from before. That large man drew her but frightened her all at the same time, but then she was afraid of most people. She'd found it safer to trust no one. Her thoughts scattered and then coalesced with a collection of memories that caused her heart to pound. She pushed the memories away, until she could focus once more on her purpose.

She'd gone as she did every morning to check on the red-haired child, but he wasn't there. She shivered. His mother was there, but the child was not, and he should have been. His mother never let him out of her sight. She was a good mother, unlike … but even as the old anxiety rose to overwhelm her, her mind took over and blocked the memories.

She started to breathe easier. That was before. This was now. Most of the time, she could keep things straight, but every once in a while confusion set in. She took a dainty sip of her now cold coffee and a tiny bite of pastry, thinking hard for a few minutes. She snorted, a very lady-like snort to be true, but a snort all the same. Something was going on at her coffee shop, and she was going to keep a sharp eye about her until she knew what it was.

The previous night, she'd heard the sirens and come out to see what was happening. At the sight of the fire billowing from Lani's kitchen window, she'd frantically tried to break into the house, only to be stopped by a fireman. It had been so many years since another human touched her, she'd recoiled, retreating to the end of the yard, breathing hard until she'd seen that Kit was safe.

Oh yes. Something was definitely up. She'd watched that young man leave the shop earlier that night, and she'd followed him. Oh yes. She was going to have to keep a sharp eye out. No doubt about it.

Rachel burst into the hospital room she was sharing with Kit. Lani was curled up on the bed playing Go Fish with her son.

"Lani, heads up. I was out in the hallway trying to hunt down a cup of coffee, and I saw the old Bi ... " Rachel's eyes flickered Kit's way, and she revised her words, "your ex-you-know-whats are on the way. They didn't even see me, but I've gotta say this looks serious. She's wearing the pearls."

Lani's face turned white, but she smiled in spite of herself at Rachel's description of the imminent invasion.

Rachel tossed her head, long hair swinging around her shoulders. "That's the spirit, Girl. I'll be right here with you, okay?"

Kit looked back and forth between his mother and Rachel, clearly confused, but also showing no sign of interest beyond his card game.

He reached out and pulled on Lani's sleeve. "It's your turn. We can't stop now, I'm winning."

Rachel grinned, pulled her robe tighter, and cinched her belt. "Hey, Kit kid, move over, and let me play too."

Clearly delighted with another prospect to fleece, Kit squiggled over so that Rachel could sit cross-legged on the end of the high hospital bed.

"Deal, sir," said Rachel, adding in a lower voice. "Don't let her get to you, Lani, okay? It's not worth it."

Less than three minutes later, Judith and Richard Emerson swept into the room. No better term existed for their entrance, thought Lani. They truly swept, and it was clear that if Lani hadn't been on one side of the bed and if Rachel hadn't been sitting on the bed next to Kit, they would have swept right down on the small boy, ignoring Lani and Rachel completely. As it was, Rachel presented a large barrier, and so they were forced to slow down.

Richard hovered in the doorway, a piece of paper in his hand. Judith stood off to one side of the bed. Sure enough, she was wearing her pearls and some sort of jade silk pantsuit beneath her black wool coat.

"Oh Christopher darling, I've been so worried. Are you alright?"

Kit looked at his grandmother with a timid smile. "Hi, Grandma. I'm fine. We're playin' Go Fish. Do you want to play too?" His eyes filled with hope. "I can move over and make more room so you can sit on the bed too."

"No, I certainly do not want to play a card game when your very life is in jeopardy." Judith turned and said in her most imperious voice. "Richard, the papers."

She stood back while Richard moved forward, a glint in his eyes, muscles clenched in his cheek, and his lips nearly invisible due to the pressure he was exerting upon them.

Lani started to breathe faster, her heart thumping wildly. This was serious. She lay her cards face down on the bed.

"Mama," protested Kit. "It's your turn, and I'm still winning."

"Not now, Honey Bug. I need to talk with your grandparents. We'll play later."

"But Mama," Kit whined.

"Hush, sweetie. I'll play you two games later, okay?" Rachel leaned over and gave him a quick peck on the forehead. Kit clutched his cards in one small hand, while he slid his thumb into his mouth. His eyes moved from his mother to his grandfather to his grandmother. He reached out for Rachel, who cuddled him close.

"I'm afraid there will be no time for card games, Christopher. Your grandmother and I have come to take you home with us."

Kit's eyes widened, but he said nothing, just sucked harder on his thumb, while he reached out and clutched Rachel's robe with his other hand.

Lani shot to her feet, the hospital bed a barrier against her in-laws.

"Oh no, you're not."

Judith looked down her nose at Lani. "Tell her Richard." She stepped aside and looked out the window, ignoring the other occupants of the room as she smoothed her leather gloves over her fingers again and again.

"Melanie, it's been very clear to me, that is to us," he said, glancing for a moment at his wife's rigid back before turning to face Lani more directly, "that you have neither the ability nor the resources to care for a child."

"What the hell are you talking about?" spit Lani, her eyes green fire.

Richard shook his head sadly. "That's the sort of thing I mean. But profanity in front of a child is one thing. Wanton neglect is another."

Rachel's eyes narrowed, but she said nothing.

"I've, that is, we've had our suspicions before, with your wild stories about Kit's accidents, but this week alone, he has been in severe danger no fewer than three times. First, you leave him alone and he witnesses a murder."

Lani opened her mouth, but she could find no words that expressed her feelings. No words that she could use in front of her son anyway, especially after the reprimand she'd received.

Richard kept talking.

"Then, he is almost run down by a car. Now, according to

Mac, you allowed the pilot light on your stove to go out, and if the gas poisoning hasn't damaged him irreparably, the resulting explosion and fire almost killed him. My God, woman, what is wrong with you?"

Judith broke in from her position at the window. She didn't turn to face Lani, she just kept smoothing her gloves.

"We refuse to take any more chances, Melanie."

"Mama?" Kit whispered looking at her over Rachel's shoulder. "Mama?"

For once, Lani didn't respond immediately to her son. She laughed out loud. "You refuse to what? When are you going to realize that you have no power here? Kit is my son. Stay out of my business. At this point, with the way I'm feeling right now, I don't care if he ever spends any time with you."

Richard shook his head. At the look on his face, Lani felt the blood drain from her own. He had something up his sleeve, and she knew Richard well enough to know that he never bluffed. He hadn't gained the reputation as one of the most successful prosecutors in Minneapolis by losing his cases.

Judith turned, head held high, triumph flashing from eyes so like Kit's that Lani couldn't understand why in one case dirty ice came to mind and in the other warm honey. "Show her the papers, Richard."

Richard handed a sheaf of papers to Lani. "I met with Judge Sheridan this morning and explained the situation. Fortunately, he agreed that Christopher is in danger if we leave him with you. These papers give us temporary custody of our grandson. We'll be taking him home right now. We'll talk about supervised visitation in a few days, and there will be a formal hearing in a couple of weeks."

"You can't do this. You have no right." Lani reached for Kit, pulling him from the bed, and clutching him close. He wrapped his legs around her waist and hung on tight. "Besides, Mac said he wanted to keep Kit in the hospital for observation."

Richard looked at her with indifference. "Mac will help us hire a home nurse."

Lani's voice rose. "I'll never let you take him. Never."

"You will, of course, want to hire your own lawyer, but it's rather late on a Friday afternoon. You may have trouble getting any real legal work done until Monday. I can recommend a few good lawyers for you. They're expensive," a flash of spite appeared and vanished from his eyes, "but they do good work."

Lani gulped. "You know I don't have that kind of money. You know ...." Words failed her, and in spite of her best efforts, tears filled her eyes. She blinked furiously. She never cried. Never.

Rachel stood. Even in her bathrobe she was an impressive figure. "You're going to have to do much better than wave a bunch of papers in our faces before we'll let you take Kit. I'm sure that as his grandparents you're not going to want to traumatize him any more than he's already been traumatized. I suggest you leave."

Judith refused to look at either Rachel or Lani and smiled a regal smile as she turned to her husband.

"I was pretty sure this would be your response. Richard?"

Richard walked over and opened the door. A county sheriff walked in.

Lani tightened her arms until Kit protested.

"Mama, you're squeezing me to pieces. It hurts."

Lani tried to relax her arms and found that she couldn't let go of her son.

Chapter 11

Lani shoved the door of the shop open with all her strength, causing the chimes above the door to whirl and clash in dissonance. She didn't care. She didn't care if she smashed every one of the stupid chimes until not a note of music remained.

Her eyes flashed around the shop. It was empty, empty of customers and empty of part-time assistants who had promised that they would not leave their posts. This time the shop door wasn't even locked. Well this time, she had had it. Michael was through. He was toast. Only, he wasn't anywhere in sight to hear what she thought.

Outside, the winter sky was black with early evening. No stars shone through the clouds. No sign of the moon.

Panting, and more than a little frightened of the rage surging through her body, Lani finally sank into the peacock chair in the window, until, remembering that this was Mac's favorite spot, she lunged out of that chair and into another on the far side of the shop. She wanted nothing to do with him. How dare he cozy up to her so that he could go and tell lies to Judith and Richard?

A sob caught in her throat as she remembered Richard and Judith opening the door to the sheriff. She'd pleaded and threatened, but the sheriff just kept repeating as he looked at the ceiling, at Richard, at Judith, and everywhere but her that she'd have her time in front of a judge to tell her story. When she refused to let go of Kit, the sheriff, still not looking at her, said that he would have thought she'd behave herself better in front of her son.

She'd looked down into Kit's frightened face.

"Mama, don't leave me. Promise you won't leave me." Tears had welled up in Kit's eyes, and he'd tightened his arms around her neck until she'd thought she'd choke, but she didn't tell him to let go, she just hugged him back—until Judith sniffed—audibly.

Lani had turned to look around the room. Rachel stood next to the bed, and for the first time since Lani met her, she was speechless, her face ashy and strained. With a pang, Lani realized that Rachel was still recovering. Judith was putting Kit's clothes together. Richard was standing by the door, conversing in a low voice with the sheriff and waving his arms, his invisible lips pressed tight together. Remembering Paul's comments about how his father's lips disappeared when he was angry, a tiny giggle escaped Lani's mouth before she could stop it.

A flash of rage sparked in Richard's eyes.

"That's it. I've had more than enough of you, Melanie. Give Judith the child."

"No, don't leave me," Kit's voice was shrill, just short of panic.

Lani looked down into his face and made her decision. They would not get her son for long, but for his sake and until she could find out who was trying to hurt them, he'd be better off with someone else, anyway. She gulped.

"Honey Bug, we're going to play a game. You like games, don't you?"

Kit nodded, but tears started to stream down his soft cheeks, until Lani thought her heart would break. "But Mama, I only like to play games with you and Aunt Rachel. I don't like Grandma and Grandpa anymore. I don't want to go with them."

Judith snorted again and said in an aside to Richard. "See, she has even poisoned the child's mind against us."

Lani ignored them. "Here's what we're going to do. Aunt Rachel is going to play too, aren't you, Rach."

Rachel moved over and put her arms around both Lani and Kit, resting her head against the tops of theirs. "You betcha. This is going to be so fun, er, you explain it, Lani." Her voice was still raspy, exhaustion clouding her eyes.

"Yes, well, you see, here's the deal. Aunt Rachel is going to go back to bed and get better—because she's gotta be ready to kick the next bad man right in the you-know-whats."

Kit giggled, and his tears slowed. "I know, I know, right in the testicles, right? Balls is a bad word."

Judith gasped, and Lani was certain that if she turned around she'd find that Richard had no lips left at all.

"Yes, Honey Bug, used in that way, balls is not a good word choice. So, Aunt Rachel is going to go rest. I'm going to go check out our shop and make sure that all the burnt places are fixed up, and for a little while, you're going to go play at Grandma and Grandpa's house."

"That's not a game. I don't want to go."

"I know Baby. Here's the game part. You can pretend that you've been kidnapped by ogres, big ugly, bad ogres, and that I'm gonna come and rescue you, and we're going to escape together. Oh, and Aunt Rachel is going to be the fairy godmother who gives us a magic wand so that we can … but wait a minute. That's the part of the game you get to make up."

"I do?" Kit's eyes were wide, and his tears had stopped.

"You do. You get to choose what magic we can do, and you get to choose how we escape," Lani had turned with a fierce look directed at Judith and Richard, "from the evil ogres."

Kit laughed in delight. "Grandma and Grandpa, right?"

Lani smiled as broadly as she could, "Right."

"Oh for the love of God," said Judith. "Give me the child."

Lani ignored her. She set Kit down on the bed and kissed the top of his head. "Start thinking, Baby. I will come and get you as soon as I can."

She'd picked up her purse and coat, put her arm around Rachel, and led the way out the door, stopping only to say in a low voice to Richard and Judith as she passed. "Enjoy your visit. It's the last you'll ever see of your grandson."

Rachel spoke in loud tones as they passed. "Oh Lani, did I tell you what Jeremy does for a living? He's a lawyer—and he's really great. He specializes in divorce and child custody. Let's go call him."

"Mama, Mama, don't leave me," Kit shrieked. "I don't want to play this game."

But Lani had walked out of the room, leaving her son behind, ignoring his cries, as he pleaded with her not to leave him.

With every step she took, her anger built and her rage grew until by the time she reached the Tropical Bean Coffee Shop she was ready to spit nails at anything or anybody who got in her way.

Michael was lucky he was nowhere in sight. Puzzled, Lani looked around. Usually one of her regulars was in the shop at this time of day. They often stopped by on their way home from work. If she'd ever needed the business, that time was now.

Unwelcome thoughts pounded against her mind. What if she couldn't raise enough money to retain a lawyer? What if Richard and Judith were successful in proving she was an unfit mother? Only she wasn't an unfit mother. She was a good mother. Life was so unfair. She was doing the best she could to raise her son with no help from anyone, and she was proud of Kit and his development.

The old phrase, "possession is nine-tenths of the law," waltzed around and around in her mind. She'd lost possession of her son. Richard may have been a jerk as a father-in-law, but he knew a whole boatload of lawyer tricks—and he was well acquainted with all the judges in town.

These thoughts pounded against her brain. Her fears were so pervasive that Lani didn't hear the real pounding for several minutes. When she realized that the pounding was coming from her apartment upstairs, she leapt to her feet and tore up the steep steps to find all of her regular customers working at one task or another.

Michael looked up, a streak of soot across his face and smiled at her.

"Lani, Honey, come on in," greeted Mr. Ambrosiak who was busy pulling down debris and charred wood from the kitchen wall. "We are making progress. Michael really knows what he's doing. Did you know he used to work in construction?"

Michael blushed and looked down at the floor, but a silly smile almost split his face. He ducked his head, and then looked back up at her. "See, I even b-b-borrowed these construction lights so that we c-c-can k-k-keep working no matter what t-t-time it is."

"Never you mind about that old fire, Lani." Dot Scheuneman panted as she tried to pull a recalcitrant nail from a stud that still looked pretty solid. "We are making progress, and we're not going to stop until we get your home back in shape."

It was too much. Lani sat down on the floor, and for the first time in years, she cried. She couldn't help it. Her customers—no her friends—gathered around her in concern.

Shirley sank down on chubby knees and put her arms around Lani. "Oh don't cry, Honey. We'll get things fixed up. I already took all your clothes over to my cousin Louise. She owns a dry cleaning establishment you know, and she's always bragging about her business. So, I told her to get every bit of smoke out of your clothes. I told her it was *gratis*. So don't cry, okay? In a few days, we'll have everything back to normal."

Mr. Ambrosiak broke in, "I have nothing more important to do than helping you get things back to normal. I've got two weeks of vacation, and I have to take it or I'll lose it, so you're really doing me a favor."

"Oh, Mr. Ambrosiak …"

"Pete, Honey. My name is Pete."

Michael broke in, "I still h-h-have to m-m-make up for t-t-taking off early the other n-n-night." His stuttering was worse than it had ever been. Lani regretted how angry she'd been with him.

"You're all so wonderful. I don't deserve it. Only, I'm not crying because of the fire. I'm crying because of Kit."

For the first time, everyone seemed to realize that Kit was nowhere to be seen. Lani watched the color fade from Dot's face. Shirley's hand flew to her mouth. Pete Ambrosiak opened his mouth, but no words followed, and suddenly Lani realized what they were thinking.

"Oh no, no, no, physically he's fine. A little too much smoke, but he's going to be just fine, really." The tears streamed faster down her face. "Only my in-laws told a judge that I was an unfit mother and got papers giving them temporary custody, and I've never been apart from Kit since the day he was born, and he cried so hard when I left him, and … "

Here she broke down and sobbed.

Dot patted her back briskly. "You can come and stay at my house, Lani. I've got an extra room. I'd be happy to have you."

"That's a really kind offer, ma'am, but Lani's coming home with me. We've got some serious work to do." Mac's head poked through the open window leading out onto the landing.

At the sound of his voice, Lani leapt to her feet, "You SOB. I'm not going anywhere with you. You're a jerk. You're a traitor."

"Yeah, yeah, yeah, I know." Mac grinned. "Wait until you really get to know me, Mighty Mouth."

"Mighty Mouth?" repeated Shirley in her soft voice. "Oh my. I've never heard that one before. What a strange nickname."

"Who are you?" Dot was more aggressive, biting off every word as it left her mouth. "My guess is that you do not know that Lani has alternatives. Besides, we don't know you."

"Ma'am, I'm a friend of Lani's."

"No, you are no friend of mine," said Lani. Standing with her feet planted wide apart, she swiped her sleeve across her nose.

Mac's eyes softened as he grinned at her. She gritted her teeth.

She didn't need his help or his sympathy, not after what he'd done.

"Oh Lani, give it a rest. I don't know what they told you, but you've got to know that I'd never help anyone—even Judith and Richard—take your son away."

Pete broke in with a puzzled look on his face. "Excuse me for interrupting, but who are you? If Lani doesn't want to go with you, then she certainly doesn't have to. She has us to rely on, you know."

Michael threw an anxious look Lani's way and said with a strange sort of urgency, "You know, what we c-c-could do? We could set up a cot in the shop at n-n-night. You've got a sink and refrigerator, and you c-c-could stay ... "

"Can it, Kid. Lani's coming home with me." Mac set his teeth and looked at each of Lani's neighbors with a challenging stare.

Michael opened his mouth to argue, but Lani cut him off.

"Get out, Dr. Mac."

"Oh I love it when you say my name like that," Mac grinned at her again.

Lani's face turned pink. She sputtered as she tried to think of something mean enough and clever enough to tell him what she thought of him. "You, you, you are ... "

"A concerned friend who understands what you are going through and who wants to help," finished Mac, his voice serious now. "Lani, I can help you get Kit back. We need to talk. You haven't got any other resources that I know of."

Dot, Shirley, and Pete Ambrosiak moved to form a line between Mac and Lani. Dot looked at the other two who nodded at her. "You're wrong, Dr. whoever you are. Lani has us. We won't abandon her."

Lani's eyes filled with tears again. She'd been fond of her neighbors, her customers, but she'd never thought of them as friends before. She'd always thought she was so alone, and the strange little trio before her touched her heart with their steadfast support.

Michael spoke up. "I still think you could c-c-camp out downstairs, and that w-w-way you'll always be … "

"You're right. There is absolutely no reason why I shouldn't stay here. I can put up a cot and be perfectly comfortable." Lani turned her back on Mac and walked over to push against a charred two-by-four.

As Mac opened his mouth to respond, his cell phone went off. He pulled it out of his pocket and barked, "Hello?"

In spite of herself, Lani turned so that she had a clear view of Mac's face. Michael and Pete Ambrosiak were pounding away again to dismantle her kitchen, but Dot and Shirley had stopped work to watch her watch Mac. When she glanced their way, they made a show of pulling out nails and tearing down charred boards once again.

"Call the police, and Janet, don't let her leave the hospital with Johnny. Not this time. In fact, if I have anything to do with it, she'll never lay hands on her son again." Mac's face was stone. His eyes flashed with a dangerous light, and his expression was a carbon copy of how he'd looked the first day Lani brought Kit to his office. Mac turned and seemed to look right through her. For a moment it was as though she didn't exist. Lani took a step back in spite of herself.

"I'll be back as soon as I can. This can't wait, I'm sorry."

Lani sniffed.

"Don't bother." She turned her back to demonstrate how much she didn't care if he ever came back. For some reason, she felt a perverse let-down when she heard him going down the stairs.

Letty tucked the folded paper under the windshield wipers on Lani's car. There, she'd done what she could to warn her, but even so, she would never give up her post, no matter how cold it was. She pulled the black rags close and headed back to her corner under the stand of pine trees that edged the side of building next to the Tropical Bean Coffee Shop. She'd hollowed out a space in the snow and lined it with old newspapers. It kept the wind off of her, and while no one could see her, she could keep an eye on both the front door and the sidewalk leading to the back.

If only she'd been here the night of the fire. She wouldn't fall down on her responsibilities again. Her thoughts blurred with events from more than twenty-five years in her past, each clamoring for attention. Her eyes filled with tears. In the end, everything had been her fault. She hadn't been brave enough or strong enough, but now, as always, it was as though her memories were made of the finest spider webs, and as she began to remember, her mind sparked a fire and the webs evaporated until the tears in her eyes dried and she once more felt the cold.

Letty looked around her tiny cave. Why was she there anyway? She couldn't remember. Never mind. It was time to go home now. She tottered to her feet and began to make her way down the sidewalk. In spite of her earlier resolve, she never saw the shadow hover and move against the door of Lani's house.

Michael shivered. Lord he was cold. He was also determined. It was time to make a difference. He was not going to screw things up again. Everyone else had finally gone home, and Lani was alone in the shop. He'd seen Letty emerge from behind a large shrub and watched her move down the street. Good. He'd grown to like the old woman. It was better if she were nowhere around when things went down.

Lani rolled over on the air mattress that Dot Scheuneman had loaned her. It was only 10:30, but the December night was dark and deep. In spite of her exhaustion she lay stiff and tense, furious with herself for losing Kit, worried that he was frightened and wondering why his mother never came to pick him up. She knew that he had very little understanding of time. All he would understand was that his mother had abandoned him. A small sob caught in her throat. She choked it back and rolled over to stare up into the darkness.

Shadows and light chased each other in crazy dances across the ceiling of her shop. Outside, cars sped by, wheels crunching against the snow and ice that had collected on the pavement throughout the day.

Earlier in the evening, it had seemed like a good idea to camp out in the shop for a few days until she could get her apartment back to some sort of order. Strictly speaking, it was against the health code for her to be sleeping in the shop, but as Michael pointed out to her, who would know? Somehow, even though the Tropical Bean was where Lani spent most of her time, tonight the space was filled with foreign sounds and shadows she'd never seen before.

Lani's thoughts turned to Mac. She clenched her jaw together until she could hear her teeth grind. She didn't care. A call had come into her cell phone at about 8:00, but she'd resisted answering it, sure that it was Mac. She wanted nothing to do with him. The big buffoon. How dare he tell lies about her to Judith and Richard? Remembering his assertions that he hadn't told them anything, she relaxed her jaw, wondering if she'd been unfair to him. He'd been so supportive that morning. Was it just that morning that she'd all but thrown herself into his arms?

In the darkness, Lani felt her cheeks burn. She clenched her jaw again. Besides, he was a liar. He said he'd come back, and he hadn't. Mac had access to her son. Judith and Richard had access to her son. The only person who didn't have access was his mother, and that was wrong. She'd get Kit back if it was the last thing she ever did, and she didn't need anyone to help her do it either.

A board creaked in the hallway outside leading down to the basement. Lani tensed, her breath caught in her throat. Her feet were ice cold, but her heart was suddenly heavy and pounding furiously in her chest. What was wrong with her? How silly. She'd never been afraid of the dark.

The same board, or one that sounded very much the same, creaked again. Lani's heart slammed against her ribs, and a rushing sound filled her ears. Her mouth was dry, and her body rigid beneath her borrowed quilt. Another shadow flashed against the ceiling, only it was unmixed with light, and it hovered rather than flashed as the others had done.

Lani sat up slowly, rolling to her knees and moving until the top of her head was level with the counter. She peered over, expecting to see someone trying to break into the shop. Nothing. No one. The stoop was empty.

She took a deep breath, feeling the tension in her body drift away. Lani lay back down. "You fool. This is your home. It's Northeast, for God's sake. Nothing bad happens here. It's safe as houses … "

The crash in her hallway brought Lani to her feet in one smooth motion.

Chapter 12

Mac glanced on the clock on his dashboard and smacked his hands against the steering wheel in frustration. The entire evening had gotten away from him and it was already 10:15. Lani must be thinking he'd forgotten all about her. He'd tried to call her cell phone, but she hadn't picked up his call.

He smiled, a feral smile demonstrating satisfaction with his evening's work. With Mac's testimony, Johnny Kazmarik would not be going home—hopefully, ever again. Working with the police and Child Welfare to secure Johnny's safety had taken much longer than he'd planned, but he was sure Lani would understand once he'd explained. Besides, he also had a report for her on Kit, which was the other reason he was so late.

He understood that in spite of the anger she'd directed at him earlier, she was heartsick over losing temporary custody of her son. Well, that's all she'd lost—temporary custody. Mac had seen her with Kit. He knew that she would never willingly let anything happen to him. He had wanted more information about these earlier "accidents" that Judith kept bringing up, and he had been determined to get some answers from her.

Dressed in a red velvet dressing gown, pearls still in place, Judith had been her most regal self when he dropped by. She bristled at Mac's questions about Paul's interaction with Lani and Kit prior to his illness.

"I am appalled that you would even question Paul's loyalty and love for his son," she said with an injured look on her face. "You grew up with him, Mac. He was like a brother to you."

"Judith, all I'm saying is that Paul was taking some pretty nasty stuff before his accident. Drugs like that can cause violent behavior."

"Mac, you don't understand. Paul is gone, and now we have his son. That's all we care about. You can be sure that Richard and I will do everything we can to protect Paul's son."

Mac looked around the room. "Speaking of Richard, where is he? I want to talk to him."

Judith shrugged her shoulders. "He's locked up in his study. He got a call right before you arrived and closed his door like he does when he doesn't want to be disturbed. He'll be out in a few minutes, I suspect."

Mac's frustration rose.

"Well, here's what I have to say, and I'll say it again to Richard. Kit isn't just Paul's son, he is Lani's son, too, Judith. He needs to be with his mother."

Judith walked up close to Mac, her eyes clouded with worry. In spite of himself, Mac's heart softened. She was the most imperious woman he'd ever met, and yet, when he'd needed a home, she had opened her own to him. She was also a shrewd woman. She immediately noticed the softening in his eyes.

"Mac, you have worked so hard all these years to help children who are in danger from their parents. Remember Robbie? If there had been someone to help him, maybe things would have turned out differently for your whole family."

For a moment, Mac was twelve years old again. Images of that night crept out of the dark corner to which he'd banished them. In spite of himself, he shuddered. He rarely let those memories loose anymore.

"Dr. Mac, Dr. Mac, did you come to take me home from the evil ogres?"

Mac pushed the memory aside and looked up to where Kit stood at the top of the stairs, his red hair tousled, his face flushed from sleep. He ran down the stairs, and pulled at Mac's hand. "I want to go home now."

"Kit, Darling, you should be in bed. It's 9:30, and you need your sleep." Judith's voice was gentle, but she was clearly frustrated with Kit.

"No, I want to go home. Please Dr. Mac. Take me home." Kit's eyes filled with tears. "I'm afraid Darth Vader is gonna hurt my Mama."

A chill chased itself down Mac's back, and his need to get back to Lani surfaced again. Too many unanswered questions rose in his mind. He stepped over to the hallway, and picked up Kit's *Star Wars* saber.

Lani had run after him earlier as he was leaving, and in a gruff voice had said, "I know you can see Kit, even though I can't. Give him this, and tell him I love him."

"Tonight, you need to stay with your grandmother, Kit. But your mama sent this for you." Mac handed Kit the toy, and the child's face lit up.

"She said I could choose any magic I wanted to escape from the evil ogres. She sent my weapon to help, didn't she, Dr. Mac?"

Mac was concerned about the pallor in Kit's face. At that point all he wanted to do was check him over to ensure that he was past any danger from the smoke he'd inhaled the previous evening.

"Your mama said this was your favorite toy. She also said to tell you 'she loves you 29'. Okay, how about we go into the kitchen so you can hop up on the countertop and let me check out your lungs, okay? We should probably also get rid of those stitches we put in your head the other day, eh?"

Kit lifted his arms, his brown eyes filled with trust, his russet hair, darker than Lani's, a deeper shade of red that caused so many memories to slam through Mac's mind that he closed his eyes for a moment and swallowed hard. If he could only turn back time just for a minute. What might his life have been like—not only his life, but also …. He swallowed hard again, the familiar discipline taking over. He didn't need to go there. It was too late. But he was damn well going to do everything he could to exert some control over his future.

Mac swung Kit up into his arms and galloped into the kitchen to plop him onto the counter.

Kit laughed in delight, waving his *Star Wars* light saber in the air.

"So, what's all this about evil ogres and magic, Kit?"

Judith snorted and coming from her the sound was so unfamiliar that Mac looked up in surprise.

"Oh," she said, tossing her head and fingering the pearls at her throat. "His mother has been filling his head with fairy tales, telling him lies about his grandfather and I."

"My mama never lies. I don't either." Kit thrust out his chin and looked Judith square in the eye. "You and Grandpa are the evil ogres, and I want to go home, now."

The child had a lot of his mother in him, Mac thought, and when Judith explained why Kit was calling both she and Richard the evil ogres, it had been all Mac could do not to laugh out loud. He felt a sudden urgency to get back to the small woman with the mighty mouth who was beginning to absorb all of his waking thoughts, not to mention many of his dreams as well.

Kit checked out fine. Mac finally convinced Judith that he didn't need to stay in bed the next day and a private nurse was an unnecessary extravagance. Kit refused to go back to bed unless Mac carried him upstairs. He lifted his arms again, and when Mac picked him up, he dropped his head onto Mac's shoulder. Mac inhaled the scent of small boy. Something clicked inside of him, releasing a surge of protective instinct from some internal reserve. Mac wrapped his arms securely around Kit. As he carried him to bed, he rested his cheek against the soft hair on the boy's head, resolving that he would do everything in his power to protect him.

Kit demanded a story, but he was clearly wearing out. Mac was only part-way through *Are You My Mother?* before Kit fell asleep. Mac pulled the comforter up around the child's shoulders, faintly disturbed at his new feelings and yet, somehow relishing this desire to care for a child. For the first time in his life, Mac thought seriously about what it would be like to be married with children of his own. Lani's image filled his thoughts. He smiled.

He heard the doorbell ring and wondered who would be visiting so late in the evening. Judith was opening the front door as he ran down the stairs.

"Jennifer darling, thank you for coming. I need you to talk to Mac. He thinks Kit belongs with his mother, but he doesn't know about her fits of anger. Tell him what Paul told you before he got sick."

Jennifer arched a perfect eyebrow at Mac, and tucked a hand through his arm, golden eyes gleaming with humor. "I came to take you to a late dinner, Mac. Judith says you've been working too hard, and besides, it sounds as though we need to talk."

She was stunning, thought Mac, totally unmoved. It was all he could do to not pull away from her. He chafed at the delay, but he couldn't walk off and snub her again.

"I'm sorry, Jennifer, but I have another engagement. I only have a few minutes before I have to leave."

Ignoring his assertion that he had to be leaving, Jennifer calmly removed her gloves and coat, and laying them across the cherry wood banister that curved toward the second floor, she once again tucked her hand through his arm. Her perfume rose, cloying and thick to Mac's nostrils. He suppressed an urge to sneeze.

"Mac, I think Judith is trying to tell you about the danger Kit has been facing," she said looking into his eyes. "This has been going on for a long time."

Judith smiled, visibly relieved. "I'll go get some coffee, decaf, of course. You two sit down and get comfortable. Jennifer, tell Mac about the first time that Melanie attacked Kit."

Annoyed, Mac pulled away from Jennifer and sat down in one of the wing chairs next to the fireplace.

Jennifer dropped with her usual grace into the chair opposite his own and stretched one slender foot toward the warmth emanating from the fireplace.

"Mac, have you ever wondered if Lani could be involved with these 'accidents' that keep happening to Kit?"

"No way. Jennifer, if you are implying that Melanie Emerson is capable of hurting her son in any way, you are definitely off base."

"Mac, look at the evidence."

He snorted. "What evidence are you talking about? I scarcely think she engineered that car accident. And, she'd have to be pretty desperate to burn down her house and endanger her business."

"But that's the point, Mac. She didn't burn down her business. Now she has nowhere to live, so everyone is feeling really sorry for her. Even Judith had a few pangs earlier this evening."

"Look, Jennifer, I don't know how you got involved in all of this ... "

Jennifer looked away, fingers pleating and then smoothing the cream silk of her slacks. "Well, Paul and I were ... involved. From the start, his marriage with Lani was a mistake, but then, Kit was born, and he felt guilty about leaving her."

"You're saying that Paul was involved with you while he was married to Lani?"

Jennifer flushed. "You don't need to sound so surprised, Mac. I knew Paul almost as long as you did. We were always attracted to each other. I think he felt sorry for Lani from the beginning, and I was young and not ready to settle down."

She leaned forward in her chair, the firelight glinting in the gold at her ears and wrists.

"Even when Kit was a baby, things kept happening. Once, when he was about six months old, she left him alone in the bathtub and he toppled over. Paul rushed into the bathroom and saw him thrashing, his face underwater. Another time, he rolled his walker over the edge of the stairs and fell all the way down to the landing. He got a concussion that time. But the worst was the night when he was two years old. It was right before Paul got hit by that drunken driver."

"Jennifer, Paul was the driver who was inebriated, and it wasn't alcohol, he was high on coke. Paul hit the other driver. It was a miracle that woman wasn't injured."

Jennifer shrugged her shoulders. "Paul did use drugs recreationally on occasion, but not to excess. The point I was trying to make is that a couple of weeks before his accident, Lani lost it one night with Kit. Paul said it turned out Kit had an earache, but they didn't know it, and when he woke up screaming in the middle of the night, Lani couldn't get him to stop crying. Finally, she started to shake him and shake him. As a doctor, you know what can happen when a young child is handled like that. Paul grabbed him away. He told me that he intended to divorce Lani and get custody, but then, he had the accident."

Mac looked at Jennifer. She spoke with conviction as though she had no doubt about anything she'd relayed. "Jennifer, did you ever think that maybe Paul twisted the facts around?"

"He most certainly did not." Judith entered the living room, balancing a large tray filled with a china coffee pot, cups, and a plate of cookies. She carefully set the tray down on a low table near the fire, and turned to him. "Mac, you've got to help us. Kit is in danger."

Heart pounding, Lani moved toward the door to the hallway and stairs that led to her apartment, listening hard, trying to hear above the rushing in her ears. Part of her wanted to grab her coat and flee to the safety of Pete Ambrosiak's house across the street. The other part of her wanted to tough it out.

This isn't the movies, she thought, embarrassed at her sweaty palms and racing heart. Walk into the hallway, turn the light on, check things out, and you'll see. A cat got into the house during all the comings and goings after the fire. That's all. Just a cat.

She pushed the door open. The smell of smoke was much stronger, and the shadows were darker without the large shop windows, which let in the bright light from the stores across the street. She flipped the light switch. Nothing happened. She was puzzled because all the lights had been working when she turned in earlier. Her heart started to pound again.

A faint scuffling to her right caused Lani to whirl around. Nothing. She tried to swallow, but somehow the saliva in her mouth had dried to glue, and she gulped instead.

I can't see anything, she thought, reaching out to feel her way forward. She banged her hip against the chest freezer that was snugged into the space beneath the stairs leading up to her apartment. Ouch. She heard another scuffling sound.

Lani started to breathe faster, her heart slamming against her chest. A bead of sweat gathered on her temple and trickled down the side of her face.

I can't see anything. Wait. The freezer has a light inside.

She turned back and scrabbling at the top of the freezer with her hands, she found and disengaged the lock, swinging the lid up against the wall. For a moment, the glare of the freezer light blinded her, and she blinked furiously against the red and green spots clouding her vision. She felt, rather than saw, a shifting of space behind her, and as she started to whirl, she caught a glimpse of what lay stuffed into the cavity of the freezer.

A woman's body sprawled atop frozen pizzas, vegetables, and hamburger packets, her skin a dull gray-blue, frost riming eyelashes and hair. Eyes drained of all but the faintest color, and frozen hard as marbles.

Lani screamed, slammed the freezer lid down and whirled back toward the shop, hands out, groping toward the door. Her fingers scraped against the old wood, and the edge of her right hand snagged against a nail that had popped loose. Her left hand brushed against something warm and pliable. Skin.

This is getting to be a habit, thought Mac as he pulled into Lani's driveway. He'd wasted 29 precious minutes listening to Jennifer's bullshit and Judith and Richard's pleading. They were convinced that Lani was systematically injuring Kit so that she could be the center of attention.

As Mac locked his Camry and pocketed the keys, he turned toward Lani's old clunker. He noticed a wad of paper tucked under one of the windshield wipers and curious, he pulled it loose. It appeared to be a note folded around several hard disks that clanged softly when he shook it. He tilted the note so that he could read the words slashed across the paper in sloping letters: *Protect the little fox.* Odd. Maybe Lani would know what it meant.

He tucked the note into his pocket and jogged towards the front of Lani's building. He paused in front of the shop door. It was black inside, and for a moment he wondered if Lani had decided to go home with Dot Scheuneman after all. Then, as his eyes adjusted to the darkness, he spied the end of a mattress protruding beyond the counter. He raised his hand to knock on the glass, and then thought better of it. After all she'd been through, Lani didn't need to wake up suddenly to see a strange figure pounding on her door. He backed away and jogged around to the back door. As he raised his hand to press the doorbell, thinking it would sound more formal and less frightening, he realized the door was ajar just as it had been the night Rachel was attacked.

Alarmed, Mac pushed the door open and slid inside. He heard a short, hard gasp, feet shuffling against the old floorboards, and then Lani screamed.

"Lani, where are you?" Mac rushed forward, eyes straining against the darkness as he tried to find her. He heard a grunt and then a soft thud. Lani cried out. The door into the shop slammed open spilling light into the hallway. Lani sprawled against the freezer, but Mac could see no one else.

In two steps he was at her side. He pulled her into his arms. "Lani, are you okay? Did he hurt you?"

"No, no, you came in time." Lani grabbed the front of his coat as though she would never let go. Mac put his own hands over hers and squeezed hard. "Wait here, Love."

He charged into the shop in time to hear the musical explosion of broken glass. A man leapt out the window and into the night. Lani was right on his heels. Mac grabbed her around the waist.

"Let him go, Lani. The police can chase him." Mac pulled out his cell phone. Lani paced back and forth the whole time Mac talked to the dispatcher.

"That bastard. The only part of my house that is still standing, and he has to smash a window. I can't believe it. *Bastard.*"

She backed up abruptly, bumping into Mac as a man's figure loomed in the window of the shop. Mac thrust her behind him and looked around for a weapon.

"Who was that g-g-guy?" stuttered Michael. He bent at the waist to enter the shop through the broken window.

"Did you get a good look at him?" Mac fired the words at Michael, eyes boring into the younger man's eyes.

"Uh, n-n-no, not really," Michael's cheeks flamed red.

"Okay, kid," said Mac. "What gives? You've been acting pretty strange the past few days. Why are you here at this time of night, anyway?"

Michael turned and looked outside as though he longed to flee. He took a step toward the door. Mac grabbed him and swung the younger man toward one of the chairs in the middle of the shop.

"Sit."

Michael sat. "It's not wh-wh-what it seems. I don't even know where t-t-to b-b-begin."

"Spill it, kid. What's going on?"

Sirens split the night, and a patrol car roared up to the curb. Lani and Mac both turned toward the front of the shop to see two policemen approach the door. Mac turned back toward Michael.

"You sit tight. I want some answers."

But Michael was gone.

"Michael," his partner's voice hissed through the telephone, "that is the name you're still using, isn't it?"

"You don't understand. Things keep changing," he said, resenting both the tone and the way he cringed inside whenever his partner used that tone.

"What do you think you're doing? We went over all of this earlier tonight. I'm beginning to think you can't even follow the simplest instructions. I fail to see how I could have made them any simpler. My first and most important instruction was to find a way to eliminate one—not two, not three—just one old man. Now we've got how many bodies? How many, *Michael?* Five or is it six? I can't keep count. I want to see you, and I want to see you immediately."

"What's the big deal? I did eliminate your one old man, and I did it in a way that keeps all suspicion away from you. I've been all over that Lani woman, too, like white on rice. At least I am when that Mac character isn't hovering all over her."

Silence.

"What did you say?"

"I'm saying that we have an added complication with that Mac person hanging around like a leech all the time."

His partner's voice sharpened with what sounded like annoyance. Heavy annoyance. "Don't worry about Dr. Mac. I'll take care of him."

"Fine. So, now maybe you can get off my back and quit complaining." He didn't need to take this kind of shit from anyone.

"I'll get off your back when you quit being so stupid," his

partner thundered in a voice harder than ice.

He shivered in spite of himself.

"You will do what I tell you to do going forward, no more, no less. Do you understand me? I want that woman taken care of. I want you to do it while her son is not with her. One woman. One body. Only one. Do you hear me?"

He nodded. There was nothing wrong with his hearing or his ability to take care of business. It wasn't the woman who was the priority in his mind, though. That kid was his number one priority. He knew for a fact that the kid saw him, and he'd heard the brat yammering away about Darth Vader. It wouldn't take a rocket scientist to begin to piece things together. The mother was on his list, but the kid was gonna be history in the very near future. There was nothing his partner could do to stop him. It was his ass on the line. He was going to do whatever it took to keep himself safe and get what he wanted. Whatever it took.

Chapter 13

Lani shivered, her face pinched, brow furrowed.

"Cold?" said Mac, instantly reaching over to take one of the fists she held clenched at her side into his warm hand.

Lani shook her head. "No. I can't get the image of that woman out of my mind."

"I know. The police will find out who did it, Lani. In the meantime, I'm not letting you out of my sight."

"Mac, where did Michael go? It was as though he's afraid of the police."

"I don't know where he went, Lani, but he's been acting strange from the beginning. Who is he, anyway?"

"All I know is that he said he was Jonathon Sutton's son," said Lani, an arrested expression on her face. "He showed up one day, and he was so good with the customers, I hired him on the spot. He's also been wonderful in helping to put my apartment back together. Did you know that he's the one who organized Dot, Shirley, and Pete Ambrosiak?"

"No, I didn't know that, but I don't trust him. He's up to something, and with everything else that's going on, I don't want you to be alone with him."

Mac turned back to the stove, pulling out the broiler to check on the porterhouse steak. He poked a fork into the meat, and deciding it was fit to eat, he turned off the stove, pulled plates out of the cupboard, baked potatoes out of the microwave, and canned asparagus from the pantry.

"Lani, could it have been Michael who attacked you?"

"I don't know. I don't think so, but it all happened so fast. What I can't figure out is how I'm linked to all this. The only connection seems to be Kit and whatever it was he saw in Jonathon's room that night. I didn't see anything, so why would I be a target?"

"I don't know, Love. But we're going to figure it out, and, I'm not letting you out of my sight until we do."

"Mac, you don't even know me."

He turned and looked into her eyes. "We know each other, Lani. Somehow. We know each other."

She looked into his eyes for a moment and smiled. Not a big smile, but it was a start, thought Mac.

"Come on, sit down and eat. You've been shivering for the past two hours, and I have a hunch that you've been so worried about Kit that you didn't eat anything much all day."

"Don't fuss. I don't need it," Lani said tartly, but she slid onto one of the stools at the kitchen island. She took a deep breath. "Sorry, I didn't mean to snap at you."

Mac sat down on the stool next to her and grinned. "Lady, if that's what you call snapping, I don't mind at all."

The smile slid off his face as he remembered the stiff, blue body crammed into the freezer. "Besides," he said more soberly, "I think I know how you feel. I saw her too, you know. Poor little woman."

He reached over and pulled Lani against him in a quick hug. "Eat up, now. Doctor's orders. If you clean your plate, you can stay up late and have dessert. I've got chocolate chip cookies."

Lani's smile was thin, but she obediently took a bite of the steak. She closed her eyes and chewed. "Oh, this is really good. I have to actually use my teeth, and I don't taste even a hint of cheesy noodles."

"So, macaroni and cheese isn't your very best favorite?" asked Mac.

"Huh?"

"I heard Kit say it was his very best favorite the day I put those stitches in his head."

"Oh, well, it may not be my favorite, but it doesn't cost much, Kit loves it, and it isn't so bad in terms of nutrition."

Mac raised an eyebrow.

"Well, it isn't," she said flushing, "Especially if you have something green with it. We always have something green with our macaroni and cheese." She started to laugh. "Don't you dare say what you're thinking."

Mac grinned. "How do you know what I'm thinking?"

The pink deepened in her cheeks, and she laughed again. "I know, I can see it."

"Well, you did conjure an image of something fuzzy and green like a big, fat caterpillar." Mac reached out and tucked a curl behind Lani's ear. "Eat your dinner. Every bite."

They ate in silence for a few minutes. Mac's eyes never left Lani's face. He couldn't remember when he'd so enjoyed seeing someone eat. As Mac looked at Lani, his heart turned over in his chest at the memory of her scream. What if he hadn't arrived in time?

The police had no trouble identifying the body, since the woman's purse had been thrown in on top of her, containing her employee ID card for White Oaks Nursing Home. After a few pointed questions to Lani, it was a no-brainer to connect those murders to the attacks on Rachel, Lani, and Kit. In spite of the grilling they put Lani through, though, the only connection they could find was when Kit ran screaming from Jonathon's room babbling about Darth Vader. If that was the only connection, he would be the one in danger, not Lani.

"Mac, I'm glad that Kit isn't with me. He's bound to be safer with Judith and Richard. What I can't figure out is what he actually saw that night." Lani shivered, her eyes enormous. "He was so scared, and all he could talk about was Darth Vader. Why? What did he see?"

Mac frowned. "He said something about Darth Vader tonight, too. He said he was afraid that Darth Vader was going to hurt his mama."

Lani's eyes filled with tears. Mac reached over and took her hands in his own. "We'll get him back, Lani. He belongs with you." Mac's voice was gruff. He cleared his throat. "You know I didn't agree to help Judith and Richard, don't you?"

Lani looked deep into his eyes, and he looked back steadily. She nodded.

"It's just that I'm not used to anyone wanting to help me. I've been alone for so long." A tear slid down Lani's cheek, and she dashed it away with her hand. "Oh God, I hate women who dissolve into tears. I don't really feel sorry for myself, you know. Things are going fine. My shop has been drawing customers, and I'm almost out of the red and making a profit, and ... " her voice broke, "my shop, Mac. They've put yellow tape all around it. I'm really out of business this time."

"For a few days, Lani, that's all. You'll be up and back in business by this time next week."

Another tear slid down Lani's face. She dashed it away even more brusquely. "I'm fine."

"Sure you are, but everyone needs someone once in a while," he said pulling her closer. She resisted, but Mac dragged her stool closer. He reached out and pulled her into his arms. "I need someone, Lani. I didn't think I needed anyone in my life, but I'm discovering that all I can think about is you."

Mac slid one hand beneath the mass of Lani's hair and stroked her neck, rubbing and kneading the taut muscles. He slid his other hand down to the curve in her waist, pressing her against his own body. Lani moved closer wrapping her arms around Mac's torso and rubbing her cheek against his chest.

"Lani," he whispered hoarsely against her hair, inhaling her scent. "I know this isn't the right time, but I need you."

Thoughts of Kit, the potential danger he was in, the murders at the nursing home, the fire, and the attacks she and Rachel had experienced spun through Lani's mind. It felt so good, so safe in Mac's arms. She wanted to close her eyes and forget everything outside of this moment.

"I need you, too." Lani pressed closer, sliding her hands up the length of Mac's back. She sighed a tiny sigh. "Mac, we've only known each other for a few days. How can this be happening?"

He stroked her hair, silent for a moment. "I don't know. Maybe we knew each other in another life or something. I feel as though I've known you forever. I don't want to let you go."

Lani stood and moved into the triangle space between Mac's legs. She slid her hands beneath his shirt, feeling the warmth of his skin. Mac reached down and tilted her face toward his. He looked down into the deep blue-green of Lani's eyes, searching for a moment. She didn't look away. Instead, she reached up and traced the edge of Mac's jaw with one slender finger.

Mac lowered his face to hers, his lips brushing the tender skin beneath each eye, and tracing gentle kisses down to the end of her nose. His lips connected with hers. Soft, her lips were so soft. With the tip of his tongue, he probed gently, and Lani responded with the tip of her own. Lightning flashed to the core of his body, and he deepened the kiss.

Lani moved closer still, pressing her lips against Mac's throat, running her hands over his face, and threading fingers that were suddenly not quite so gentle through his hair.

She sighed as Mac swung her up into his arms. It had been so long since anyone had held her, since she'd felt a man's hands on her body. Mac carried her without speaking into his bedroom at the end of the hallway, and pausing next to his bed, he looked into her eyes, a question in his own.

In answer she twined her arms around his neck and pulled his head down so that she could kiss him, leaving no doubt about her desire. Mac swept the covers off the bed and deposited Lani with a little bounce right in the center. He smiled and she smiled back, watching as he started to unbutton his shirt.

Lani got to her knees and pushed his hands away. "Let me," she said softly. She pushed his shirt away from his shoulders and Mac shrugged, allowing it to fall to the floor.

"My turn," he said gruffly. Reaching out to thread his fingers through Lani's thick hair, he cradled her head in one large hand while he brushed kisses across her brow and cheekbones, his nose rubbing softly against hers, fingers kneading the back of her neck.

Nerves Lani didn't even know she possessed started thrumming at the touch of his hands and lips. When Mac stepped back, she murmured in protest. He ran his thumbs along Lani's collarbone, and then slowly slipping his hands beneath Lani's t-shirt, Mac stroked her back and sides for a moment before pulling the shirt over her head. Cool air stirred against her hot skin.

Mac leaned forward and kissed the slope of her breast, and Lani closed her eyes and slid her hands into the thickness of Mac's hair as he nuzzled her breasts. Mac reached behind Lani to unhook her bra and drop it to the floor. Suddenly shy, she closed her eyes and leaned forward pushing the fullness of her breasts against the crisp black hair of Mac's chest. Her eyes flew open as her nipples tightened against the heat of his body. Mac pushed her away.

"Let me look at you. God, Lani, you are so beautiful."

He reached out to stroke the sides of Lani's breasts with light, butterfly fingers. Lani groaned deep in her throat, and Mac leaned down to take one hard nipple into his mouth and suckled gently. Heat exploded in Lani's groin, and with a sudden urgency, she pushed Mac away so that she could reach his belt buckle. He helped her, shedding khakis and boxers in one motion and standing naked before her.

His eyes met hers, and suddenly her shyness fell away and she looked at him. All of him. Of their own volition, her hands reached out and rubbed against the rasp of his evening beard. Moving lower, she stroked the width of his chest, tangling her fingers in the black hair and tracing the line down to his flat belly.

Mac pushed Lani back onto the bed with an urgency of his own and lay down beside her. Pulling her into his arms he once again stroked her the length of her back, hands dipping into the curve of her waist and out again over the fullness of her hips. He pushed her back against the pillow and lowering his head, he took first one and then the other nipple into his hot, wet mouth.

"Mac, oh Mac," moaned Lani, her face flushing with heat, her body hot and heavy. Mac lifted his head for one short moment to meet her eyes, and then lowered it again to begin kissing his way down Lani's torso and across her stomach.

A quiver spiraled through Lani's belly as Mac's lips brushed and nibbled their way lower and lower still.

"Ahhh, Lani." He inhaled her scent and brushed the hot, tip of his tongue against her and then gently grabbed the center of her sex with his teeth and pulled gently until the spiral grew and spun and Lani began to gasp his name as explosion after explosion rocked her body and mind.

"Mac, oh Mac."

Mac turned and opened Lani to him, draping her legs over his shoulders and entering her with one long thrust. He rocked back and forward, his movements awakening new sensations, his body growing tenser and tenser until with a shout and one final thrust, Mac pulled Lani into his arms.

"You're mine," he said fiercely, burying his face in her hair and pulling her head down onto his shoulder. "You are mine."

Lani wrapped her arms around Mac's waist, took a deep breath and felt her body relax. Her breathing grew even, and the last thing she thought before falling asleep was that Mac was right. They knew each other. Somehow, in that special way that happens only rarely between a man and a woman, they knew each other. She felt as though she'd come home after a very long absence.

Light pressed against Lani's eyelids, but she didn't want to wake up. She was warm, her body nestled in softness, and outside she could hear the wind shrieking against the side of the house, ice pelting the window.

She yawned, thinking I've got to get up and open the shop. She stretched, and her foot encountered a warm leg. Her eyes flew open, and the first thing she saw was Mac's face turned towards hers, his eyes filled with amusement and understanding.

"Good morning."

Lani sat up, the quilt falling away from her shoulders and baring her from the waist up. Damn it was cold. Her teeth started to chatter. Mac reached for her, pulling her back down against the warm length of his body. He wrapped his arms around her waist, one hand reaching up to cup her breast. He stroked the side of her breast with the very tips of his fingers. Lani moaned, closing her eyes and giving herself up to the sensations fluttering to life in her belly. She rolled over to put both of her hands on Mac's face, stroking the bristles that had emerged over-night, relishing the crisp rasp against her fingertips.

"Make love to me again, Mac. I want you."

Mac lowered his face to hers, rubbing the edge of his nose along the plane of her cheek and then dropping soft kisses along her jaw. His lips found her ear lobe. He nibbled gently and then pulled it into his mouth to suckle.

Lani groaned and turned her face into Mac's throat. She started her own assault of kisses, rubbing her nose against the scratchy new beard. Mac swallowed convulsively, and said in a thick voice.

"I need you, Lani. I need you." He ran his hands up and down her back, stroking the soft skin over and over.

Lani started the coffee, and Mac cracked eggs into a blue ceramic bowl, whipping them to a lemony froth. He added a dash of garlic, salt, and pepper, threw in a handful of green peppers and cheddar cheese, and poured the mixture into a hot frying pan.

As the coffee dripped and gurgled into the aluminum pot, Lani wandered into the adjoining living room attracted by a small framed photograph on the mantelpiece. She reached out and picked it up.

"Oh my God, he looks like Kit."

Mac looked over at her, nodded, and looked back at the eggs he was stirring in the pan. He cleared his throat. "I know. It struck me the first day I met you, and then again when you brought him into my office the day that crazy driver tried to run you down."

Lani picked up the photograph, studying it. The child was looking up at a young Mac, clutching a child-sized baseball glove and bat against his chest, an enormous smile lighting his eyes.

"Mac, you couldn't have been much more than twelve years old. That little guy looks like he worshiped you. Look at his eyes."

"His faith was misplaced. I couldn't save him."

Mac's voice was gruff, his eyes stony as he looked at Lani. She shivered. Mac hadn't looked at her like that since the first day in his office.

"Mac, what happened to him?"

He didn't answer. Instead, he reached out and pulled two plates down from the cupboard. Lani came back into the kitchen carrying the photograph with her. She sat down at the island, and waited silently. Mac filled the plates with mounds of scrambled eggs, slid slices of whole-wheat toast onto each plate, and plopped the plates down on the island. Lani watched him, but still said nothing. Mac grabbed a carton of orange juice from the refrigerator and sloshed some into a couple of small glasses. His movements were precise, but his mind seemed focused outside that room and outside that kitchen.

"Tell me what happened, Mac." Lani reached out and touched the back of his hand. He finally looked at her. "Come sit down, and tell me what happened."

Mac joined her on a stool, and forked an enormous pile of eggs into his mouth. He chewed, swallowed, took a sip of juice, and then leapt to his feet.

"I forgot the coffee."

Lani pulled him back onto the stool and slid off her own. "I'll get the coffee. Talk to me, Mac." She filled two mugs with the amber brew and sat back down next to Mac. She pushed one of the mugs across the counter and waited.

Mac reached out with gentle fingers and touched the photograph. "Robbie. He was my little brother, and in this picture he was five years old. He wanted to play baseball like I did."

He laughed, harshness easing away from his face, light returning to his eyes. "Robbie wanted to do everything I did. I used to call him my copy kid, and every time I called him that, he'd giggle and say, 'copycat, not kid, Mackie'. Then, he'd laugh and laugh at his own joke. Robbie was the only person who ever called me Mackie. My friends used to tease me about it, but I didn't care. He was my little brother, and I loved him more than anyone else on this earth."

Mac stopped, clearing his throat. He closed his eyes. Lani reached over and took his hand, saying nothing, waiting for him to continue.

"Mom took this picture of the two of us on Robbie's fifth birthday. I gave him a little kid's baseball mitt and bat. He was so proud of them that he insisted on sleeping with them that night." Mac chuckled. "My mother tried to get him to put them under the bed, but Robbie insisted that it was more comfortable to sleep with the glove under his pillow, and he said that the bat was protection against burglars. I don't have a clue where he picked that one up."

Lani smiled. "It reminds me of Kit and his *Star Wars* light saber."

"I know. That's exactly what I thought the first time I saw Kit—that and the red hair reminded me of Robbie, big-time."

Mac reached out and picked up the photograph, studied it for a moment, and then gently put it back on the counter. His eyes were dark with memories, and two, deep vertical lines changed the contour of his forehead. Lani had never seen Mac so vulnerable before. She'd seen him angry. She'd seen him tender. And, she'd seen him fierce, protective, and funny. But he'd never looked right through her as though she were not even in the room with him.

She reached up and touched his face. "Mac, what happened to Robbie?"

Mac blinked several times, his eyes shiny with moisture. "He died. My father was off on some business trip the night of Robbie's birthday. He was always gone, and we were so much happier without him. The night after Robbie's birthday, my father came home. It was obvious to all of us that his trip had not been a success. My father wasn't the pleasantest person at the best of times. That night was not one of those times.

"My mother kept walking around shushing us and trying to please him. I was trying to stay out of his way, and Robbie was dogging my heels everywhere I went. When my best friend, David, called and asked if I'd like to stay overnight at his house, I leapt at the chance."

Mac slid off his stool and paced over to the window, looking out at the snow blowing through the yard.

"I never saw Robbie alive again. I don't really know what happened that night. I can only guess, because my mother fell apart and ended up in the hospital. All I know is that Robbie did something, got in my father's way somehow, and my father hauled off and hit him. When he did, Robbie fell and hit his head against the edge of the fireplace." Mac's voice broke. "He was so little. If I'd been there, it wouldn't have happened."

"Mac, you don't know that," said Lani fiercely. "You were only a kid. I was an adult, and I almost lost Kit the same way."

Mac's head jerked up.

"Oh yeah," said Lani bitterly. "I'm sure you've heard Judith's version of the famous abuses my son has endured."

Mac shook his head, "Lani, I never believed … "

"Oh, yes you did. Don't deny it. The first time I brought Kit into your office, you all but accused me of abusing him."

"I'm sorry, Lani. Something comes over me when I think a child is being abused, but you've got to believe me. I never thought you'd hurt Kit. Not really. The minute I saw you with him, I knew you were a good mother."

"Well, Judith never believed me when I told her that Paul was beginning to lose it big time with Kit." Lani's voice was passionate, and she started to wave her hands all about. "Paul was using drugs more and more often. I didn't know how to get him to stop. One night he came home late. I don't know where he'd been, but the look in his eyes scared me. Kit had an earache all that day. He woke up screaming right after Paul got home."

Lani shuddered. "Paul marched into Kit's bedroom and snatched him out of his bed before I could stop him. He started to shake him. I'm not a doctor, but I know what can happen to a small child's brain when their head is snapped back and forth. I grabbed Paul's arm, but he knocked me down. I screamed at him, and when he wouldn't stop shaking Kit, I grabbed a lamp and smashed it against his head. He fell to the floor, dropping Kit."

"Paul wasn't really hurt. I don't care what his mother says. I took my son that night, and we moved in with Rachel until I could find a place for us. That was two years ago, and I haven't regretted leaving Paul for one moment. I had no choice. Now, Judith and Richard are trying to take my son away from me. That's not right. I'm a good mother."

Mac pulled Lani into his arms. "They won't get your son, Lani. I'll testify. No judge in his right mind ever assigns custody to a grandparent when the mother is able and willing to take care of him."

Chapter 14

"Christopher Emerson, you put those mittens right back on."

Kit spun around to see his grandmother standing in the back door. "Ah Grandma, I can't fight the evil guys with my mittens on."

Kit swung his light saber in a half-circle, lunging forward to stab first one and then another of the enemies of the empire. He wanted to rebel against everything his grandma told him to do. He wanted to make her so mad, she would finally let him go home to his mother.

Even though the early morning sun was shining bright it was cold outside. This was the first morning his grandmother had even allowed him to play outside since he'd come home with her from the hospital the previous week, and she'd said he could play for fifteen minutes, no more.

"Please put them on or come back inside. It's freezing outside this morning."

Grumbling to himself, Kit pulled his mittens back on and held his hands up high so that his grandmother could see.

"Thank you, darling." Judith ducked back inside the house, and Kit turned and got back to business.

"Take that you evil alien." Kit enthusiastically jabbed the air with his light saber.

"Kit, hey Kit."

Kit stopped killing evil aliens and looked around, but he saw no one.

"Psst, Kit, over here behind the garage. Your mom sent me with a message."

Kit turned toward his grandpa's garage, and when he saw the man standing there, he smiled and moved forward. Kit knew that he wasn't supposed to talk to strangers, but he knew this man.

"My mama sent me a message? Where is it?"

"Shhh, come closer. Your mom told me to whisper the message in your ear so that your grandma can't hear it."

Obediently, Kit moved right up next to the fence. The man reached over, grabbed Kit under the arms with his large hands, and hoisted him over the fence.

"Hey, wait a min …" yelled Kit, but before he could finish his sentence, a large white cloth came down over his face. It smelled sweet and funny, and Kit didn't like it. He held his breath, and kicked as hard as he could to get away. His right boot connected with the man's stomach.

"*Oomph.* You little bastard."

Big hands pressed the white cloth harder against Kit's face until finally he had to take a breath. A whooshy wind blew through Kit's mind. His stomach started to spin. Kit tried to kick the bad man in the stomach again, but somehow his legs wouldn't do what he wanted. Black spots filled his vision until he knew no more.

"Well, the police sure made a mess," said Rachel in disgust, vigorously wiping down the counter around the cash register. "What did they think they were going to find in here, anyway?"

"I don't care how messy everything is. I can finally open up shop again. It's been five days. If I don't get things up and running again pronto, I'm going to be out of business," said Lani.

She swiped at one of the glass tables, wiping it clear of the black fingerprint powder the police had sprinkled liberally throughout her shop and the hallway beyond. Mac ran the vacuum cleaner by the front door. Things were beginning to be presentable again. Mac had even arranged to have her front window repaired.

He looked up and his eyes met Lani's. They smiled at each other.

"Sweet," said Rachel acknowledging the interchange. "About going out of business? Not in this lifetime. I've never seen so many people rally around someone before. You've got a lot of friends, Kiddo."

"I know. Don't think I take it for granted, either. The upstairs is almost livable again, thanks to Michael."

"I'm still not sure I trust him. He ran out of here pretty fast the other night when the police showed up."

"Michael explained that, Mac. He was hanging around outside the shop because he was worried about me being alone. I think you scared him when you started yelling, and that's why he took off. Only, he's too embarrassed to admit it."

Mac snorted. "Well, while he was 'hanging around' why didn't he see an intruder break in through your back door?"

Lani shook her head and shrugged as Mac hauled the vacuum to the other side of the shop and continued working.

"Speaking of angels, where is the man? I haven't seen him since last night when he was managing the crew. Isn't that Dot Scheuneman just the cutest thing with a tool belt slung around her waist?" Rachel wiped her perspiring forehead with the back of her arm. "Whew, isn't it hot in here?"

Lani looked at her with concern. "No, it isn't hot. Rachel, sit down and rest. The doctor told you to take it easy for a couple of weeks. I think you're working too hard."

"Hey, I cancelled my date with Jeremy the hunk for tonight. Anyway, I don't mind not seeing him. He's cute, but a bit of a bore lately. I like my men cute—and smart."

Rachel moved out from behind the counter. "Besides, we're going to get this shop up and running by the end of the day, or it's the last thing we're going to do."

"Thanks Rachel. I don't know what I'd do without you."

"So, what's the news on the Kit kid?"

"The court date is set for next Wednesday. Mac is sure that I'll get him back, but Rachel, what if I don't? I haven't even been allowed to see Kit for the past three days. The worst thing is whenever I call him, he cries for me to come and get him. Kit is too little to understand what's going on, Rachel. He thinks I've abandoned him."

"No, he doesn't, Lani. He knows how much you love him. Kids have an instinct." Rachel pulled her hair back, twisted it into a knot, grabbed a pencil from below the display counter, and shoved it through her hair to anchor the heavy mass. "So, how is it going with, uh, you know?" Rachel jerked her head towards Mac.

"Fine," Lani blushed.

Rachel pounced. "Spill it. Don't you dare leave anything out; I want all the details."

"Shhh, he's going to hear you."

"So, what?" Rachel tossed her head. "If you don't tell me how things are going, I'll just ask him."

"You wouldn't dare," said Lani with a sudden grin.

"Sure I would," said Rachel reasonably. "Hey Mac, I have a question."

Mac turned at the sound of Rachel's voice, and over the vroom of the vacuum cleaner, he shouted, "I might have an answer, try me."

Rachel stepped forward, and Lani grabbed her arm, pulling her back. She started to stammer, "What she really means, that is, uh, what Rachel wants to know, er, that is … " Lani's eyes flew desperately around the shop as she struggled to come up with an answer that Mac would buy. She spied his black cashmere coat slung over the back of a chair, and snatching it up, she said,

"Rachel wanted to know if you minded if we hung up your coat in the back room so that it doesn't get covered with all this fingerprint powder."

Mac frowned, his brows meeting in the middle of his forehead, clearly wondering what the big deal was. Then he started to smile, and his eyes met Lani's again. "Sure, that's fine. Uh, thanks, Rachel, for thinking of it. Any other questions?"

"Well as a matter of fact ... *ouch*. Hey, watch your elbows, Lani, they're out of control." Rachel was smiling too. She exchanged a look of understanding with Mac.

Lani turned with Mac's coat in her arms. Feeling lighter than she'd felt in days, she sent a pointed look her friend's way. Rachel looked nonchalantly at her nails, ignoring her friend's glare.

As Lani stepped toward the back room, a white homemade envelope fell out of Mac's coat. It split open, spilling three beer bottle caps onto the floor.

"Hey Mac, what is this?" Lani read the crude scrawl of letters out loud, a puzzled look on her face. "It says, 'Protect the little fox. He is in danger.'"

"Oh shit," said Mac, flipping off the vacuum cleaner. "With everything that's been going on, I completely forgot about it. I found that note under the windshield wiper of your car, Lani, the other night, when you were attacked."

Lani reached out with one foot and poked at the beer bottle caps.

"Huh?" said Mac, coming over to take a look. "Beer bottle caps and a warning. Who would leave you such a thing?"

Rachel exchanged a meaningful glance with Lani. "Letty must have left the note."

"Letty?" Mac looked confused. His face cleared. "Oh, you mean that tiny street lady that comes in here sometimes?"

"She's Lani's lady in black rags and string," nodded Rachel. "She always leaves a beer bottle cap or two as a sort of tip. I swear she thinks they are gold doubloons or something."

"Kit means baby fox," said Lani slowly. A chill raced up her spine. She hadn't spoken to Kit since early that morning. Suddenly, she needed to hear his voice. She dropped Mac's coat onto a chair.

"Mac, can I borrow your cell phone?" Her voice shook with sudden urgency.

"Sure, Lani, go ahead. It's in my coat pocket."

Lani pulled out Mac's cell phone. Her hands shook. Mac pulled it away from her and dialed.

"Judith? Good morning, it's Mac. Can you put Kit on the telephone? Lani would like to speak with him." He pushed the speaker button so that Lani and Rachel could hear Judith.

"Oh, Mac, is this really necessary? She spoke with him earlier this morning, and he cried for thirty minutes afterwards. Lani needs to leave him alone so that he can begin to adjust to his new life."

Lani grabbed the telephone from Mac. "He doesn't need to adjust to a new life, Judith. He is staying with you on a temporary basis—that's all. Now, please get my son, I need to speak to him. Now."

"Well, we'll have to see how things turn out, won't we?" Even through the telephone airwaves, Lani could hear Judith's imperious sniff, and she could imagine with no difficulty whatsoever the toss of her ex-mother-in-law's head.

"Please Judith, please for once, for once in your life do me a favor," said Lani, her desperation growing as each minute passed, "Get Kit."

"Oh, all right. He's playing outside with that ridiculous sword thing. He won't let it out of his sight. Hang on."

Lani clutched the cell phone, holding her breath. Her sense of urgency continued to rise. Mac moved close and wrapped an arm around her, brushing a kiss against the top of her head. For once Rachel remained silent, no quips, no sass. They waited listening to the silence on the other end of the telephone.

"Christopher, where are you darling? Your mother wants to talk with you." Judith's voice was faint, but the three of them could hear her words.

Lani's heart started to slam against her ribs.

"Christopher, please answer Grandma. Stop hiding, darling, it's not nice."

Lani turned in Mac's arms, "Mac, something is wrong. I can feel it. Kit wouldn't hide. I know he wouldn't."

Without a word, Mac grabbed his coat, snatched Lani's off the chair she'd flung it into earlier that morning, and tossed it to her. "Let's go."

Rachel grabbed her coat and followed without uttering a word.

"He was here less than half an hour ago. I fed him his lunch. He insisted on macaroni and cheese, and even though I made it with a blend of cheddar, asiago, and parmesan, he wouldn't eat it. He said it didn't taste like the macaroni and cheese his mother makes. In fact, he actually said it smelled bad."

Judith was babbling and so distraught she didn't even seem to realize she had been running her hands through her hair, causing it to stick up in all directions.

"Judith, where's Richard?" said Mac looking around the room. "Is there any chance he took Kit with him somewhere?"

"No, he went into the office early this morning. I haven't spoken to him since."

Lani's teeth chattered. She'd never felt so cold before in her life. Mac hovered, never leaving her side.

"Ma'am, when did you last see the child?" The older police officer, Ridley, asked the questions, while the younger one, Szymanski, took notes. Mac recognized them both as the officers in charge of the nursing home murders.

"Just a few minutes ago, I swear." Judith whirled toward Lani, pointing her finger. "Ask her. She's been hurting my grandson for years now. For all we know, she's taken him so that everyone will feel sorry for her again." Her voice broke.

Ridley turned to look at his partner. Their eyes met, and they both turned to look at Lani. "Ma'am if you know anything about where your son is, now is the time to tell us."

Lani gritted her teeth. "This is bullshit, and you know it, Judith. Who put these ideas into your head? We are wasting time. I want my son."

Mac opened his mouth, but Judith cut him off. "Officer, this isn't the first time Kit has been in danger. Tell him, Mac."

"Lani has been with me, Officer, for the past twenty-four hours. Now, let's stop wasting time and find the boy."

Ridley turned to Judith. "When is the last time you saw the child, Mrs. Emerson?"

"I saw him a few minutes ago. I swear I didn't leave him alone for more than fifteen minutes. I told him that was as long as he could stay outside because it was so cold." Tears flowed down Judith's cheeks, smearing her mascara, and leaving pale trails through the blush and foundation she carefully smoothed over her face every day.

Lani glanced at the indoor/outdoor thermometer that sat on the hall table. On the drive over to Judith's the radio announcer had predicted a blizzard, and already the temperature was starting to plummet. Her baby was lost outside somewhere in the cold. She had to find him.

"You don't think this has anything to do with those nursing home murders, do you?" Lani couldn't stop shivering. She reached for Mac's hand.

"There's no way to tell, ma'am. It's too soon."

A brisk knock sounded on the front door, and a petite policewoman entered. Lani's eyes flew toward the object the woman held in her hand.

"That's Kit's mitten. Where did you find it? "

The policewoman looked away from the pleading look in Lani's eyes. "I found it on the other side of the backyard fence. Your neighbor, ma'am," she looked at Judith, "said that she saw a young man loitering behind the garage. She thought he was a friend of the family."

"I found this, too." Her eyes met those of her colleagues as she held out her hand. In the center of her palm lay a gum wrapper. An old-fashioned Clove gum wrapper.

Lani's eyes flew from Ridley to Szymanski and then back to the policewoman whose name she couldn't remember. "What? What does that wrapper mean?"

The older policeman started toward her. "We can't go into details, ma'am, but we found a similar wrapper at the nursing home under Jonathon Sutton's bed. We have to assume your son is in trouble."

Kit opened his eyes and groaned.

Before he could do more than register the fact that his tummy hurt, a spasm twisted through his small body. Turning onto his side, he retched, heaving the remnants of his breakfast waffles all over the floor.

Flushed and sweating, Kit lay still for a few moments confused and panting. Tears trickled down his cheeks. Where was he? The last thing he remembered was brandishing his light saber in his grandparents' back yard, daring Darth Vader's evil aliens to try and catch him. Then, someone had called his name.

His heart started to pound hard inside his chest. He shivered. Now that he was no longer throwing up, he could feel the cold from the floor seeping through his jacket. He still had his snow boots on, but he'd lost one of his red mittens.

Kit stuck his bare hand into his pocket, sat up and looked around. He'd had the strangest dream. He'd felt someone leaning over him and then lifting him to put something soft beneath his head. He turned and looked down at the heap of rags he'd been lying on.

He knew it was still day outside because he could see light

leaking through the windows over his head. The room was so big that shadows filled the corners. Kit got to his feet, and turned in a slow circle carefully avoiding the vomit at his feet.

McDonald's hamburger wrappers, still bearing bits of grease and cheese littered the floor, and a red French fry packet lay in one corner. Kit's stomach growled. His mouth watered at the thought of a hot cheeseburger. Beer bottles, some whole and some smashed to amber shards, lay among the wrappers. The walls were stone and the air smelled funny, like his grandma's basement. Painted pipes crisscrossed the walls, ending halfway down above long wooden tables. Here and there wooden benches lay among the broken glass.

Kit was starting to shiver now. He was cold. He was colder than he ever remembered being, and he wanted his mother. He'd settle for Aunt Rachel or even his grandmother, but he wanted his mother. The tears on his cheeks had dried, and his heart wasn't beating so fast anymore. He was going to find a door. Then, he was going to get out of this place.

Chapter 15

Damn, it was cold. It was cold, but it sure was satisfying to see everyone scurry around trying to find that kid. No doubt about it. He had them by the short hairs. He wasn't afraid of any of them either, not his partner, surely not Lani and company, and not even the police. In fact, why not prove just how in control of the situation he was? He sat up straight, deep in thought, mouth twitching in a crooked smile.

"If you won't come to Papa, Papa will come to you," he muttered under his breath. This was going to be a lot of fun. Sliding out of his car, he turned to grab a white box from the back seat. Hunching his shoulders into his coat, and lowering his head against the wind, he trudged toward the shop. He was so intent on keeping his head down, he almost didn't see the police car as it pulled up to the curb at the side of the Tropical Bean. If it hadn't been for an ambulance streaking down the road, sirens blaring, he would never have looked up in time.

"Shit," he muttered, starting to turn back to his car. He paused. A smile spread across his face. He wasn't afraid of anyone. He turned, hoisted the box onto his shoulder, and started walking toward the Tropical Bean.

"Did you hear what they said on the radio?" Lani stood in the window of her shop, eyes fixed on the sky.

Mac and Rachel sat at a table nearby.

Lani shivered. "The wind chill is 10 below zero now, and it's only going to get colder." She turned to face Rachel and Mac. "How long can a child survive outside in this kind of cold?"

Rachel walked over to Lani, and gently pushed her into a chair. "Sit, and drink that hot tea. You won't be any good to the Kit kid if you collapse."

Lani shivered again. "I can't sit still. I need to be moving."

"Okay, so move, but drink the tea."

Lani held the ceramic mug close to her chest, as though the warmth could bring her comfort. Suddenly, she stood up straight and leaned forward to peer out through the falling snow. An indecipherable sound left her lips, and she dropped the mug to the floor where it rolled unbroken in steaming liquid at her feet. All color left her face, and she swayed.

Mac jumped to his feet. As he reached Lani's side and put an arm around her, he could see the two policemen walking solemnly toward the door from their squad car.

Rachel grabbed the edge of the counter with both hands, her eyes fixed on the door.

Lani clutched Mac's shirt. "They found Kit. Oh God, Mac, I think they found Kit."

"Lani, you don't know what they found." Mac pushed Lani into Rachel's arms and unlatched the door.

"Ms. Emerson?"

"Officer Ridley, right?" Lani said nothing else, waiting to hear the worst.

"Yes ma'am." The older police officer took off his hat. "We don't have any more information about your son, but something has come up. We're hoping that you can answer a few more questions."

Lani took a long breath, wrapped her arms around herself, and closed her eyes. "I'll answer anything you ask, only please find my son." She opened her eyes and looked wildly back and forth between the younger and the older police officers. "First, I want you to tell me something, and I want you to be honest. Kit has been missing since nine o'clock this morning—and now it's four. What are the chances of a little boy surviving outside in this weather? I want the truth."

Officer Ridley looked her straight in the face. "None, ma'am, in all honesty. If, that is, your son were outside this whole time. If you want me to be brutally honest, being outside is not the scenario we're concerned about at this point. If Kit was kidnapped, in all likelihood, he is not outside."

Mac cleared his throat. "What do you want to know? The quicker we answer your questions, the quicker you can get out there and find Kit. Talk to us."

Mac led Lani back to her chair, and pushed her gently into it. The police officers followed, while Rachel moved behind the counter and poured out two large cups of coffee to go. She shoved one at each of the officers, who looked at her gratefully.

Wind chimes pealed and frigid wind whooshed in.

Lani's head turned so fast toward the door that a small bone cracked in her neck. When she saw who it was, she pressed her lips together and turned back to the policeman.

"Hello, everyone, late pastry delivery, here."

Rachel gestured to the counter, scribbled her signature across the invoice, and muttered thanks. The deliveryman took his time closing the metal holder over the invoice and looking around the room. A smile quirked the edges of his mouth, but no one noticed.

Szymanski pulled out his notebook and sat with pen poised. Ridley took a sip of coffee. He placed the cup down on the table in front of him and raised his eyes to meet Lani's.

"How did you meet Michael Sutton?"

Lani looked puzzled. "Michael? You don't think he has

anything to do with Kit's disappearance do you? Although," her brow furled, "he was acting really strange the other night?"

Mac nodded. "Yeah, and when I tried to question him, he bolted."

Ridley's head jerked up. "When was this?"

"It was the night Lani was attacked here in the shop."

Lani said slowly, "He was acting really strange that night when we were getting ready to close, and he disappeared right before the patrol car ... before you two showed up." She turned to Mac. "I still think he ran off because he was afraid of how angry you were. He was back the very next day, and he apologized for disappearing so fast."

Szymanski looked at her steadily. "Why didn't you say something that night?"

A look of confusion passed over Lani's face. "I don't know. Michael can't be part of all this. He can't. Kit loves him, and he's gone out of his way to help rebuild my apartment, you know."

"How did you meet him, ma'am, and when?" asked Szymanski.

"Well, he just showed up in the shop and asked for a job one day. I'm not really sure exactly when it was. Do you remember, Rachel?"

Rachel nodded. "He showed up the day after I was attacked. I remember because you told me not to worry about taking time off when you came to visit me in the hospital. You told me how much he wanted the job and how Letty responded to him, remember?"

"No offense intended, ma'am, but why would Jonathon Sutton's son want to work in a coffee house so badly?" Officer Szymanski cleared his throat as he looked around the shop. "Even one as nice this?"

Lani shook her head. "I don't believe Michael is involved in any of this. I think he wanted to work here because I knew his father. He told me one day when we were working that it helped him to hear about his father. I used to tell him about Kit and Jonathon. Kit loved Jonathon, and I think Jonathon was just as fond of Kit. When Michael was a teenager, some rift occurred between he and his father. I don't know what happened, but afterwards, Michael refused to speak to him. I got the impression that he'd finally decided to respond to Jonathon's attempts to reconcile. Only, he was too late." Lani reached out and Mac took her hand in his and held on tight.

"Who knows, maybe he's angry that his father connected so well with your son." Ridley turned to face Lani directly. "Ma'am, we believe your son did see Jonathon Sutton's murder. That said, we can't seem to find any link between the White Oaks murders. The only connection is you, including the attack on Ms. Rachel, the murder of Shari Peterson, the other attacks on you and your son— we believe all of it is connected. Somehow, Jonathon Sutton and his son, Michael, are central to everything that happened. Unless someone we don't know about is connected somehow."

They all jumped at the loud clatter, but it was only the deliveryman who had dropped his clipboard to the floor.

Rachel tossed her head, long hair flying back over her shoulders. "Was there anything else you needed?"

'Uh, no, no, I'll see you tomorrow." He turned and fled into the storm, wind chimes crashing as he slammed the door.

With an impatient jerk of her shoulders, Rachel turned back to the officers and rubbed her forehead with the back of her hand. "I don't understand. Why do you think Michael had anything to do with these murders?"

"Michael Sutton stands to inherit his father's entire estate."

Lani looked confused. "Well, that's the usual situation when a father dies, isn't it?"

"It's also a motive for murder."

"Well, then why on earth would he waste his time working here and asking questions about his father?" asked Mac.

"That's the six-million dollar question, alright."

When the knock sounded against the window, they all jerked toward the door. Outside the wind blew bits of ice and snow against the window. Snow streamed toward earth so fast and thick they could see nothing but streaming white. Mac pulled the door open, and icy wind howled into the room whisking the napkins on the table into the air and slamming them against the wall.

A cry escaped Lani's lips. She darted forward to pick up the object lying in a drift of snow on the stoop to the shop.

Kit was lost, and he was cold. He'd been wandering through the old building ever since he'd awoken. The hallways were long and dim, the rooms filled with the detritus of an abandoned business, wads of cardboard and paper, dust, broken glass, and odd pieces of wood and equipment.

As daylight waned outside, what little light existed streaked in through chinks in the boards covering windows set high in the walls, casting long shadows that swayed and crept. Scrabbling noises sounded inside the walls as Kit passed by. His stomach twisted with each scritch and scratch.

Kit reached over his shoulder for his light saber. He wanted to feel it in his hands. He knew the light saber wasn't a real weapon, but somehow it made him feel safer to hold it in his hands.

"Where'd you go?" He frowned and reached back further, thinking that maybe his weapon had fallen down inside his coat. He hunched his shoulders, but he couldn't feel the familiar poke against his back. He unzipped his jacket, reaching as far as he could over his shoulder. Nothing. The light saber was gone.

Kit's shoulders drooped. His teeth started to chatter. The light seeping in from the windows was grayer than it had been, and he could hear wind whistling and pulling at the old building. Kit zipped his jacket back on and reached for his mitten. He was so cold.

Ahead the hallway split into two directions. He turned right and as he passed an open door, a shadow appeared on the floor in front of him. The shadow lurched forward larger and larger. Kit gasped and turned to run, but before he could take more than two steps, the bad man swooped out of the door and grabbed him, lifting him off the floor.

"Aha, I've got you now," the man snarled, warm stinking breath steaming the side of Kit's face, filling his nostrils. "You were supposed to stay right where I left you.

"Let me go," he grunted, all the air squeezed out of him by the strong arm clamped against his stomach.

The bad man laughed. "Not on your life, bucko."

Tears started to leak out of Kit's eyes. His mom said it was okay to cry when he was afraid or sad. He remembered what his Aunt Rachel said once to his mom when she was crying about something that happened. Aunt Rachel said she was so mad she could spit nails, and even though the tears were spilling down her cheeks, Kit could tell she wasn't just afraid, she was mad. He sniffed loud, because his nose was all filled up with snot, mucus his Mama called it.

Then he started to get mad too. Just like his Aunt Rachel. He remembered something else. He remembered that if anyone tried to take him away he was supposed to yell, loud so that people could hear him and come and help.

So, even though he was being bounced all around as the bad man ran down the hallway, Kit started to scream and kick. The man lurched to a stop, and as Kit heaved himself from side to side screaming shrilly, the man dropped him. Kit fell down onto the concrete floor. It hurt, but he didn't care. He jumped up and started to run away.

"Get back here, you little shit."

Kit kept running, he didn't look back, but no matter how fast he ran, he could hear the bad man getting closer and closer. He was laughing, big ugly laughs that scared Kit more than the yelling. The bad man reached out and grabbed Kit by one arm and jerked him right off his feet and into the air. Kit screamed from the pain of being held by one arm, and he started to kick again. He was mad.

He was so mad, he was going to kick the bad man right in the balls.

"Aieeeeeeeee, Shit that hurt, you little bastard." The man dropped him again. Kit scrambled to his feet and ran, leaving the bad man writhing on the floor behind him. He came to another junction in the hall and swerved left around the corner, frantically searching for a place to hide.

Over on the far wall, he saw a door through the fading light, and he ran for it. He tried to turn the handle on the door, but his mitten slid uselessly against the metal. The bad man quit groaning, and Kit heard him roll over in the grit and dirt on the floor. His heart started to beat faster, and he pulled his mitten off, reaching for the doorknob again. The cold metal burned his hand, and when he tried to twist it, nothing happened.

"You might as well give up, kid. It's only a matter of time before I get my hands on you, and the longer it takes, the madder I'll be." Kit heard the man grunt, and then say in a mean voice, "I'm already pretty pissed off at you, you little shit. Come out, come out wherever you are," sang the bad man, a catch in his voice.

Now the bad man didn't sound mad. He sounded like he was playing a game. Somehow that made everything even scarier. Footsteps crunched through broken glass right around the corner of the hallway.

A tiny squeak left Kit's lips. Turning, he twisted the doorknob one last time, throwing his body against the door. It opened with a loud screech, and he fell inside. He streaked across the vast room and through another door set into the wall on his right. In the instant it took for him to turn and slam the door, he saw a mattress in one corner and a wooden crate that held ... his eyes widened ... a mug from The Tropical Bean.

"Come out, come out wherever you are," the man was closer now. Kit whirled back to the door pushing it closed and sealing himself into darkness. He felt for a button on the back of the doorknob. Nothing.

"Okay kid, we can play games if you want." Kit heard the man's feet crunching through the debris on the floor, his voice booming louder and louder as he approached. Suddenly, Kit heard a jingle of music. It sounded like his mother's cell phone. The crunching footsteps stopped.

"Now? You want me to come now? Look, I'm kinda busy ... no, wait a minute. You don't know what's going on. I *am* taking care of business."

Kit backed away from the door, trembling. His heel banged against a cupboard, and he dropped into a crouch, breathless, waiting.

Abruptly the bad man stopped speaking. "Hold on a sec, I'll call you right back. I may have found the solution to our problem."

"Hey you little bastard, I can hear you." The man's voice was low and sing-song. His voice came closer and closer.

Kit started to sob, and he put his hands over his mouth, trying to stifle the sound. Suddenly, something brushed past him, moving toward the door, and he heard a tiny click. He opened his mouth to scream, but before he could utter a sound, arms lifted him off the floor, and a warm hand covered his mouth. Kit went rigid, and then started to struggle. The arms around him tightened.

The doorknob rattled. "Hey kid, cut the crap. I don't have time for this. If you're in there, open the door." Kit heard a thud against the door, and then another. The wooden frame around the door creaked. The bad man kicked the door again with a dull thud. Kit heard a crack of wood.

The arms holding Kit pulled him back into an iron embrace and dragged him across the darkness and into another room as the bad man broke through the door.

"Where the hell are you, you little bastard. When I get my hands on you ... "

The musical jingling started again.

"Hello? Now what? Ah, shit. Whatever you say, Partner. Alright, alright, I'll be there. Relax, will ya? There's no need to get your undies in a bundle. I'm taking care of business like I said I would. I repeat. I am on my way."

Thump. Kit cringed. Another thump. It sounded like the man was kicking a wall, and then he laughed.

"Hey Kid, don't go away, I'll be right back. I've locked all the doors so you can't get out. Besides, there's a blizzard going on outside. Step into that and you're dead in 15 minutes. So go ahead, save me the trouble of taking care of you myself. Or, wait until I get back, and we'll have some fun." The man laughed, his voice fading away.

Kit struggled and the arms holding him suddenly let go. He tripped and fell hard to the floor. Looking up, Kit's eyes widened.

"Oh my God, it's Kit's light saber. He never lets this out of his sight." A flash of gold caught Lani's eyes, and she leaned over and plucked three beer bottle caps out of the snow. Oblivious to the wind, and the spinning snowflakes, Lani stood in the doorway of the shop, hugging the toy to her breast, laughing and crying all at the same time.

She whirled to the others. "Mac, look. Oh my God, Kit's okay. Letty has him. I know she would never hurt him. He's okay, he's okay. Oh, my God, he's okay." Tears streamed down her face.

"Love, come inside," Mac drew her back into the shop, closing the door against the blizzard, which seemed to be gaining force with every passing minute.

"Why would Letty take Kit?" said Rachel.

"I don't know. It doesn't matter. I just know she would never hurt him."

"Ma'am, slow down," said Officer Ridley. "Who is Letty?"

Mac broke in, "She is a homeless woman who comes in sometimes. She leaves beer bottle caps as tips."

"Well, then let's go get your son," said Officer Ridley. "You can ride with us ma'am."

Lani's hand convulsed over the golden metal disks. She looked up, eyes stricken, voice small.

"I don't know where she lives."

Chapter 16

He pulled up to the elegant apartment building with a screech of rubber and slammed the car into neutral. It was about time his partner learned who was in charge of this particular operation.

Lips tight, he swaggered his way through the lobby and into the elevator. He was surprised his partner had suggested meeting at Sutton's apartment, but what the hell. The police were so stupid, they wouldn't think of looking for a clue in a place they might actually find something. Turning the key in the lock, he burst into the apartment.

"It's about time."

His partner was sitting in the sunroom, surrounded by a warm pool of light from a Tiffany lamp and nursing a glass of what appeared to be the best brandy in the place.

"You know, I'm getting pretty sick and tired of all the orders." His voice squeaked, which pissed him off. His partner always had this effect on him. He could be feeling on top of the world, in charge of his universe, and within sixty seconds of proximity to Jennifer Sutton, he started to stutter and defend himself.

"Sit down. I poured you a glass of brandy. It's time we talked."

She was always so cool and assured, but then, why wouldn't

she be? He was doing all the planning, all the wet work. He was taking all the risk.

He took a breath, his confidence surging back. "Yeah, sure."

He crossed over to the sunroom and dropped into the big bamboo armchair. Outside the sky was dark and snow spit its way down to earth in icy clumps.

Inside, every surface glowed with lamplight. He could feel the tension begin to seep out of his body. Settling into the chair, he reached for the snifter. He tossed back a gulp of the amber liquid, and then took another to prove that nothing was too strong for him to handle.

His partner smiled, and the muscles in his back tightened at the sight. He swigged another gulp. His eyes fell on a gold box filled with chocolate truffles.

"Here, take one. I brought these for you."

He reached out and grabbed a chocolate, popping it into his mouth.

"Mmm, not bad." He snatched up two more and leaned back in his chair to enjoy them between sips of brandy.

"So, I thought I told you to leave the child out of this. I need you to tell me where he is."

"Yeah. I know you told me to leave the kid alone. Here's the deal though." He leaned forward in his chair, crossing one leg over the other and letting his right hand dangle loosely over one knee. Too bad he didn't have a cigarette he could hold between his fingers. He cleared his throat, taking his time to make up for the squeak he'd let loose a moment before. It was always important to be the one in control. In spite of his unease, he smiled.

His partner smiled back.

Encouraged, he leaned forward. "You see, Jen, the kid saw my face. No one sees my face and lives to tell about it."

The smile on Jennifer's beautiful face never faltered. "Why didn't you say so?"

Gratified, he put both of his feet on the floor, slapping his hands on his knees. "Well I did keep trying to tell you, Jen, but you just wouldn't listen." His words slurred together. His tongue felt thick.

"So, now you can tell me where you left the child. I'd like to know."

He was having trouble holding his head up. He hadn't eaten all day, that's what was wrong. "I left him at . . ." He tried to chuckle, but his throat wouldn't cooperate.

"You left him at ... " she encouraged in a soft voice.

As he looked at Jennifer, his eyes blurred. He blinked, and then blinked again hard, trying to focus.

She smiled again. "Tell me where you left him, Ryan."

"You said ... " he gasped, "that we shouldn't use our real names ... "

"I think we're past worrying about your real name now, Ry." Her voice thickened, "Where is the kid?"

"I left him ... left him ... bre ... brew ... ery." A spasm crossed his face, and when he tried to speak again the only thing that left his mouth was a long string of saliva.

Jennifer looked at him in distaste, "God, Ryan, can't you do anything right? You should have lasted a little longer than this." Her smile was no longer beautiful. Her eyes were cold as a wild cat's. When he tried to speak again, her smile grew. Reaching for a strand of hair hanging over one shoulder, she started to twirl it around her finger. "Give it up, Ry. You're finished."

"Robbie," the tiny woman hunkered down and started to pat him all over as though she feared he'd hurt himself when he fell out of her arms. "You're okay now. He's gone now. He can't hurt us anymore."

Kit had never heard Letty speak before. Her voice rasped like ripping silk in the cold room. He looked up, reassured by her familiar form. He wasn't afraid of Letty.

"I want to go home."

"I know, Love, I know," she crooned in her raspy voice. "Come now. You must be hungry."

Letty held out her hand, and Kit allowed her to pull him to his feet. She led the way into the smaller room. Reaching inside the old milk crate, she pulled out a box of matches to light the candles on top. She dug in one large pocket and pulled out a crumpled napkin wrapped around the remnants of the scone she'd gotten from Lani the day before.

"I want to go home."

The tiny woman smiled. "Robbie, Love, you're always joking with your mama, aren't you? We are home, and we're safe. No one will find us here."

"You're *not* my mama. I want to go home. I want to go home, *now*," his lip quivered.

Letty frowned for a moment at his words. A tree branch struck the side of the building, and at the sound she swiveled her head, listening to the roar of the wind slashing snow and ice against the windows. Her face cleared. She looked down at Kit.

"I know, Love. I want to go home too, but it isn't safe for us at home right now."

When he heard Lani say his name, Michael paused at the door leading into the shop.

" … Michael can't be part of all this. I don't care what the police think, Mac. He just can't. Kit loves him, and he's gone out of his way to help me since the fire."

Michael pulled back from the door leading into the Tropical Bean Coffee Shop. He'd come in the back door using the key Lani had given him, intending to spend an hour or two spackling the new sheet rock they'd all hung before Kit's disappearance.

Hard physical work helped him think. It freed his mind to roam through all the facts he'd gathered since his father's murder.

The work also helped him deal with the fact that he'd come home too late to reconcile with Jonathon.

After his mother died, it was weeks before he was willing to read all the letters his father had sent him over the past few months. It took two weeks more to make a final decision to come back to Minnesota. Michael closed his eyes for a moment and bowed his head. As his mother lay dying of the cancer eating its way through her body, she'd made him promise to make peace with his father.

"Darling, it's time to let go of your anger. Your father isn't a bad man. He never was."

"He hated me, Mom. I could never do anything right in his eyes."

His mother looked at him and shook her head. "No, Michael, he doesn't hate you. If he did, he wouldn't be trying so hard to reconnect with you. You won't even read his letters," she chided.

"He was rotten to me, and he was rotten to you when he had that affair. Mom, I was there. He broke your heart."

His mother got a faraway look in her eyes. "You know, something? I've had a lot of time to think since I've been ill."

"What do you mean?"

"I'm not sure he *was* unfaithful. I think I had a little help jumping to some pretty impulsive conclusions. That's the trouble with anger. Sometimes you say things, and afterwards the emotions you experience and the words you say lay like boulders in your path, and it's hard to put them aside. I said terrible things, and when your father tried to tell me he'd never had an affair, I called him a liar." Tears rolled down his mother's face. She rarely cried. "I think I may have been wrong."

"Oh, Mom," said Michael with a catch in his voice.

"I'd had enough, that was part of it, enough of all the lonely days and holidays because he had to work. I felt rejected, unlovable, and so angry. I refused to believe anything he said. I just packed up our bags and hightailed it home to my family in

Milwaukee."

"Well, he didn't listen very well to either of us. The only person he ever listened to was Jennifer."

"Yes," she said simply. "Jennifer was always there right in the middle of everything, wasn't she?"

Michael's lips twitched. "She sure was. She wrapped Jonathon around her little finger whenever she wanted something, and he let her do it. She used to tell me to stay out of her way because she didn't like to share. Mom, I was such a screw-up. I wanted Dad to notice me, too. That's all."

His mother chuckled. "Well, you were particularly gifted at being, now what's the word I want? Maybe a little bit geeky. You were so smart, you didn't seem to understand how to make your way in the world. You tried so hard, and I know he loved you. He was too busy to give you the attention you needed to feel more confident, that's all."

That was the truth, thought Michael. His father was a busy executive. He never had much time to spend with a geeky, clumsy son.

Michael jerked back to the present at the vehemence in Lani's voice.

"No, I refuse to believe that Michael could have anything to do with Kit's disappearance."

Michael's heart warmed at Lani's confidence in him.

"The fact is, though, Lani," said Mac, "you don't really know him. Everything the police said implicates Michael in his father's death."

Michael couldn't blame Mac for suspecting him. He frowned. If he were in Mac's place, he would have had the same suspicions.

His mouth went dry, and his heart started to pound. Someone had done a most excellent job in setting him up. What he couldn't figure out was any connection between the four people who died that night at White Oaks. There had to some connection, and what about that girl, Shari, who ended up in Lani's freezer. She'd worked at the nursing home. So, somehow, she had to be connected too.

"It doesn't matter, not right now," said Lani. "I don't care if Michael murdered his whole family. I need to find Kit before it's too late."

Michael leaned forward so that he could peer into the shop.

"Okay, let's think. If Letty has Kit, at least we know he's safer than he would be if someone else had him. But why did she leave his light saber on the doorstep?"

"Yeah, and what about these beer bottle caps?" said Mac, flipping one high into the air and catching it. "They're perfect. They look brand new."

"Think," said Rachel. "She has to have a ready supply. Where on earth could she find brand new beer bottle caps in the dead of winter?"

"Oh my God," said Lani. "The old brewery. Could she have Kit at that old, abandoned brewery? It's just a few blocks away."

Michael backed up so fast, he tripped over the broom he'd left leaning against the wall. Out of the corner of his eye, he saw Mac jerk around. He was out the door, blinking against the blinding snow and skidding down the icy driveway in his car as Mac appeared in the back doorway.

Enough, thought Jennifer. The old adage "if you want something done right, do it yourself," ran through her head. Ryan was a fool. He'd always been a fool. Even so, she'd thought he could be a useful tool, allowing her to stay one step removed from all the ugliness she wanted to happen and yet still close enough to watch everyone squirm.

She stepped on the gas. She knew exactly how to find the old brewery on Marshall Street, although why Ryan had chosen that place to dump the kid she would never know.

It wasn't supposed to be like this, she thought, but she wanted Jonathon's money, and it was too bad that Paul's kid had to get in the way. Only God knew what Ryan had said or done, and she couldn't take a chance Kit knew something that might implicate her.

Letty tilted her head. At first Kit heard nothing, and then he heard it too, the sound of feet crunching through broken glass, coming closer and closer.

Kit turned to look at Letty, his eyes wide. Streetlight spilled through the broken boards over the windows, and wind whipped branches to and fro causing shadows to leap and fall against the walls.

"The bad man," he whispered. "It's the bad man." Frantically, he looked for a place to hide.

Letty put a tiny gnarled finger to her lips. "Shhh, now," she whispered back, gesturing for Kit to stand behind the door of the small room.

Golden candlelight flickered behind him. He crouched, watching through the crack in the door as Letty glided silently across the room and climbed up onto the old work table next to the door, an empty beer bottle in her hand. She flattened herself against the wall and waited.

Trudging through knee-deep snow, Michael tried the door to the loading dock at the back of the old building. It wasn't locked. Someone had obviously preceded him, and from the deep gouges around the doorframe, it wasn't anyone who was authorized to seek entry. He plunged through the entryway and into the hallway beyond.

What Michael had grossly underestimated in his rush to find Kit, was how dark it would be inside the building and how confused he would become as he floundered through the labyrinth of hallways.

Stumbling across a stairway, Michael decided to search the

second floor of the old building. At the top of the stairwell, he stopped to listen. The sound of wind slashing ice and snow against the roof filled his ears. Streetlight from a broken window at the end of the hallway chased shadows into darkness so deep it hurt to look at them. He closed his eyes and tried to listen past the wind and rain for any sound that would help him move in the right direction. Nothing.

Where in all this space would he ever find one small boy?

The instant he'd heard Mac and Lani mention the beer bottle caps they found with Kit's light saber, Michael had been sure he'd find Kit at the old brewery. What he hadn't been sure about was whether Kit would be alone or with his kidnapper.

As Michael tramped down one hallway after another in stygian blackness, he weighed the chances of finding Kit against being overhead calling for him. He'd take his chances, he thought clenching his hands into fists. He refused to fail Lani in finding her son.

He hadn't been around to save his father, but he was going to do everything in his power to ensure Kit was safe if it was the last thing he ever did.

"Kit," called Michael in a low voice. "Kit, c-c-can you hear me? I've come to t-t-take you home."

Lights turned red all the way down Marshall Street until Jennifer thought she would rip her hair out in frustration. The roads were empty and the snow falling so fast, it was hard to stay in the right lane. Damn it. She never would have been in this position if Ryan had followed her instructions.

Well, she didn't have to deal with him any longer. As the light turned green on Eighth Avenue, Jennifer pressed her foot to the accelerator and twirled a strand of hair around her forefinger, the smile she never used in public spreading across her face.

She pulled into the parking lot and plowed through snow as

she cruised around the building. She'd forgotten how enormous the complex was. She didn't have a clue where to begin to look for Kit inside. She thought of turning around, going home, and letting nature take its course. If the kid was locked up somewhere, it would only be a matter of time before the cold killed him anyway. Then, she noticed the rear unloading dock and the small white Corolla parked next to it. She pulled over to a dark corner of the lot, parked beneath a huge overarching blue fir, and got out of the car, lowering her head against the buffeting storm, wondering who on earth could be inside.

A siren split the silence of the night as another car skidded through the snow into the parking lot. Mac leapt out of one side and Lani out of the other.

"Lani, stay here," ordered Mac. "We don't know who that car belongs to or whether the kidnapper is inside."

"Not on your life," snapped Lani, not breaking stride. "I'm going to get my son."

Silently, Jennifer drifted back toward her car. As Lani and Mac disappeared into the brewery and a police car's strobing light appeared a block away, she headed toward a back lot exit. It was nearly impossible to drive without lights, but she didn't switch them on until she turned right onto University Avenue.

"Kit, where are you? It's Michael. Kit, can you hear me?"

Michael stopped to listen again, but beyond the raging storm outside, he could hear nothing. He trudged down the stairs to the first floor.

Images of finding Kit hurt—or worse, filled his mind.

Blinking against the darkness, Michael thought his mind was playing tricks on him when he saw a faint light seeping through a doorway at the end of the hall.

"Kit?" he called rushing forward.

Kit heard Michael calling to him, and without hesitation he ran out into the big bottling room. Letty perched on top of the workbench next to the doorway, but Kit didn't stop his headlong rush toward Michael's voice.

"I'm here, I'm here," he shouted, small legs pumping, propelling him closer to the hallway.

"Kit, thank God," muttered Michael appearing in the doorway. He stretched out his arms, stepping into the room.

Kit looked up in time to see Letty raise her glass bottle weapon high over her head.

"No, no, don't," screamed Kit as she smashed the bottle against the top of Michael's head.

"Lani, slow down," shouted Mac as she ran ahead of him. "You don't know who we might run into."

"I don't care. Listen to that siren. The police are right behind us," she panted, twisting the door lever and propelling herself inside.

"Dammit," muttered Mac, looking behind him for an instant to see the police car careen into the parking lot and slide for a good 10 feet before stopping. Ridley and Szymanski leapt out.

"Here," he yelled, not waiting for them to catch up. By the time he entered the building, Lani was no longer in sight. Following the sounds of her running feet, Mac caught up to her. Miles of yawning black hallways confronted them and as they hesitated they could hear Ridley and Szymanski blundering their way forward.

Mac yelled out again. "This way, and if you've got a light, we could really use it."

"Which way, which way?" Lani stopped, clenching her fists in frustration.

"Shhh, stay still and listen," said Mac, an arrested expression on his face.

An eerie voice echoed down the hallway to their right.

"Kit, where are you?"

"That's Michael," said Lani, launching herself forward, following the faint sounds as Michael called out to Kit.

Behind her she heard a crash and a terse exchange between the police officers.

"Ma'am, please stop. It may not be safe." Somehow Ridley was on her right, and he tried to grab her arm. Szymanski followed right behind, strong light beaming a path before her from the flashlight he held in his hand.

Lani shrugged off the officer's hand and never stopped running. Mac was right beside her. Far ahead she could see flickering golden light emanating from a doorway.

A mile away, Jennifer settled back in her seat and frowned. Everything should be fine, she thought. She'd been careful. No one would suspect her of being involved in Jonathon's death. She may not have been able to follow through on her plan to implicate Michael, but her back-up plan was just as good. Besides, she thought, maybe she could still point the cops in Michael's direction.

Lani and Mac careened into the bottling room guided by the flickering candlelight. Ridley and Szymanski followed an instant later, each wielding powerful flashlights sending bright swaths of light beaming before them. As the paths of light crisscrossed the room, Kit's small figure flashed before Lani's eyes for a second, but that was all it took. She launched herself at her son, gathering him into her arms.

"Kit, Kit, are you okay?" She rubbed her nose and lips against the warmth of his head, tightening her arms until he squeaked in protest.

"Mama, you're crushing me to bits and pieces."

Lani laughed and cried all at the same time. "I'm sorry, Honey Bug. Tell me you're okay."

"I'm okay," he said obediently, "but Mama, look. Michael's hurt. He came to find me, and Letty hit him over the head with a beer bottle because we were so scared."

Ridley sent his beams of light flashing everywhere across the room. For an instant, light flashed across the small street woman's face where she crouched against the far corner of the cavernous room.

Mac gasped. "Hey, shine that light back over to the left."

When Ridley complied, no one was there.

"It couldn't be her. My mother disappeared so long ago." Mac muttered, shaking his head. "Give me that light." Again and again he flashed the light around the room, searching, only to find it empty except for the small group huddled over Michael who groaned and sat up holding his head.

"What happened," his eyes cleared and sharpened. "Kit, where's Kit? Is he okay?"

"Michael Sutton, you are under arrest," said Office Szymanski, wrenching a set of handcuffs from his belt.

"Wait, wait, you can't arrest Michael," said Kit indignantly from the safety of his mother's arms. "He's not the bad man."

Chapter 17

"Kit, stop. You're going to wear Dr. Mac out, poor man," laughed Lani from her position on the couch. She and Kit had been spending the past few days with Mac at his townhouse.

"I'm not Dr. Mac, you infidels," he roared in a deep voice. "I am an enemy of the empire. You *must* follow my orders."

Kit leapt in front of Mac, waving his light saber. "Oh, no we don't. Take that, you evil enemy."

Mac's cell phone rang on the table next to Lani.

"Lani, will you get that for me," he said in his evil enemy-of-the-empire voice. "I'm otherwise engaged at the moment."

"Absolutely." She scooped up the cell phone. "Hello, Dr. Mac's house."

Behind her Mac roared again. "Give in, you measly human. You can't win against the Lord of the Realm."

Kit squealed with laughter. Lani smiled. "Hello? Is anyone there?"

When no one answered, she clicked off the cell phone and knelt with her arms along the back of the couch to watch Mac and her son roll around on the carpet. Kit had accepted Mac as a kindred spirit without hesitation, and Mac's response to her son was so warm and enthusiastic that Lani thought she would burst from happiness.

The day after tomorrow they would appear before the judge, but with Mac beside her, she could only feel optimistic. She had done nothing wrong, Kit was her son, and the outcome was inevitable. At least that's what Mac kept telling her, and she believed him.

"No one was on the line," she said. "So, it was either a wrong number, or it was one of your patients, and I scared 'em off."

"If it's important, they'll call back," mumbled Mac as he wrestled with Kit.

Jennifer clenched her cell phone for a moment before pushing End Call. She set it down very gently on the kitchen table.

A frown wrinkled her brow, and her golden eyes clouded with thought. Things had been progressing so well with Mac until he met Lani that night at the nursing home. With a grim expression, Jennifer straightened her shoulders and tossed her head. She would not allow history to repeat itself.

She'd dated Paul Emerson several times before he met Lani at the university where he was a teacher's assistant in the math department. He'd taken one look at Lani and never looked back.

When Paul succumbed to the coma, Jennifer had taken a sharp, mean pleasure in planting the thought with Paul's parents and Lani that Paul had been intimately involved with her for years. It never happened. Paul was a drug addict, but he'd been in love with Lani, no one else. Deep in a coma, Paul couldn't do a thing to refute her claim.

The embellishments she'd added about how Lani was hurting Kit were another way to get even. Jennifer did not like to share.

Judith bought right into her lies. Richard hadn't been nearly so quick to believe her, but after a few well-timed stories, even he began to accept her claims that Lani was not a fit mother.

A small chuckle bubbled up in Jennifer's throat. People were so easy to manipulate. Many art forms existed. Knowing how to make people believe what you wanted was definitely an art form, and she had been a master since she was a child. Her philosophy was, "If you want something, figure out who can help you get it, and then figure out how you can manipulate that person into wanting to help you."

Jennifer learned how to manipulate people before she hit puberty and firmly believed it was the only way she survived her childhood. Her mother was a loser who always had her head in the clouds and no means to support them.

When Jennifer was eleven, she and her mother moved in with her Uncle Jonathon and his family so that her mother could "get back on her feet." Instead, she'd been murdered one night as she sat writing her poetry in the tiny cubicle at the University of Minnesota where she worked as a parking lot attendant so that she could focus on her art.

Early one morning, a few days after her mother's funeral, Jennifer slipped into Jonathon's office where he sat working at his computer.

"I wish you were my daddy, Jonathon. Michael is so lucky." As she spoke, she placed a steaming cup of coffee on the desk where Jonathon was already responding to emails and working on a customer report.

Visibly startled at her words, he looked up from his papers. "You don't have to worry, Honey. You have a home here as long as you want."

She'd smiled sadly. "But I don't have a daddy, and now my mother is dead too."

"You will always be part of my family, Jen." Jonathon, usually undemonstrative to the max, had reached out and pulled her into a quick hug. Releasing her, he took a sip of the coffee. "Wow, this is the best coffee I've ever had. Thank you."

Jennifer got up and brought him coffee every morning after

that. She also listened for the sound of the garage door opening and met him with a hug and a huge smile every day when he walked into the house after work. She had a plan. Even as a child it was obvious that Jonathon wielded a lot of power. She was drawn to that power and what he could do for her.

Eleven months later, Jonathon and Elizabeth Sutton officially adopted her.

Her Aunt Liz didn't really get in her way much beyond trying to make up for the loss of her mother by lavishing attention on her. Jennifer was not impressed. She knew who held the power. It wasn't Liz.

Michael, she loathed. She didn't like to share, and as his son, Jennifer understood that Michael had the priority claim to Jonathon.

One day, a few months after her mother died, Jennifer noticed the wistful look on Michael's face when Jonathon thanked her for his morning coffee with a warm smile and hug. The next day she asked Michael he if wanted to bring his father a cup of coffee for a change. Michael grinned and simply nodded. Even at nine he was shy—and even more important from her point of view—as clumsy as any nine-year-old can be.

So Jennifer filled a cup with steaming hot coffee—just the way Jonathon like it. She filled it so full that Michael could focus on nothing but the hot brown liquid sloshing against the rim of the cup as he slid his feet forward in tiny steps across his mother's off-white carpet. With the tip of his tongue poking out of one side of his mouth and his brow fiercely wrinkled in concentration, Michael never saw the stack of books she'd left on the floor next to Jonathon's desk. When Michael tripped over the books, coffee flew out of the cup, scalding Jonathon and spraying his keyboard and the customer presentation laying on his desk. She'd had to bite her lip to keep from laughing out loud.

"Michael, how can you be so clumsy," roared Jonathon, leaping to his feet. "Damn it, I worked all night on that presentation." When Jonathon tried to print another copy, he discovered that his keyboard was no longer functioning. "I want you to stay out of my office from now on. Do you hear me?"

Michael cringed, tears running down his face and dripping off his chin.

It became a game to see how often she could compel Michael to take an action that would get him into trouble. Michael fell into her traps over and over. Jonathon never suspected a thing.

She achieved her magnum opus when Michael was fifteen. He had decided to create a slideshow presentation for his final project in world studies. The night before his presentation, he invited the whole family to sit down and watch his stupid slideshow about how one village in Africa had become afflicted with a strange sickness, which turned out to be bacteria in the water. As part of his presentation, he'd described the food eaten by this tribe, their customs, and the garb they wore.

Jennifer did not like the interest Michael's parents displayed in his work. That night, she crept downstairs after everyone was asleep and changed out one of the URLs in his presentation. The next day, Michael came home from school visibly upset, but he wouldn't tell his mother why.

The telephone rang right after dinner.

"Hello, Sutton here." Silence as Jonathon listened, a frown growing on his face. "Michael did what? No, that doesn't sound like something my son would do." A long pause ensued while Jonathon's face turned dark. "Yes, I understand. Three days? I will definitely speak with him immediately. Thank you for calling."

He hung up the phone and turned to face his son. Michael's face was the color of chalk.

"Dad, I d-d-didn't d-d-do it. I d-d-don't know h-h-how ..." Michael stuttered.

"Jonathon, what happened?" Liz rose to her feet and moved over to stand behind Michael.

"Your son presented his slideshow in school today, which by

the way," he turned with a sarcastic look at Michael, "was apparently brilliantly conducted. Then, the students started to snicker and there for the whole class to see was a bunch of naked women—not from Africa, but from some porn site, according to the principal. Apparently, this was not the slideshow he presented to us last night.

"B-b-but D-d-dad," started Michael.

"No more, Michael. You have been in so much trouble the last few years. You can't do anything right. You've been suspended for three days. Go to your room, I can't stand to look at you."

Outwardly, Jennifer was all perfect decorum. Inwardly, she was holding her sides and laughing with glee. It had been one of her finest moments.

She knew at once when her Aunt Liz began to suspect that all the things that kept happening to Michael might not have been of his own making. She began to hatch another plan.

It was so easy to manipulate people. A little perfume on her uncle's overcoat. A crumpled note left in the pocket of a suit jacket her aunt was taking to the dry cleaner. It hadn't been difficult at all to convince Aunt Liz that Jonathon was having an affair.

In the end, it had only taken a few weeks to get rid of her aunt, and when Liz left she took fifteen-year-old Michael with her. Finally, Jennifer had Jonathon all to herself.

She stretched. Things pretty much worked out the way you wanted them to if you were just smart enough to know how to manipulate people.

Now, she wanted Mac, and she would not allow history to repeat itself. He belonged to her.

Her cell phone started playing *Moonlight Sonata*. Judith Emerson's face came up on the screen.

"Good morning, Judith. How are you?"

"Jennifer, I apologize for calling so early, but I need your help this morning." Judith's voice was filled with determination. "Richard is being difficult, and I would like you to come with me to Melanie's when I go this morning to pick up my grandson. I still have custody, and I intend to bring him home."

"Of course. I'll pick you up at ten o'clock." Jennifer looked over at the small, golden box of truffles sitting on her table, which she had carefully refilled and rewrapped the night before. She slid it into her purse and went to take her shower.

"Poor bastard. Someone obviously didn't have a high opinion of you, did they," muttered Officer Ridley, looking down at Ryan Kramer's contorted body. He turned to the coroner. "So, what's the verdict, Doc?"

"Obviously poison, and I agree with you. Someone definitely didn't want this guy around anymore." The coroner held up an evidence bag containing a smeared brown substance. "Looks and smells like chocolate. I'm guessing it had so much poison in it, this guy expired within minutes. In my opinion, you're looking at one cruel perp."

Officer Szymanski sat in the black leather chair behind the desk, looking through a stack of papers. He picked up a notebook, and flipped through it, his fingers clumsy in latex gloves. A frown flickered, disappeared, and flickered across his forehead again.

A young police officer appeared in the doorway and held up a silver bracelet.

"Sir, we found this on the window ledge over the kitchen sink. What was the name of that body that turned up in the Emerson woman's freezer the other day? Take a look at this four-leaf clover thing."

"It's called a shamrock, you ignoramus," grunted the coroner from where he squatted on the floor next to the body.

"Call it whatever you want. See, it says *Shari* with a little heart over the i. Why do chicks always dot their i's with a little heart, anyway?"

"Shari Peterson," said Ridley without missing a beat. "Now

what do you think of that?"

"I think the pieces are starting to come together for those nursing home murders. Listen to this," said Szymanski. He read out loud from the notebook he held. "It's all about KISS really, Keep It Simple, Stupid. Professional CIA agents understand that if enough work goes into the planning, the actual wet work will go off without a hitch."

"Wet work? What is that," snapped Ridley.

"According to what he wrote on the inside cover, it's *The Assassin's Playbook*, and you ain't heard nothing yet. This guy was a lunatic." Szymanski shook his head, "This, uh, playbook reads like a bad novel, a bad novel written by a moron.

"Here, listen to this." He read some more. "My partner isn't doing any of the hard stuff. It's all up to me, but I have a plan that is perfect. No one is ever gonna find out who really offed Old Man Sutton. If I'd left it up to my partner, we'd have used poison. I mean, really? A good assassin would never choose poison as a weapon." Szymanski held up the notebook, "It just goes on and on. He really thought he was king of the assassins."

"Who the hell was this guy?"

"Wish I knew. I also wish I knew what was on the missing pages." He flipped through the book, pointing at the jagged edges, indicating a number of pages had been ripped out.

The coroner flipped open the wallet he'd pulled out of the dead man's pocket. "Michael Sutton. The poor bastard's name is Michael Sutton. Must be related to the guy who owned this place, eh?"

"No way. I don't know who this guy is, but he is not Michael Sutton.," said Ridley.

"Hey, wait a minute," Szymanski flipped back to the front cover of the notebook, turning it toward his partner. "See, the name here is Ryan Kramer. So, how do you suppose Sutton and this Kramer guy are connected?"

Chapter 18

"**H**ey, you lazy woman," said Rachel with a bright look in her eyes. "What have you been doing all morning? I didn't think you'd ever get here today."

"Thanks, Rachel, for running the shop these past few days. I really appreciate it." Lani hung up her coat and turned to help Kit.

"Michael's been in and out helping as well. The police keep calling him in, poor man, but it's clear to me that he would never do anything to hurt you or Kit."

Lani nodded with vehemence.

"Besides, you needed time with the Kit kid, Lani. I wish I could have done more," Rachel's voice was gruff.

Lani walked over and put her arms around Rachel. Standing on tiptoe, she kissed her forehead. "You are the best."

"Hey, who wants a cup of coffee?" smiled Mac from behind the counter. He filled a small aluminum pitcher, twisted some switches, and steamed milk into a thick froth.

"Well, would you look at that," said Rachel. "Who woulda thought you'd make such an accomplished barista."

"Mais oui," said Mac with feigned hauteur. "I pay attention to everything. Not only do I know how to make you an excellent cup of coffee, I know how you take it. Voilà, Mademoiselle, your latte straight up, no flavor added." He finished off his masterpiece by swirling the thick, creamy milk mixture over the top of the coffee and sprinkling a dash of nutmeg on top with a flick of his wrist and an added bit of flair.

He held Rachel's eyes as he handed her the cup. "Seriously, Rachel, you are a good friend. Thank you."

Rachel smiled and tasted the coffee. "Superb, Dr. Mac. If you get tired of doctoring, I think you have an alternate path to fame. This is a most excellent latte."

Two customers who had smiled all through Mac's antics waved goodbyes as they opened the door to exit the shop. Frigid air swirled into the room, but for the first time in days, the sun outside was shining bright.

Lani turned to find Kit. Since his kidnapping, it was all she could do to let him out of her sight for even an instant. She relaxed as she watched her son roam around the shop stopping at one table after another to say hello to the customers who smiled and said hello right back to him. They were used to seeing Kit around the shop.

Lani was so focused on Kit, she never heard the chimes ring. She whirled around at the sound of her ex-mother-in-law's voice.

"Melanie, I have come to take Christopher home with me." Judith stood in the doorway, carefully pulling off one glove, and then the other. "Get his things together for me, if you please."

Jennifer Sutton stood behind her, and when Lani's eyes flew toward her, she shrugged her shoulder as if to say, "Hey, I'm only along for the ride."

Judith slid out of her coat, and Jennifer accepted it, sauntering across the shop, her persimmon Coach bag swinging gently at her side. She glanced out of the side of her eyes at Mac as she passed, but he had eyes for no one but Lani. Jennifer's mouth tightened.

"No," said Lani, her face white. "You can't take him."

Mac stepped behind Lani and put his hands on her shoulders.

"Oh Lani, hear me out," said Judith dropping into a chair and holding up one finger in Rachel's direction. "I will take a cup of your dark roast, if you please."

Rachel promptly came out from behind the counter. "Not in this lifetime."

Judith sniffed, pulled her pearls straight, and turned back to Lani. "Really, Lani, there is no need for a repeat of the performance you gave at the hospital."

Kit ran up to his grandmother. "I won't go, and you can't make me, can she, Dr. Mac?"

"I have legal custody of you, Christopher, at least until we go to court tomorrow." Judith smiled triumphantly. "After that, well, I have no doubt that the judge will make the right decision."

No one saw Jennifer slip a golden box of chocolates out of her purse and onto a chair at the back of the shop next to a display of Rachel's ceramic mugs. The chair presented a clear line of sight for a small child who might be rummaging around in the toy box sitting next to it. She hung their coats on the rack and sauntered back across the shop.

Mac reached for Kit's hand. "Kit, I think it's best if you stay with your mama and me." Kit, snuggled up against Mac, a look of trust on his face and not a hint of worry as Mac turned to say, "I won't support you, Judith. You know that. I think you should leave."

"Well, I've called Richard and told him I'm here. We'll wait." Judith settled back into her chair. "I'd really like a cup of coffee. It's bitter cold outside in spite of the sunshine."

With a mutter, Lani snatched a mug off the shelf, and filled it with coffee. She turned to Jennifer, "I suppose you want something too?"

Jennifer set her large purse down on the table next to Judith and sank into a chair. "Oh no, I'm fine, actually, thanks." Amusement and something else filled her eyes, but Lani was too distracted to notice.

The chimes over the door rang in the entrance of another customer.

"Lani," beamed Pete Ambrosiak. "it is so good to see you and Kit back where you belong. I've missed you these past few days. Hey Kit, did you find what we brought you?"

The chimes jingled again, and Shirley Dubrovnik crowded into the shop, wrapped from head to toe in a down overcoat that threatened to overwhelm her short figure.

"Lani, we have missed you so much. How is Kit? Did he find the loot we brought over yesterday? We thought for sure you'd be home."

Dot Scheuneman followed close on her heels.

"Here I am, Mrs. Shirley." Kit ran over to the two ladies and Pete, a look of interest lighting his face. "What loot?"

Dot's sharp eyes swept around the shop, pausing first at the sight of Judith sipping a large cup of coffee, and then at Jennifer who was watching everyone with a smile on her face as she wound a strand of silken hair around her finger. Dot raised an eyebrow at Lani before turning back to Kit.

"We brought you important stuff, young man," said Dot. "Behold." She pointed with one long, skinny finger at a small pile of brightly wrapped objects next to the register.

Rachel smacked the side of her head "Gosh, it's been so crazy around here," she said with a glare toward Judith who kept sipping her coffee in total oblivion. "I forgot to tell you, Kit. Look what our friends brought you while you were away."

"Here, open mine first," said Pete, holding out a package gaily wrapped in red and white stripes.

Kit tore the wrappings from the package. When he saw what was inside, he grinned.

"Mama, look, look, it's just what I need." He held the Han Solo action figure high above his head.

"Well, now," said Dot. "Is this one of the good guys or one of the bad guys?"

"It's Han Solo, Mrs. Dot. He's a good guy because he's smiling, see?" said Kit, holding out the toy.

"Well, then," said Shirley, pointing toward another small package with a red ribbon wrapped around it. "I guess you need a bad guy, too, eh?"

"Or, maybe two bad guys," smiled Dot, handing him the other box wrapped in silver paper with a blue ribbon. "Although, maybe you really needed another good guy to help you get rid of all these dudes."

Kit turned to Lani. "Is it my birthday, and did you forget to tell me?"

"No, Sweetie. Everyone is just so glad we found you and that you are okay."

Satisfied, Kit turned to his loot and proceeded to rip the paper and ribbons to shreds.

"Mama, Mama, I have Jabba *and* Darth Vader." Shouting with joy, he turned to Dot and Shirley. "Thank you Mrs. Dot and Mrs. Shirley. Don't worry, it's okay if I have two bad guys and one good guy. Han can fight off anyone. He's the best. Besides, I have Luke over here to help."

Kit dashed off to his corner of the shop, and scrabbled among the toys in the toy box until he found the small figure of Luke Skywalker. Engaged in more important things than chatting with friends and customers, he turned and began to orchestrate a war of the Empire.

Michael stood outside the Tropical Bean and watched the tableau inside. His eyes settled on his cousin as she sat twirling a strand of hair around one finger. Something was wrong. He couldn't have said how he knew it, but he did. Something just wasn't right.

He turned at the sound of a car pulling up to the curb, and his heart sank when he saw Officers Ridley and Szymanski get out and walk toward him.

"Sutton, what are you doing here?"

"I work here," he muttered. "That is if I still have a job after all the time you've caused me to be absent from it."

"We need you to come down to the station. We have a few more questions, and they really can't wait," said Officer Ridley.

"Not again," groaned Michael. "Come on guys, don't you have anyone else to harass?"

The door behind him opened with a clash of chimes and a rush of warm, coffee-rich air.

"Michael Sutton," said Rachel in a stern voice. "I thought you worked here. It's about time you showed up." She reached out and pulled him through the door, ignoring both policemen on the stoop.

They followed her into the shop.

"Ms. Rachel, ma'am," said Officer Szymanski. "We're here to take Michael Sutton down to the station. We have some more questions we want to ask him."

"Well, then ask him here." Rachel turned and looked at the young policeman, her eyes starting at the top of his head and wandering slowly all the way down to his toes and back up. She pointed a finger at a table in the corner. "Sit. I'll bring you complimentary coffee, *if* you behave yourself. This is a place of business, this is where Michael works, and I expect you to show him some courtesy. From what he's told me, you've had him down at the station more often than not these past few days. Enough."

"But ma'am," said Szymanski, his face turning an interesting shade of red. He looked to his partner for help.

Ridley grinned. "You heard what the lady said. Sit, be a good little officer, and we'll get a free cup of coffee." He turned to Rachel and said with gentle sarcasm, "If it's all right with you ma'am, we do have a few questions we need to ask."

"Of course," she said graciously. "That will be fine in a few minutes. I need Michael's help first."

Rachel swung her hips and her long hair as she sauntered to the counter, snagged a couple of mugs, filled them with fragrant dark roast, and returned to plop them down on the table before the officers.

Szymanski's eyes followed every move she made, and if he hadn't been so fed up with all the questioning, Michael would have laughed at the expression on the young officer's face.

At that moment, Lani looked over and waved. "Hi, Michael."

"Hey Kid, it's good to see you," said Mac.

"Michael," yelled Kit. "Where have you been? Is your head still broken? Letty didn't mean to hit you with that bottle. She thought you were the bad man."

"Oh Michael, I don't know how to thank you for rescuing Kit," smiled Lani as she rushed over to hug him.

Michael hung his head, "I didn't do much, Lani, except get my head bashed in.

"Exactly," said Lani as though it made perfect sense to her that a head bashing was a prerequisite to saving Kit. She looked at him as though he'd saved Kit's life, when actually, Kit was fine by the time he'd arrived at the brewery.

Michael's heart swelled. He felt as though he'd come home. He had a lot he wanted to say to Lani and Rachel, and he wanted to say it soon. His eyes darkened as he nodded at his cousin.

"So, the prodigal son returns," murmured Jennifer.

"Hi Jen. Long time no see," said Michael quietly looking her in the eyes.

He pulled off his gloves and coat. He felt the police officers' eyes watching him the entire time he walked to the back of the room to hang up his coat. He wasn't guilty of anything, but he knew they suspected him of something. What that something was exactly, he didn't know. He was feeling so self-conscious, he didn't see the toys Kit had spread out on the floor, and he tripped against the table, knocking over a chair.

Michael's face reddened as he heard a titter from Jennifer, but then he straightened his shoulders. He was no longer a child, and she no longer had the power to torment him.

"Hey, what's this?" He scooped up a small golden box and held it up." He saw Jennifer watching from the other side of the room, twirling a strand of hair and smiling as though she were especially pleased. The hair on the back of his neck stood up.

"Look, another present. Is this one for me, too?" Kit held up his hands, and Michael dropped the box into them with a smile.

"Must be," he said.

Kit tore off the gold ribbon, and opened the box. "Oh Mama, look, can I have one?" He ran over and held the box up for Lani to see.

Lani leaned over the box. "Wow, these are the best chocolates this side of Belgium. I want one, too."

Michael started wiping the counter. The shop was empty of customers for the moment. Judith was sipping her coffee with delicate little sips, dapping carefully at her lips from time to time. Jennifer sat at her side, eyes fixed on Lani and Kit. The hair on the back of Michael's neck stood up again. Officer Ridley held up a hand and then pointed at the vacant chair by his side.

As Michael started over to sit down by the policemen, he kept his eyes on Kit. The box of chocolates sat on the table before him. Kit stood with one hand poised over the box, obviously searching for just the right piece of candy.

"People have been dropping things off all week, haven't they, Rachel?" Michael tried to relax. What could possibly go wrong with all of them together here in the room? Besides, with two officers of the law swigging coffee and watching everyone in the shop, he felt an added measure of safety.

"That's for sure. Hey, take a look at all this stuff."

Rachel rummaged about behind the counter for a few minutes, pulling out a cellophane-wrapped loaf of banana bread, a tin of cookies, and a bag of Tootsie Pops. "Hey Kit kid, look at these."

Kit picked up a starfish-shaped white chocolate and was about to take a bite when he saw what Rachel held. "Aunt Rachel, those are my own personal favorites."

"You can have one piece of candy, Kit, so choose the one you want the most," laughed Lani.

Without another word, Kit dropped the piece of chocolate back into the box and rushed over to where Rachel was dangling the box of suckers. "Grape, please. That's my absolute best favorite."

Judith sniffed, a haughty look on her face. "Lani, I am sure you have fed the child his breakfast since you are allowing him to eat sweets at this time in the morning."

Mac smiled at Lani and neither replied.

"Well, I know exactly which one I want," said Mac. With his pinkie held high, he reached into the box and chose a dark chocolate dusted with a sprinkle of coconut. Holding it high above his mouth, he tilted back his head.

"Mac," interrupted Jennifer.

He paused, looking at her. "Hmmm, what's up?"

"I need your advice," said Jennifer patting the chair next to her. "Rather urgently, in fact," she added when he didn't move for a moment.

"Sure." Mac dropped the piece of candy back into the box, and joined her at the table. Lani looked at the box of chocolates and started to reach for one herself. The chimes above the door rang out and when she saw who it was, she pulled her hand back and jumped to her feet.

Richard Emerson walked into the room with a blast of cold air.

"Lani," he nodded at her. "We need to talk."

She stood in front of him, hands clenched. "You can't take him, Richard. I won't let you."

"I agree with you." He glanced over at Jennifer. "We still need to talk."

"Richard, I want to speak with you first," said Judith with a quaver in her voice.

"Yes, Judith. I think that would be a very good idea. You left rather abruptly this morning after breakfast."

"I will never agree to …"

"Come on, let's talk over there."

Judith stood and walked to the back of the room, her back stiff and unyielding. Richard followed her, and the two of them sat at one of the small glass tables. Judith's agitation was clear as she spoke in a low, fast voice, waving her hands to and fro. Richard listened to her with a stony expression.

Mac jumped up to join Lani. Jennifer sat alone at her table, eyes dark and stormy.

A phrase from his past swept through Michael's head as he watched Jennifer watching Lani and Mac.

I don't like to share.

"Hey, Sutton."

Michael jerked back to the two police officers sitting across the table from him.

"Do you know this guy?" Szymanski held out a photograph.

"No. That is … wait a minute." Michael took the photo and stared at it. "Wow, it's been years since I saw that face."

He handed back the photo. "His name is Ryan Kramer. We hung out for a while in high school. He was one weird dude. You remember him, don't you Jennifer?"

"Hmmm," Jennifer was staring at Mac who had returned to her table and was waiting to hear whatever it was she needed from him. It was obvious he was trying to be polite. It was just as obvious from the way his eyes followed her as she moved about the shop, that he was ready to leap to Lani's defense if she needed it.

"You remember Kramer, don't you?" repeated Michael with patience. "You know, that weird dude who used to drool whenever you walked past him. I'm convinced the only reason he ever hung out with me was because he thought you'd pay him more attention."

Jennifer's head snapped up. "Who?"

"Ryan Kramer."

She blinked. "No, I don't remember him. You had a lot of geeky friends. I don't remember any of them."

Michael jumped up and pulled the photo out of Szymanski's hand. He waved it in Jennifer's face. "You have to remember him. He was really strange, always yammering on and on about joining the CIA and writing in that little black notebook of his," said Michael. "You and your friends used to laugh about him all the time."

Jennifer glanced indifferently at the photo. "No, I can't say that I remember him at all."

Michael flung his hands in the air, and turning his back on his cousin, he stalked back to the officers. "So, why don't you two just get to the point?"

"Sure thing," said Szymanski. "We found this guy's body at your father's apartment. According to the coroner, someone who didn't like him very much poisoned him. Your name was all over his, uh, "playbook.""

"Huh," said Michael. "What playbook?"

"You tell us, Sutton," snapped Ridley. "Seems he was still writing in a little black notebook, and your name is all over it. Some pages are missing, though, and I'd really like to know what was on them." He pulled some photocopied pages out of a large leather portfolio case and handed them to his partner.

Rachel dropped the cloth she was using to wipe the counter and followed Lani as she drifted over to the table to listen as Szymanski read a passage out loud.

"Sutton brought me some more of that stupid Clove chewing gum today. In my own humble opinion, no CIA agent worth his salt ever used such a wimpy clue. Give me a break. Who in the world would ever think a gum wrapper is a clue.

He read another.

"So, I get this call from Sutton to get the job done tonight. I didn't need

any orders about not blowing it. I took care of the job, and the way I did it, no one will ever suspect Old Man Sutton was the target. That's what I mean about having a KISS plan, sticking to it, and doing what you think is the right way to go. My partner doesn't have a clue how it is out in the real world where assassins actually have to get their hands dirty."

Szymanski looked up. "KISS, you know, keep it simple, stupid." He shook his head. "This guy was a real moron."

"Yeah, that's fine," Ridley interrupted. "What we want to know, is why is he calling you his partner, Sutton? Even more to the point, why was he carrying identification claiming he was Michael Sutton?"

At their table, Shirley, Dot, and Pete were also obviously listening in on the action happening at the small glass table between Michael and the policeman.

"Hey, Ridley, why don't you lay off the kid," said Mac.

"Well, it's obvious to me. You've got the wrong Sutton. Is there a first name in that book? You know, he's not the only Sutton around town," said Rachel with a heavy dose of sarcasm, "Or, even in the room for that matter to prove my point."

"Huh, what do you mean?"

Michael knew he was clutching at straws, but he was tired of all the questions. "If it's a Sutton you're looking for, why don't you harass my cousin over there. She's a Sutton too, you know."

Everyone at the table turned to look in the direction Michael was pointing. Jennifer was sitting alone at her table across the room from them. Kit stood next to her. Her voice was low, but in the sudden silence they heard her say, "You are a lucky boy to get all these presents. Especially these chocolates. I bet your Mom wouldn't really care if you had just one."

Michael stiffened at the eerie, yet familiar tone in Jennifer's voice. As she talked with Kit, she twirled a lock of hair around her finger.

Lani looked on, "I guess for once it won't kill him to have too much candy."

Kit reached into the box and plucked out the white starfish. "This is the one I want." He smiled up at Jennifer, and she smiled back as he raised the candy to his mouth.

"No," shouted Michael, leaping to his feet and across to the other table in two big leaps. He knocked the candy out of Kit's hand. "Don't eat that, Kit. It will make you sick."

He turned in fury to face his cousin. "It was you, wasn't it? This whole time it was you."

"As usual, I haven't a clue what you're talking about." Jennifer all but yawned in his face.

Michael scooped up the starfish candy and held it out to her. "You take a bite."

She tilted her head and looked up at him. "I never eat chocolate."

"Make an exception this time, Jen." Michael held out the chocolate on the palm of his hand. "If this is okay for Kit to eat, show us."

Jennifer stood with dignity. "I don't have a clue what you're talking about. I have an appointment, and so I will see all of you another time."

Sketching a mocking bow in everyone's general direction, she slung her purse over her shoulder and turned to get her coat.

"Wait," said Michael reaching for her arm and catching the strap of her purse by mistake, yanking it off her shoulder. The purse fell, spewing it contents across the floor.

"Let go of me, you oaf," snarled Jennifer, but it was too late.

Michael stepped back as she scrambled to snatch up a set of keys, a small makeup bag, and a pack of Clove gum. She was reaching for a sheaf of papers when Szymanski shot to his feet.

"Leave it."

Ridley stood too and stared at the package of gum in her hand and the small pieces of paper scattered across the floor. When Michael looked to see why they were so interested in those papers, it was clear to him that they'd been torn from a small notebook.

The writing was familiar too.

"Jen, why do you have pages from Ryan's notebook?" asked Michael. He turned to the police officers. "And, why are you two guys so interested in my brand of chewing gum, anyway?"

Chapter 19

"Hey Rachel," called Lani from the upstairs hallway. "Come on upstairs. We can finish cleaning up the shop tomorrow."

Lani turned back into the warmth and light of her apartment. In the three weeks since Jennifer's arrest, with the help of her friends, her apartment was better than it had ever been.

She looked around the small kitchen, inhaling all the good smells. Pete Ambrosiak was spooning thick mushroom gravy into a small bowl. Bits of dill and garlic floated on top. It turned out that he was quite the cook. A turkey sat in its pan next to a festive china plate filled with succulent slices.

Dot was carefully loading one dish full of pierogi and in another, Shirley was arranging holopchi—tender stuffed cabbage rolls filled with meat and rice.

In the dining room, Michael was laying out the silverware next to the good china.

"Mama, are we Ukrainian?" asked Kit licking some of the mushroom gravy off his thumb. "I think we must be, 'cause I sure love this food." He was the special assistant chef in charge according to Pete, and was charged with tasting every morsel that spilled along its way to the serving dishes.

Lani laughed out loud. "Who knows, Kit? We may be. My

mama told me once that I was such a mixture she didn't know what nationalities lurked inside me. Except, she would always say to me with a hug and a little kiss right above my eye," she paused to demonstrate, causing Kit to giggle in response, "that whatever I was, it was the perfect blend."

"I'll vouch for that perfect blend bit," said Mac. "I think I have this routine down right." He leaned over and gave Lani a tiny kiss on her forehead before returning to his job folding napkins.

"Hey, everyone. Look who showed up at the front door as I was closing up the shop."

Hearing an unusual tone in her friend's voice, Lani's eyes flew to Rachel's face. She was actually blushing, a first. Officer Szymanski peered over her shoulder into the kitchen.

"Wow, what smells so good?" He turned to Rachel. "When you invited me to dinner, I had no idea it was going to be a feast. I haven't seen pierogi like these since my grandma died when I was a kid, and oh my gosh, are those really holopchi? I think I died and went to heaven."

"That's not all," said Kit with a longing look at the refrigerator. "We have Jell-O cheesecake. It's yellow, and it's really good. I got to lick the spoon."

Lani smiled. "Welcome to our home, Officer Szymanski."

Now, he was blushing. "Please, call me Dan."

"Hey, what's a feast?" Kit didn't find it strange at all that one of the officers who'd worked his case showed up at the door for dinner.

"A feast, Kit kid, is when all your friends come and you eat lots and lots and lots of really good food until you burst."

"Aunt Rachel, you are too funny." Kit laughed and waved his spoon around, but no one cared if a little gravy sprayed here and there.

Lani took another look. Yes, no doubt about it, Rachel was blushing, and her eyes were shining as she ushered Dan Szymanski into the room. The young officer was about the same height as

Rachel, with dark brown hair buzzed close to his scalp. He was wiry thin and not at all in the style of Rachel's usual dates. Hmm, thought Lani, this one may be serious.

"Okay, we're ready," said Pete. "Choose your seats if you please, and we will begin. I don't want things to get cold."

Rachel looked at Lani. "Hey, I thought you invited Judith and Richard."

"I did. She turned me down."

"Yes," said Mac. "Although, I think she is finally realizing that if she wants to see her grandson, she is going to have to mind her manners. She was furious when Richard cancelled the court date, but he told me, and I quote, 'a little boy really needs to be with his mother.'"

"Well, that doesn't sound like him," snorted Rachel with a quick look in Kit's direction to be sure he couldn't hear the conversation. No worries, though, he was busy chattering away to Shirley and Dot as he climbed up onto a dining room chair.

"Richard told me that the judge had called him and recommended that he and Judith back off. Richard may be many things, but he isn't stupid, and he really does care about Kit. I think the only reason he tried for custody in the first place was because of the grief he and Judith were experiencing when Paul finally died. After he had a little time to simmer down and reflect, he knew it was wrong."

"So, that's what he and Judith were arguing about in the shop that day?"

"Yeah, Rachel. I'm pretty sure that was it. I also think he had started to suspect Jennifer's stories may not have been true."

Steaming dishes filled the dining room table. Cream-colored candles glowed golden above an antique forest green tablecloth. A potpourri of goblets, all colors, shapes, and sizes waited to be filled with wine, lemon water, or in Kit's case, milk. Intricate stalks of tangerine, fuchsia, and lemon alstroemeria filled a crystal vase in the center of the table with a splash of color. The wood floor beneath the table gleamed with a fresh coat of varnish, and the walls were creamy white once again without even a hint of soot.

Lani took a deep breath of satisfaction and relaxed in her chair. She'd never had friends like this before. Friends … or Mac. What a difference. Michael caught her eye and smiled with the new confidence he'd assumed lately.

A couple of weeks earlier, Michael had made a proposal to she and Rachel. Turned out, he also had a master's degree in business and an entrepreneurial bent as strong as Lani's. However, unlike Lani, he also had money to invest in a business of his choosing.

Michael presented the national study he'd done on the coffee retail industry, the trends and possibilities he'd studied, and he told them he believed that the Tropical Bean Coffee Shop was unique and an excellent place to invest. He'd asked with hardly a stutter if they would consider allowing him to invest some of his inheritance in growing their business into a series of franchises for the Midwest to begin with, and then expanding with the profits into the Northwest as well. He believed in Lani's concept of a warm, tropical getaway for those who couldn't afford an expensive holiday, and for those who could but would still love the ambiance.

Lani and Rachel were both excited at the possibilities, and the three of them had already talked with a lawyer about how to set up the partnership. Michael's stutter had all but disappeared as his confidence grew with the approval of all his new friends.

"Okay, so here's what I want to know," said Rachel suddenly. Around the table, silverware stopped clinking, and everyone stopped talking as they waited to hear what she had to say.

"What," prompted Kit, "what do you want to know?"

"I don't understand why she did it."

Michael cleared his throat. "Because she could, that's why."

"Huh," said Dot. "I want a BMW, but I don't go out and knock the first person I see who owns one over the head to get it."

Michael smiled. "Well, the first thing you have to understand is that Jennifer cared about Jennifer, and that was pretty much the only person she cared about. Whenever anyone got in her way, she would think up elaborate plans to remove any obstacles. She was so charming and devious, it took me years to figure out what she was doing, and I lived with her full-time."

"But why Jonathon?" said Lani. "He adored her."

"Yeah, he did. Something must have happened."

"Whenever she walked into a room, I always felt so, oh, I don't even know how to explain it, lacking somehow." Lani grimaced. "I figured it was my own insecurity."

"No, she had her ways, subtle, but effective." Michael shook his head. "I was about nine years old when Jen and her mother moved in with us. My aunt Nadine was my father's sister. She was a bit of a dreamer, but the problem was that her dreams had a tendency to lead her in directions best not taken. At least that's the story I heard Dad tell my mother over a glass of wine one evening."

"What happened to her?"

"She and Jennifer were only supposed to stay with us for a couple of months until Nadine got on her feet. My aunt found a job right away as a parking lot attendant at the University of Minnesota." Michael smiled sadly as he remembered. "She claimed it was the perfect job because she could write her poetry whenever she wasn't busy. She said she didn't care about worldly possessions because she was committed to becoming a published poet. Then one night, a junkie high on PCP approached her booth, demanded all the money in her till, and shot her in the head after she handed it over."

"Oh, my goodness," said Shirley. "That poor little girl was left all alone."

Michael nodded, a wry expression twisting his lips. "Not for long. My mother and father adopted her within a year of her mother's death."

"Poor little girl, nothing." Dot shook her head. "Losing your mother to a violent crime is a terrible thing, but it doesn't give you permission to hurt others."

"Anyway, back to your question, Rachel, about why she did it?"

Lani glanced at Kit. His plate was clean, and he was beginning to wiggle in his chair while listening to every word they said.

"Hey Honey Bug, would you like to go watch a video while the rest of us keep stuffing our faces with all this good food? I'll call you back when it's time for dessert, okay?"

"Don't forget, Mama. I want some of that yellow cheesecake."

As Kit left the room, Michael continued.

"Jennifer doesn't like to share. She used to tell me that. She'd say it over and over again. That's why she went after Lani and Kit, I think." Michael tilted his head toward Mac. "Maybe you didn't realize it, but I think she'd set her sights on hooking up with Dr. Mac there, and you got in the way. I get that part, but the part I don't get is why she ever went after Jonathon."

"Oh, I know the answer to that one," said Dan Szymanski. A euphoric expression flitted across his face as he bit into a forkful of pierogi filled with cheesy mashed potato and drenched in mushroom gravy.

"Well by all means, keep us guessing." Rachel removed the fork from Dan's hand despite his protest. "You'll get it back when you quit tantalizing us with innuendo while stuffing your face."

He looked with longing at his plate filled with holopchi and pierogi. "Okay, here's what I know."

He gently tugged his fork from Rachel's grip and laid it across his plate. He took a sip of his chardonnay, and cleared his throat. He looked across the table at Michael.

"Your cousin has some serious issues. At first when we brought her in she was all poise and polish. She refused to answer any questions without her lawyer. All we could get her to say was that she didn't have a clue where that box of chocolates came from. As far as the papers in her purse? She claimed you put them there to frame her."

"B-b-but, I d-d-didn't." It was the first time Michael had stuttered in weeks.

"We know, Michael, we know. Although, I have to say, your fingerprints were the only ones on the box."

"She left it there for me to pick up. Somehow, she knew she could get me to do it."

"But Michael, there was no way she could know you'd be at the Tropical Bean," said Dot.

"My guess is that she had no clue you were going to show up. She didn't care who picked it up because she'd already wiped it clean. No, I don't think she could count on you, although based on what she finally did admit, you were the target to begin with along with your father. She figured she'd frame you for the murder of your father and rid herself of both of you at the same time.

"What gave her away in the end, the one thing she couldn't talk her way past—and let me tell you that woman is unbelievably smooth—was the pack of gum and the contents on the notebook paper we found in her purse, which *did* have her fingerprints all over them." Dan stopped to take a quick bite of holopchi in spite of Rachel's disapproving look.

Lani spoke up. "But why did she want to kill Jonathon?"

"Let me guess," said Michael. "My father found out something, and he was either going to cut her off or tell the world that she wasn't who she has always pretended to be."

"Close, very close," mumbled Dan through another mouthful of holopchi. "When we confronted her with the contents of the notebook, she finally crumbled." He shook his head. "No, crumbled is not the word. She exploded. Turns out she ran into that Kramer guy at a class reunion about six months ago, and he tried to hook up with her."

"No way. She wouldn't have looked twice at Ryan. He was a creep in high school, and I can't imagine he'd improved with age."

"She thought she could use him. She tried really hard to get us to believe that you and he were partners. What she didn't count on was that he kept notes on everything in that little black playbook of his. The deal was supposed to be that they never referred to each other by name. She figured she'd be safe that way. But Kramer was crazy as a loon, and thought he was some kind of assassin extraordinaire, and he liked to write about it."

"So he wrote about Jennifer in that notebook of his?" said Pete.

"Yep. In most of the entries, he called her, "my partner." But the idiot slipped from time to time and called her Jennifer instead of Sutton. Those were the pages that she'd torn out of the notebook. When she knew we had all the information we needed to get her put away for a very long time, she lost it, and started screaming that no one ever understood her."

"My father finally figured her out, didn't he?" said Michael. "When my mother died last year, she made me promise to contact my dad. For years she believed that my father had an affair. She walked out on him when she found a note and a pair of women's lacy underpants in one of his coat pockets."

Around the table, faces stared at him in astonishment.

"I'll bet you anything, Jennifer was behind it. She wanted my father all to herself. I know my father reached out to my mom after his accident, and I also know they corresponded. She was too sick from chemo to visit, and he wasn't able to come to her, but my guess is that she convinced him Jennifer was behind their breakup, right?"

Dan nodded. "That about sums it up. Your cousin was pretty bitter about a certain conversation she had with your father. Seems he'd been subsidizing her lifestyle."

"I always wondered how she was able to afford all those clothes and that condo," murmured Mac.

"She didn't. Sutton told her that he was going to stop subsidizing her lifestyle. I think that's basically all he threatened, but her devious little mind filled in some blanks that probably would never have happened. She assumed he would tell everyone that she was a fraud. So, when she ran into Kramer she figured she could make use of him, take you out, Sutton, and inherit the whole shebang."

Dan turned to look at Lani. "You got in her way, because … "

" … she doesn't like to share, and it was obvious to everyone that Mac has eyes for no one but Lani," said Michael.

Lani's eyes flew to Mac's, and he put one hand over hers. "Well she was right about that at least."

Lani cleared her throat. "Michael, if you hadn't knocked that candy out of Kit's hand … " Her voice broke and Mac's hand tightened over hers.

Michael shook his head, but Dan nodded. "She's right, Sutton. That whole box of candy was filled with poison. That's how she took out Kramer."

Dot picked up her spoon and clanked it against her wine glass. "Okay, I want to make a toast." She raised her glass. "To friends who stand by each other in bad times and good. How lucky did we all get to be?"

Smiles broke out across everyone's faces.

Kit poked his head back into the dining room. "Can we have the yellow cheesecake now?"

Lani closed the door after the last of her guests and turned back into the shop. Mac pulled her into his arms.

"Dot really had it right when she said, 'how lucky did we all get to be.'" She looked up into Mac's face. "Have you heard anything more today about Letty?"

Mac shook his head. "No, but I won't stop looking until I find her.

Lani settled her head into the hollow of Mac's shoulder and wrapped her arms around his waist. He lowered his face, lips searching for hers.

They jerked apart as they heard a clink and a soft knock. Lani flew to the door, pulled back the latch, and opened it. Outside snow fell soft and thick, blurring the harsh lines of the world upon which it fell. On the stoop lay a small wadded up piece of paper. Mac scooped it up and eased it open, taking care not to tear the damp paper. Inside they discovered a large smiley face scrawled across the page in thick black ink and three golden beer bottle caps.

Dedication

As always, thanks for all your support and encouragement, Bob. You are the best. Many thanks also to Bonnie for your wonderful editorial insights and Renee for your creativity. Kerry—as promised long ago, this one's for you.

www.ingramcontent.com/pod-product-compliance
Lightning Source LLC
Chambersburg PA
CBHW030142200626
46812CB00015B/849